THEY WERE TH
JOHNSON COU
THEIR STORY WOULD BE WRITTEN
IN BLOOD . . .

JAKE COLBY: Some thought he was an outlaw. Others said he was a hero. Once he worked for Johnson County's biggest rancher. Now, he's going up against an army of hired guns, including one man who used to be his friend.

TOM HORN: He'd served with Jake Colby and General Crook as an Indian Scout in Arizona. But somewhere along the line a good man went bad—and now he's a gun for hire.

DOYLE HUNTER: As the county's biggest landowner, Hunter wants to crush everyone around him. And with a new state law and his very own army, he might just get his way.

ELLA WATSON: Nicknamed "Cattle Kate," this frontier madam was a pro with any kind of gun. But once she started dabbling in stolen livestock, she was marked by the Cattle Barons to die.

LAURA PLACE: The beautiful young woman was forced from her home in Tennessee into a life of prostitution in the Wild West. Then she met a good man, and faced the prospect of losing everything again.

RANGE WARS

Robert Vaughan

St. Martin's Paperbacks

RANGE WARS

Copyright © 1997 by Robert Vaughan.

All rights reserved. No part of this book may be used or reproduced in any manner whatsoever without written permission except in the case of brief quotations embodied in critical articles or reviews. For information address St. Martin's Press, 175 Fifth Avenue, New York, N.Y. 10010.

ISBN: 0-312-96334-3

Printed in the United States of America

St. Martin's Paperbacks edition/November 1997

10 9 8 7 6 5 4 3 2 1

★★★

Author's Foreword

In Wyoming they still refer to it as the Johnson County Range War. As wars go it wasn't much of a war. In terms of human drama, however, it epitomizes the classic tale of the Old West: big cattlemen with their sprawling acres, thousands of head of cattle, and scores of cowboys pitted against blizzard, drought, Indians, wild animals, nesters, sheep men, small ranchers, and rustlers.

Although the ''Cattlemen's Invasion of Wyoming'' happened over a period of only a few days in 1892, telling that story as a singular event would be like playing a Beethoven symphony with only one instrument. It is the full orchestra that makes this tale resonate . . . from the early days of Tom Horn as an Indian scout, to the trying days of small ranchers bucking the odds to survive against corporate ranching, to the lynching of Ella Watson and Jim Averill, to the ''invasion'' conducted by the big ranchers' private army, to the hired killers the big ranchers brought in to ''weed out'' the rustlers, and, finally, to the trial and hanging of Tom Horn.

Corporate ranching was king of the western ranges at the close of the nineteenth century, and bankers and entrepreneurs from back east, many even from Europe, were investing heavily in huge cattle conglomerates. But when the big ranches began losing heavily, the ranch managers and heavily financed owners were faced with the problem of justifying these losses. Actually, most of the losses were due to poor management and the caprice of nature, such as droughts in the summer, blizzards in the winter, prairie fires, and grass-eating insects. But rustlers were also taking their toll, and they were a handy excuse for the big ranchers to give to their lenders.

The heavy losses and the real presence of rustlers also provided the ranchers with vindication for any action they wanted to take. Their steps to stop rustling included an agreement not to allow any of their employees to own cattle. This measure actually backfired against the big ranchers, because it prevented the small ranchers from obtaining much needed part-time employment. As a result, many an otherwise honest small rancher had to resort to just what the big ranchers accused them of all along—rustling.

Those who didn't rustle adopted the legal practice of rounding up unbranded calves—called mavericks— from the open range. To counter this, the big ranchers forced the "maverick law" through the Wyoming State Legislature, making every unbranded stray calf on the range the property of the Wyoming Stock Growers' Association. The WSGA then sold the calves to the highest bidder. This meant that the small ranchers couldn't claim their own strays and, in many cases, couldn't even afford to buy them back from the association.

When their losses persisted, the Wyoming Stock Growers' Association declared war against the rustlers and the small ranchers, for by now the terms "rustler" and "small rancher" were synonymous in the lexicon of the big ranchers. In desperation the WSGA hired and equipped a private army to invade Johnson County, a county that was very near Hole in the Wall, a known hideout for outlaws. Johnson County was also the home range of several small ranchers. These small ranchers, the Wyoming Stock Growers' Association insisted, were the root of all their problems, for they were either stealing cattle themselves or providing a ready market for the cattle that someone else stole. This invasion came to be known as the "Johnson County War," and though it had the tacit backing of the state government, it ended badly for the big ranchers.

The wealthy stockmen's next step was to hire professional assassins to take care of their enemies, and this met with considerably more success. Rustlers and small ranchers began turning up dead, either shot or hanged, and rustling decreased dramatically. The big ranchers pointed to the decrease in rustling as proof that they were right.

The most notorious of these hired gunmen was Tom Horn, a man who had already achieved fame for his work as a scout for the army against the Apache, as a United States marshal, and as a private detective for the Pinkerton Agency. Tom Horn was a professional gunman who killed with grim efficiency, drawing no more distinction between the rustlers and the small ranchers than did the Wyoming Stock Growers' Association. He marked "his" dead by the use of a unique calling card—a rock placed under the head of his victims.

Then one of those rocks turned up under the head of a fourteen-year-old boy. Drunk, Tom Horn was tricked into a confession . . . a confession he quickly recanted as soon as he was sober. Despite his protestation of innocence, he was brought to trial for murder.

The national fame he had already attained, as well as the fact that he was in the employ of the Wyoming Stock Growers' Association, made his trial a cause célèbre, as closely followed in its day as the more famous trials have been followed in ours.

The stock growers, anxious about what might come out during the trial, raised a great deal of money for Tom Horn's defense. However, they put as much distance between themselves and their hired killer as they possibly could. Privately they agreed that it would be best if their hired killer could be found guilty, then hanged quietly, without involving them.

That is exactly what happened. Tom Horn went to the gallows protesting his innocence—insofar as killing the fourteen-year-old was concerned—but never once did he betray, or even compromise, his employers.

This book is inspired by the exciting history of the Wyoming range at the close of the nineteenth century. However, it is not a slave to events as they really happened. While I have drawn freely upon the incidents, locale, and characters of that period, the purists will note that some authentic characters have been consolidated or omitted, while many fictional characters have been added. I have also shamelessly manipulated the chronology, because I believe it enables me to tell the story more powerfully and with a smoother flow.

I know that Tom Horn's meeting with Governor William A. Richards didn't take place until three years *after* the "invasion" of Johnson County, but for my purposes I have made the meeting much earlier. And though he wasn't tried and hanged until 1903, eleven years after the Johnson County War, I have moved that event up so that it becomes a part of the whole story.

I make no apologies for my manipulation of time and

place and event. Instead I ask that the reader remember this is, after all, a novel and not a textbook. If you want the details of a specific incident, there are many good history books you can read, and I would hope that you find my story entertaining enough to inspire you to do so.

As you read this story it may help to remember that while all facts are true, not all truths are factual. It would also help if you would consider this to be an artistic rendering rather than a factual accounting of the Old West.

✯ ✯ ✯

One

The wind, which had moaned and whistled across the rocky crags and sharp precipices throughout the long night, was quiet now, and a stillness descended over the land.

Jake Colby, tall, lean, and whipcord tough, yawned and stretched to work out the kinks of having spent the night on the ground. He ran his hand across his lower jaw and felt the two-week-old beard. He actually preferred to be clean shaven, but here, in the desert, the priorities for water were clearly established. Drinking came first, for man and horses, then cooking, then cleaning, and, finally, shaving.

Jake reached for his hat, small brimmed and low crowned, shook it to make certain it was free of scorpions and, finding it safe, put it on his head. He unscrewed the cap of his canteen and took a drink, measuring the portion carefully because the nearest water was several miles away.

Behind him he heard his two campmates, Al Sieber and Tom Horn, stirring awake.

"It's about time you folks woke up," Jake said without turning toward them.

"You anxious to run into Geronimo today, are you, sonny?" Sieber asked.

Sieber was chief of scouts and oldest of the three men. He had alternately lived with and fought against the Apache for many years, nearly losing his own identity in the process. Now he wasn't fully trusted by either white or Indian, though Jake found him to be one of the most fascinating men he had ever encountered.

Al got up from his bedroll, then walked over to a large rock to relieve himself. "Tom," he said calmly as he continued to urinate, "you lyin' close to that rifle of yours?"

"Yeah. Why?" Tom Horn answered.

"Don't be too obvious about it, but you might want to roll over and take a look off to your right, just beyond that four-armed cactus, in the notch of them two big rocks. Jake, you just go on doin' what you're a-doin'."

Jake wanted to look as well, but he managed to resist doing so. Instead he returned to his own bedroll and began rolling it up.

"Do you see him?" Al asked, buttoning up his pants. He had shown absolutely no alarm, neither in the tone of his voice nor in his physical action.

"Yeah," Tom answered. "I see him."

"Kill him," Al said simply.

Still lying in his bedroll, Tom slowly cocked his rifle, jacking a round into the chamber. Then suddenly he was on his knees with his rifle at his shoulder, aiming toward the Apache who had slipped down to spy upon them.

The Apache, realizing that he had not only been spotted, but was being targeted, shouted in alarm and turned, attempting to get away.

The rifle cracked and bucked against Tom Horn's shoulder. Jake turned to look toward the Indian and saw a pinkish mist spray from the back of his head. The Indian fell, then slid several feet down the steep incline. Al Sieber was the first one to him.

"Damn good shot, Tom," he said, rolling the Indian's body over with his foot.

"Is he one of the band we're following?" Jake asked.

"I expect so," Al said.

"He is. His name is Natache," Tom answered. He knelt and placed a rock under Natache's head.

"You know him?" Al asked. He carved off a plug of tobacco and stared down at the young Indian.

"Yeah, I know him," Tom answered, still kneeling beside the Indian's body. "He's one of Geronimo's nephews. I lived with his family the year I stayed with the Apache. Fact is, I took him fishin' first time he ever went. He was a feisty little shit then, running around, dancing, chanting, talking, scaring the fish."

Tom reached out and took a rawhide cord from around the dead Indian's neck. A couple of items were hanging from the cord.

"What are those things?" Jake asked.

Tom held out a piece of carved wood about five inches long. "This here is his scratching stick," he said. "This other thing is a drinking tube, made from a horse's innards." He nodded toward the dead Indian. "These are the things carried by a novice."

"A novice?"

"That's what we would call a cadet, or a recruit," Tom explained. "Natache was too young to be a warrior yet. These things mean he was still in trainin' for it. He would've made a pretty good one, I think." Tom stood up, pocketing the items he had taken from the Indian's neck.

Jake marveled that Tom Horn could be so impassive after having just killed someone with whom he was once friends. "You think there are any more around?" he asked.

Al spat out a stream of tobacco juice, then wiped the back of his hand across his mouth. He looked toward the south. "I doubt that a novice would come here all by hisself," he replied. "He probably had a shaman with him, watchin' over him to see how he was doin'."

Jake pulled his pistol, then started looking around nervously.

"No sense in lookin' for him now. More'n likely, whoever come with him has gone back to tell the others what happened to the boy."

"They'll be comin' after us for sure, now," Jake suggested.

Al laughed. "Hell, son, they was already comin' after us," he said. He waved toward the dead Indian. "Killin' this boy ain't goin' to make 'em no madder. We're their enemy. They expect us to kill 'em, if we get the chance, just like they would us. And the boy died a good death. He'll be elevated to warrior right away, I reckon."

"What do we do now?" Jake asked.

"Why don't we get saddled up and see if we can find their camp?" Al suggested.

At half-past eight the three scouts were backtracking Natache and the shaman who had visited their camp. Then Jake caught the flash of sunlight from a distant hill. Miles away, on the other side of the trail, there was another flash, then another still, until, in all, they counted eight flashing lights.

Al spat disdainfully and again wiped his mouth with the back of his hand. He stood in his stirrups and looked at the many winking lights.

"General Miles has all his mirrors flashing again," Tom pointed out.

"General Miles and his heliographs," Al snorted. "He's got all the science of the modern world, plus five thousand armed and mounted men in the field against Geronimo. I told him, and Crook told him, there ain't no more'n twenty to twenty-five warriors with Geronimo . . . total! But Miles ain't Crook. Miles thinks the way you kill a fly is to hit it with a sledgehammer."

"What do you think he's up to now?" Jake asked.

"General Miles, you mean?" the chief of scouts asked.

"Yes."

Al rummaged through his saddlebag before he answered. Then he found what he was looking for: a bottle of whiskey. He pulled the cork and held the bottle out toward the mountains.

"The way I figure it, the son of a bitch is usin' us as bait," he said. He took several deep swallows of whiskey, then replaced the cork without offering any to either of the others. He slapped the cork down with the palm of his hand. "He's goin' to wait until we're jumped, then he's goin' to close the trap with five hundred to a thousand men."

"Why, that's ridiculous," Jake said. "Does he think Geronimo is just going to sit there and wait for him?"

"Son, you're talkin' like a thinkin' man, an' that's where you're makin' your mistake," Al said. "Miles, on the other hand, is a soldier. And that puts him at a great disadvantage in the thinkin' department."

"Crook was a soldier, too, and you liked him."

"Yeah, well, any general who would go into battle wearin' a straw hat, a canvas suit, and ridin' a mule has got my vote for common sense," Al insisted.

"Hey, Al," Tom said. "You really think ole Miles is usin' us as bait?"

" 'Pears that way," Al answered.

"You know what I've noticed about the bait that's in a trap?" Tom asked.

"What's that?"

"It nearly always gets eaten."

Al laughed. "Damn me if you aren't learnin', boy," he said. He turned his horse around. "Come on."

"Where we goin'?" Tom asked.

"We're goin' to have us a talk with General Miles."

They had ridden for about an hour, going back over the ground they had covered earlier in the morning, when Jake saw a troop of cavalry approaching them.

"Al," Jake said.

Al spat another stream of tobacco juice before he answered. "Yeah, I see 'em," he said. "I thought they'd prob'ly send someone out to meet us if we turned back."

A large cloud of dust billowed out from behind the cavalry as they approached, and Jake could hear the jingle and jangle of their equipment. The officer in charge held up his arm as they arrived, and the sergeant riding beside him turned and yelled over his shoulder.

"Troop, halt!"

"Mr. Sieber, I am Captain Jackson," the officer in charge said. "Is something wrong?"

"Wrong? What makes you think something is wrong?" Al asked.

"We observed you turning back," Jackson said. "General Miles was curious as to why."

"I'll just bet he was," Al replied.

"Is there a problem?"

"You're damn right there's a problem," Al answered.
He pointed to the mountains. "You've got your damned
mirrors flashing behind every rock and hole up there,
talking back and forth. Do you think Geronimo can't see
you?"

"Oh, we are certain that he does see us," Captain
Jackson said. He smiled. "But we are just as certain that
he doesn't know what we are saying."

"What you are saying? Hell, Cap'n, I can't read the
damn code, but even I know what you are saying. And
if I can figure it out, don't you think he can?"

"Just what do you think we are saying?" Captain
Jackson asked.

"You are saying, Use those three dumb bastards
we've got scoutin' for us as bait. Don't make a move
until the Apache attack them."

Jackson chuckled. "Well, that's not quite what we are
saying," he said. "But you do have the substance."

"Look," Al said. "If we go on like this, you are
never going to catch Geronimo. The best you can do is
wear him down until he dies of old age."

"Have you a better suggestion?"

"Yes, I do, as a matter of fact."

"Then perhaps you would share it. I'm sure the general would be glad to hear it."

"How about if me an' these two go to see Geronimo,
to offer him a chance to surrender?"

"Too dangerous."

Al laughed. "Too dangerous? Hell, a moment ago
you was willin' to let us get took as bait. Now you say
it's too dangerous for me to go talk to Geronimo."

"Suppose you did go," Captain Jackson said. "Geronimo could have come in anytime he wanted to. What would make him come in now?"

"He's tired, Cap'n. He's tired and the people with him are tired. I think I can get them to come in now, if we make the right offer."

"And just what would the right offer be?"

"No more'n what General Crook has been offering all along."

Jackson shook his head. "If they haven't come in with that offer before, what makes you think he'll listen to that offer now?"

"You got to understand the Apache mind, Cap'n," Al said. "To the Apache, fighting the good fight is as important as winning. If they had come in when the offer was first made, they would have been giving up. But Geronimo has taken no more'n a handful of men, women, and starvin' kids, and fought the whole U.S. Army to a standstill. I think he'll listen to Crook's offer now."

Captain Jackson stroked his chin for a moment before he spoke again.

"I can't make that decision, you understand," he said. "You wait here, I'll go back and ask General Miles. If he approves, I'll flash you a message."

"Are you going to leave someone here to read it to me?"

"Anderson!" Jackson shouted.

A rider broke ranks and rode forward, then reported to Jackson.

"Stay here with Mr. Sieber and the scouts," Jackson said.

"You, you want me to stay here, sir?" Anderson asked nervously.

"Don't get scared, boy," Al said. "You're just goin'

to read one of them little mirror messages to me, that's all.''

''They have seen us,'' Al said. It was late afternoon, some five hours after Anderson read the flashed message to them, authorizing their peaceful contact with Geronimo. Anderson had returned to the main body of troops, but Jake, Tom, and Al rode on. They had spent the better part of the day with white strips of cloth tied to the ends of their rifles as a signal that they wanted to parley.

''Did you see something?'' Tom Horn asked, looking around.

''No.''

''Then how do you know they have seen us?''

''I know,'' Al said simply, and his quiet conviction was enough for Jake. Now he, too, knew they had been seen. Soon they would make contact.

About fifteen minutes after Al announced that they had been seen, three warriors suddenly appeared from behind some rocks in front of them. They were on foot, and they stood in front of them, with their rifles at the ready.

''Come,'' one of them said.

''Can't be too far from here,'' Jake said. ''They're walking.''

''That don't mean nothin','' Al replied. ''Apaches ain't all that good with horses.'' He laughed. ''They're as likely to eat 'em as ride 'em.''

The three Indians moved into an easy, ground-eating lope, leading Al, Jake, and Tom through a narrow draw up the side of a mountain, away from the main trail.

For half an hour the three scouts followed the warriors. When they finally emerged from the draw, they saw about a dozen wickiups and Jake knew they had reached Geronimo's camp.

A woman, her hair cut short and her face covered with mud and ashes, came toward them. She shouted angrily at them and spat on them as they rode by.

"What was that all about?" Jake asked.

"That was Enata," Tom explained. "Natache's mother. She has cut her hair short and put mud and ashes on her face for mourning."

Jake twisted in his saddle and looked back at the Indian woman. He saw then that she was crying, and he felt sorry for her.

When they reached the centermost wickiup, a proud, defiant-looking man came out to greet them. He held up his hand in a sign of peace.

"Sibi," he said, which was as close as he could get to pronouncing Al Sieber's name. "It is good to see you in peace."

Al dismounted and held up his own hand. He nodded toward his two companions.

"This here is Jake Colby. You already know Tom Horn," Al said by way of introduction.

"I have heard that my parents are dead," Geronimo said. "Is this true?"

"Yes," Al replied.

Geronimo nodded. "I am sorry I did not return to San Carlos to see them, but I am sure they knew why I could not."

"They were proud of you," Al said.

Again Geronimo nodded, as if the praise were his due.

"Are you really the greatest warrior of all time?" Jake asked, speaking for the first time.

"Ho," Geronimo laughed. "Do you doubt it? I have

fought the entire American and Mexican armies and they have not defeated me.''

''Nor have you defeated them,'' Jake said quietly.

Geronimo looked up quickly, surprised by the comment. Then he laughed again. ''You are correct,'' he said. ''I have not defeated them.'' He looked at Al. ''Have you married?''

Al laughed. ''I'm like you,'' he said. ''No woman will have me.''

''Ah,'' Geronimo replied. ''But I have taken a wife.'' He turned and called back into the wickiup. A moment later a woman, much younger than Geronimo, appeared to stand shyly in the door.

''This is your woman?'' Al asked.

''She is called Taz-ayz-Slath,'' Geronimo said. ''She is a fine warrior, and she pleases me in bed.'' He laughed a rich, ribald laugh, and because Al and Tom laughed, Jake, following their direction, laughed as well.

''May your wickiup fill with children and your days be long and happy,'' Al said.

''Shall we drink tiswin while you try to talk me into returning to the reservation?'' Geronimo asked. Tiswin was a fermented corn drink, more like a beer than a whiskey, though able to get one intoxicated. It had been outlawed on the reservations, and its prohibition was one of the biggest bones of contention between the Indians and the U.S. government.

''How did you know I was going to try to talk you into returning?'' Al asked.

''Last night I had a vision,'' Geronimo replied. ''It was a very powerful vision, and I learned many things. In my vision I learned that you would come to speak to me.''

''And what else did your vision say?'' Al asked.

"The vision said your heart is good," Geronimo answered. "And I know that what happens will not be your fault."

"What happens?" Al said. "I don't understand. What is going to happen?"

"Many bad things are going to happen," Geronimo said. Taz-ayz-Slath handed Geronimo a cup of tiswin, and he took a drink as she passed cups to the others.

"What sort of bad things?" Al asked.

Geronimo wiped his mouth with the back of his hand. "In my vision I learned that there are two paths before me. Both paths are filled with much sorrow. If I choose one path, many will die, but some will live. If I choose the other path, all will die. One path is to stay in the mountains and fight the war forever. The other path is to surrender and go the way of peace. But I do not know which path is better."

"You know the words of General Crook," Al said. "He has promised to do many things on the reservation. He has promised to let the Apache live on ranches, or in the mountains if they wish. He has promised to take the soldiers away and let the Apache govern themselves with their own police force and their own laws."

"Yes," Geronimo said. "I have seen some of the Apache policemen. They wear soldier jackets and they fight against their own people."

"They are protectors of their people," Al said. "There are some good men who have become Apache police."

"Sibi, you are a white man, with the knowledge of the Indian. You are without fear, and though you are an old man, I have never seen you tired. Tell me, Sibi, man of war, man of peace, man of council, what do you think I should do?" Geronimo asked.

"Geronimo, I say to you in all faith and honor that if you continue to make war, you and all your people will be exterminated. It takes you ten years to make a warrior out of a ten-year-old boy. But General Miles can make many hundred soldiers in a single day. The white man cannot be exterminated. You and I have seen this when it was Indian country. We have seen it when there was no business here except getting in rations for the soldier and his horse. We have seen it from that day to this, when there are towns everywhere, and ranches and settlements where once there were only Indians. Now we see the railroad and the telegraph, and with this command is a corps of men who can signal words with a sun glass over many miles.

"You must go to the reservation now, or else make up your mind to die on the warpath and see the last remnant of your tribe die with you. Your men are brave and fearless and your influence with them is as you want to make it. Not one of them is afraid to die, but all men who are used to facing death every day of their lives like to get the best of any fight they are compelled to make. I have fought and know what the feeling is when I know that I cannot win the fight. My heart gets heavy when I know that I have to lie close in the rocks all day and creep away when the darkness comes and can take only my rifle with me and cannot tell when I may get something to eat and at times something to bind up my wounds. I cannot tell you how I feel then, but this I can say: that it is not well for any man to be so, be he white or red.

"While you have been growing weaker in men day by day and week by week, General Miles has become stronger. You know I speak only the truth. Sometimes I have made a mistake, but I have never told a deliberate lie. My advice to you, Geronimo, is that you go to Fort Apache. You know that you cannot hold out here, and from here, you have no other place to go.''

Geronimo was quiet for a moment, then he finished the last of his drink and set down the cup.

''Listen,'' he said. ''This is what I will do. Tomorrow, I will take all my people and we will go with you to Fort Apache. There, I will surrender to this new general they have sent after me.''

''You are doing the right thing,'' Al said. ''The children's children of the Chiricahua will speak your name with respect.''

''No,'' Geronimo said sadly. ''This will not be.''

''But of course it will be,'' Al insisted. ''You are a great man and will be honored for generations to come.''

''For the Chiricahua, there will be no generations to come,'' Geronimo said. ''We are finished.''

★ ★ ★

Two

When Al, Jake, and Tom led Geronimo and his tiny band of followers into Fort Apache, hundreds of people were there to watch the surrender. Most were Apache from the reservation, but there were also many whites, soldiers from the post, and civilians from the nearby towns. Camillus Fly, the famous photographer, was there, as well as reporters, not only from the local newspapers, but from the eastern press as well. Geronimo, as the last hostile Indian, had become important news over the last few years.

Some of those gathered booed, and some cheered, and some even wept, but not one person watched without feeling some emotion.

Jake rode with Al, Tom, Geronimo, and his people through the crowd of onlookers toward the headquarters of Fort Apache. Jake saw that Geronimo's head was held high, his eyes were clear, and he was looking straight ahead, paying no attention to either his detractors or his supporters.

A double row of troops formed an honor guard that led them right up to the flagpole. There, at the head of the formation, Jake saw General Miles and the officers of his staff, waiting to receive Geronimo's surrender.

"Is this some sort of trick, Sieber?" Miles asked angrily when he saw the paltry number of Indians. "You were supposed to bring in Geronimo *and* his army."

"This is it, General," Al said. He twisted in his saddle and took in the sullen-faced Indians with a sweep of his arm. "You are lookin' at his entire army."

General Miles walked around the group of Indians, looking them over carefully. There were a handful of warriors who sat on their horses with defiant pride. There were several young boys, some still wearing the scratching stick and drinking tube of a novice; and there were a few old men, beyond the age of warrior but just as proud and just as defiant. The rest were women and very small children. Some were sick and some were wounded, and those who were unable to walk or stand were sitting or lying on a travois.

No one said a word.

"This?" Miles finally asked. Again he held out his arm toward the pathetic band. "This is the enemy which has kept five thousand soldiers tied up for five years?"

"I'm afraid it is, General," Al replied.

Miles shook his head. "What a disgraceful chapter of history this has been."

Al leaned over and spat a stream of tobacco near the general's feet. "I agree, General," he said. "That's why I'm ready to help put in them changes General Crook wanted on the reservation."

"There will be no changes," Miles said.

"No changes? General, what are you talking about?" Sieber asked. "That was part of the deal to secure Geronimo's surrender."

"That was General Crook's deal, not mine," Miles

said. "I have my own plans, and they don't include mollycoddling Apaches . . . especially the likes of a murdering savage like Geronimo. I intend to see to it that he and all his people pay for their transgressions."

"General, you can't do this," Al protested. "Whatever else you might think of Geronimo, he is a man of integrity, and his word is his bond. And because his word is good, he is at the disadvantage of believing that everyone's word is good. Now, are you trying to tell me that we are going back on our promises?"

"General Crook's promises, not mine. And the answer is, 'Yes!' I'm going back on every one of them," Miles said. "I am acting in accordance with General Sherman's instructions. I know you aren't going to approve of what I have to do, but it really doesn't matter. I have my orders, and I will carry them out."

Al looked at Geronimo, and Jake thought he had never seen such sadness in anyone's eyes as he saw in Al's eyes at this moment. Al was going to have to tell Geronimo that he had betrayed him.

"Do not worry, my friend," Geronimo said, speaking first. "This comes as no surprise. I am ready for whatever Usen has planned for me. If I am to die, then it is a good day to die."

"You aren't going to die," Miles said. "You and all your people are being banished from the San Carlos Reservation."

"Banished? What do you mean, banished?" Al asked.

"Geronimo will be imprisoned on a government reservation in another location, far from here." General Miles paused for a moment. "And not just Geronimo."

"You mean those who fought with him."

"Yes," Miles answered. "And more."

"And more?"

General Miles took a deep breath. "All the Chirica-hua," he said. "Those who rode with him, and those who stayed on the reservation. The very old, the very young, the very sick, men and women, boys and girls; every Chiricahua is to be loaded aboard train cars and shipped to Florida."

"When is this to be?" Al asked.

"Right now," Miles said. "I have a train of empty cars waiting for them at this very moment. In less than a week, the Chiricahua of Arizona will be no more than displaced Indians in Florida."

"General, surely you don't mean to include the fam-ilies of my Indian scouts?" Al said.

"I do indeed mean the families of the scouts, Mr. Sieber. And your Indian scouts as well," he added.

"No!" Al bellowed. "They are our friends, our allies! Some of them are not even Chiricahua!"

"I know that some are not Chiricahua but, by their very understanding of us, they have become danger-ous."

"General, this isn't right! Without my Indian scouts, we would never have tracked Geronimo down! I won't let you betray them now!"

"You won't *let* me, Mr. Sieber?" General Miles re-plied sharply. "Captain!" he barked.

"Yes, sir!" Captain Jackson answered.

"Get all the warriors—and Mr. Sieber's Indian scouts—in chains now. When the others see that they are helpless, they will go without protest. Get them loaded into the train cars and get the train under way. By the time the sun sets tonight, they will be out of the territory."

When the Apache realized what was happening, a wail of protest started. Quickly armed soldiers rushed out to give a show of strength so that the protest never developed into anything more than the mournful cries of the women and children.

"Mr. Sieber, Mr. Horn, Mr. Colby," General Miles said.

"Yes, sir?" Al answered.

"The United States Army thanks you men for your services. You are dismissed."

"Let's go, boys," Al said to Jake and Tom.

"Mr. Sieber?" Miles called to him.

Al turned to look back at the general.

"I don't mean you are just dismissed from this formation. I mean you are dismissed from service. All of you. With Geronimo now safely in custody, there will be no more need for civilian scouts."

Disdainfully Al spat out another stream of tobacco juice. "You know, General, I've seen a few sons of bitches in my day," he said. "But I do believe you are about the sorriest son of a bitch I ever have seen."

"Captain, see to it that these . . . *civilians* . . . are escorted off the reservation," General Miles ordered coldly. "Immediately," he added.

"Yes, sir," Captain Jackson replied. The look in Jackson's face told the three erstwhile scouts that while he didn't agree with the general, there was nothing he could do about it.

"Come along, boys," Al said. "I never was one for hangin' around someplace where I wasn't wanted."

That evening the three ex-scouts sat in the back of the Silver Nugget Saloon in Phoenix, contemplating their respective futures over a shared bottle of whiskey. Jake was holding his hat, turning it around slowly in his hand.

"Jake, all this time you been with me, I been meanin'

to ask you," Al started. He tossed down a full glass of whiskey before he continued. "Where the hell did you get that pitiful-lookin' hat?"

The hat was very different in style from most of the other hats. It had a narrow brim and a short, flat, crown, as opposed to the wider brim and deeper crown of the hats Al and Tom Horn were wearing.

Jake took off his hat and looked at it. "What's wrong with my hat?" he asked.

"What's wrong with it? I'll tell you what's wrong with it. It looks like a damn piss pot, that's what's wrong with it."

Tom laughed. "You know what I think?" he said, slurring his words. "I think he was caught in bed with somebody's wife, and when he heard her husband comin' home, he had to run. Only, when he reached under the bed for his hat, he got the chamber pot instead."

"All right, all right," Jake said. "You found me out. But, once I started wearing the piss pot, I had to pretend that it was what I was wearing all along."

All three men enjoyed a good laugh. Then, when the laughter subsided, Jake asked: "What are you two going to do now?"

The smile left Al's face, and he rolled the glass back and forth between his palms as he thought about the question.

"I don't rightly know," he admitted. "I been livin' this way of life for twenty-five years. Now, the army just puts me aside, the way they might an IC mule . . . inspected and condemned. I guess I'll just drift around for a bit until somethin' else comes up."

"You could come with me, Al," Tom suggested. He poured himself another drink.

"And just what are you going to do, my fine-feathered friend?"

"Well, sir, they're havin' a ropin' and tyin' contest here in Phoenix, at the territorial fair," Tom said. "Reckon I'll enter that, then, with my prize money, buy myself a silver mine."

"Haw!" Al laughed. "The ropin' and tyin' contest is all right. Like as not you'll win that. But why you want to waste your money in buyin' a silver mine when you could spend it on whiskey and whores is beyond me. What about you, Jake? What are you plannin' on doin'?"

"I'm figurin' on somehow gettin' myself up to Wyoming," Jake answered. "See if I can get into the cow business."

"You might think about enterin' the ropin' and tyin' contest at the fair," Tom suggested. "If you win, it'd give you lots more money to start out with."

"No thanks," Jake said, laughing. "You know damn well I can't beat you. You're just trying to get more people in, so the prize'll be bigger, that's all."

"Well," Tom said, tossing down his drink, "you can't blame a body for tryin'."

Al poured the three men another round, then became quite melancholy.

"You know, boys, we've been together a good bit here, lately," he said. "I taught the two of you ever'thing I knew about scoutin', and now that you've learned . . . I'd put you up with the best scouts there is. Only, there ain't no best scouts, 'cause there ain't no scouts a'tall. There ain't no more scoutin' to do. And here, after we've faced death together, and been thirsty, and hot, and hungry together . . ."

"And whore'd some together," Tom added with a smile, making the mood a little lighter.

"Yeah, and done that, too," Al agreed. "Now, after all that, we're all three goin' our separate ways, and we ain't never goin' to see each other again."

"Oh, I wouldn't say that," Jake said. "Never is a long time."

"It may have escaped your notice, bein' as I'm as strong and spry as either one of you two greenhorns," Al said, "but I'm gettin' to be an old man. I prob'ly ain't got all that long of a time left."

"Hell, Al, you'll outlive us all," Tom joked. "Jake's goin' to wind up gored by some bull, or caught up to by the man that owns that piss pot he's wearin' as a hat, and I'll like as not get myself hung somewhere."

Al laughed, then lifted his glass. "All right, boys, then let's have one last drink together. If we don't meet on this side of that last bugle call, we'll meet again at Fiddlers' Green."

"At Fiddlers' Green," Jake said, holding up his glass as well.

"Fiddlers' Green," Tom repeated, lifting his glass.

Fiddlers' Green was the cavalryman's euphemism for the great hereafter. It was a solemn and, for them, as spiritual a moment as they were able to muster. The three men touched their glasses, then tossed down the drink in one great gulp.

★★★

Three

The solid crack of the breaking of a rack of billiard balls was the loudest sound in the posh game room of the Cheyenne Social Club. A couple of men in tuxedos were playing out a "gentleman's wager" of $100.

Doyle Hunter, also wearing a tuxedo—for that was the dress code of the club—was not playing, but he had put a side bet of $25 on the outcome. At the moment he was watching the game from a red leather stool at the mahogany bar. An attractive young female employee of the club had just freshened Hunter's drink for him, and he took a sip before continuing the conversation he was having with George Perry. George Perry was one of the other members of the Wyoming Stock Growers' Association. The Cheyenne Social Club was the WSGA's headquarters. It was to here that the members of the Wyoming Stock Growers' Association—all large ranchers—came to relax and conduct business with each other.

"I don't know about you, George," Hunter said, "but

I'm not looking forward to the next financial report I'll be sending back east. For the last two years, I've been promising my investors that things were going to turn around . . . that the Rocking H was going to begin showing a profit. So far that hasn't happened. I'm still losing money.''

"Hell, Doyle, you think you're the only one losing his ass?" Perry asked. He had just peeled a boiled egg, and now he dipped the end of it into a little crystal boat of salt and pepper. "My English investors hold so much paper on my ranch now, they could take it away from me just like that." Perry snapped his fingers. "It's the damned rustlers that are causing all our problems."

"And the small ranchers," Hunter added. "They don't have the same kind of overhead we have, so when it comes time to sell our beef, they can afford to undercut us in the market."

"Rustlers, small ranchers, same thing far as I'm concerned. You take that bunch up Johnson County, for example. There's maybe nine or ten little ranches up there, but when you put them all together, they're runnin' nearly as many head of cattle as any one of the biggest ranches. And where do you think they got they stock?"

"Stole it, more'n likely," Hunter said.

"Yeah, either that, or bought it from those who did steal it," Perry said.

"Somebody ought to do somethin' about it," Hunter said. "Our profit margin is small enough as it is. We can't afford to be stolen blind."

"I'm glad you brought that up, Doyle, because some of us have met with the governor. He's aware of our problem, and he's promised to give us all the support we need."

"Hell, rustling is already against the law. What more do you think the governor can do for us?"

"Don't sell the man short. He knows which side his bread is buttered on," Perry said. "And because he is the governor, he is in position to get a few additional laws passed that will make things harder for the small rancher and easier for the large rancher."

"Like what?"

"Like the maverick law. That's going to stop the small rancher in his tracks."

At that moment there was an exclamation of victory from one of the two men playing billiards.

"Well, now, aren't I the lucky one?" Perry said with a smile. "It would appear that my man won. I do believe you owe me twenty-five dollars."

Hunter pulled the money from his billfold and paid without protest. "Tell me about this maverick law," he said again.

"It's a little idea I came up with myself," Perry explained, pocketing his winnings. "It's a law that says all unbranded cattle belong to the Wyoming Stock Growers' Association."

"All unbranded cattle? You mean even our own?"

"Yes, if they wander off your home range," Perry said. "But not just yours—mine, Kohr's, and all the other ranchers'. Including the small ranchers."

"I don't get it. What is the benefit of a law like that?"

"Well, for one thing, it will close one of the loopholes in the small ranchers' rustling activity," Perry explained. "They all claim that's where they're getting most of their stock, when you and I and everyone else knows they're just using those unbranded mavericks as a cover for the stolen cows they are running. Besides, most of the mavericks rightly belong to us, anyway. So if we pass a law saying that the WSGA owns all the unbridled cattle, and that they are for sale to the highest bidder, it'll do two things. It'll raise money for the association and it'll squeeze the little rancher out.''

"I don't know," Hunter said. "I'm afraid that might just make things worse. I mean, if they can't have the mavericks, they might start rustling even more."

"Let them," Perry suggested. "If they do start unrestricted rustling, then we won't have any trouble at all getting the state to approve of whatever action we might be forced to take to clean up that nest of varmints once and for all."

"Is this more talk about forming a private army to go after them?" Hunter asked.

"You're damned right it is. Where do you stand?"

"You know where I stand," Hunter replied. "I'm against it. I don't feel that good about arming a bunch of men we don't know anything about. How do we know we won't just be making the situation worse?"

"Nothing can be worse than it is now," Perry insisted. "And I'm not the only one who feels this way. I've been listening to the other ranchers. If we brought it up for a vote right now, as to whether or not the Wyoming Stock Growers' Association should hire and equip an army of private detectives to go into Johnson County and clean it out, it would pass by a wide margin."

"If you feel that way, why don't you bring it up for a vote?"

"Would you vote for it?"

"No," Hunter said.

"Well then, there you go. I don't want just a majority, Doyle, or even a wide margin," Perry said. "After all, raising a private army and invading another part of the state is serious business. If we do it, I want it to be the unanimous decision of every member of the Wyoming Stock Growers' Association.''

"Do you think you'll ever get everyone to go along with it?''

"Getting you on our side would go a long way toward convincing the others who are hesitant,'' Perry said. "What do you say? Will you support us?''

"I don't know. Let me think about it for a while,'' Hunter said. "I agree that we are going to have to do something. I can't continue to send in money-losing reports to my investors without showing that I am taking some steps to turn the situation around. But I don't think a private army is the answer.''

Although Jake Colby had come to Wyoming intending to start his own ranch, he quickly saw the difficulty in bringing his dream to fruition. Going into the ranching business, even as a small rancher, was an expensive proposition, and like so many others who had shared the dream before him, he found it impossible to put together enough money to make the step. The closest he could get to ranching was to work as a cowboy for one of the big ranchers.

His employer was Doyle Hunter, and the ranch was called the Rocking H. The Rocking H was located about halfway between Casper and Buffalo, Wyoming. It was a huge ranch of over one hundred thousand acres, and it ran several thousand head of cattle.

Jake justified working here by telling himself that he was learning the cattle business. And though it appeared that he was getting no closer to his goal, he never gave up the dream. The fantasy of his own spread often sustained him when he was watching over the herd at night or on one of the many long, lonely rides to repair broken fenceline.

It was early evening in the spring, and Jake and three others had been rounding up the Rocking H cattle that had wandered off the range during the winter just passed. More than a hundred head, the end product of their work, were in the holding pen outside, waiting to be driven back to rejoin the main herd.

It had been a hard day's work, and the four cowboys were inside the line shack. The line shack consisted of one room with four bunks and a stove that both warmed the shack and cooked the food. Jake and two others were sitting at the table, playing cards, while the fourth member of the group was standing over the woodstove, cooking their supper.

"What the hell's that you're a-cookin' over there, Ollie?" one of the card players teased, smiling and waving his hand in front of his nose. "Some dead skunk you found out on the trail?"

"Listen, if you don't want to eat it, Troy, you can always rustle up your own supper," Ollie replied, stirring the pot.

"Hell, didn't say I wasn't goin' to eat it," Troy answered. "It's your bet, Dooley. You in or out?" Troy asked impatiently. Then, to Ollie: "I just said it stinks, that's all."

"In for a penny," Dooley said, sliding a copper into the little pile in the middle of the table.

"Whoa! A penny!" Troy teased. "So much money! What do you think, Jake? If you win this hand you'll have enough to start that ranch you're always a-talkin' about!"

"Troy, you're as full of shit as a Christmas goose," Dooley said. "Don't pay no mind to him, Ollie," he said over his shoulder to the cook. "You know him. He'd eat the north end of a southbound mule while the mule was still walkin'."

Suddenly Ollie let out a little grunt of pain, spun around once, then fell to the floor.

"What the hell are you doin'?" Dooley asked, laughing at what he thought was a joke.

"Boys, I been shot!" Ollie gasped.

The laughter died in Dooley's throat as bullets began crashing through the glass windows and popping through the thin board walls of the little line shack, smashing crockery, careening off the iron stove, and projecting lead splinters and shards of glass like miniature bursts of shrapnel.

"My God! My God! What is it? What's happening?" Troy shouted.

Of the four men in the shack, Jake was the only one who had ever been under fire, and while the others were shouting in alarm, he was reacting. He rolled off his chair, dropped to the floor, then crawled over to the window while bullets continued to crash and whiz through the shack.

By now the little canyon was roaring with the thunder of gunfire, and when Jake looked out the window he saw three men hiding behind rocks, firing rifles at the cabin.

"Rustlers!" Jake yelled, but there was no one left to hear him, for when he looked back inside, he saw that the other three were already dead.

Jake knew that he had to get out of here or he would be dead, too. The walls of the cabin were so thin that they couldn't stop the bullets. The only protection they could offer would be to mask Jake's movement. Using that to his advantage, Jake managed to tear out a couple

of boards from the floor. As soon as the hole was big
enough, he crawled through it to get to the ground below
the cabin.

He felt the dank coolness of the dirt, smelled its odor,
and breathed a small prayer of thanks that he had come
this far without being hit. Whoever was shooting at the
cabin did not realize that Jake had slipped away, for the
bullets continued to crash through the cabin overhead
with the intensity of a heavy hail.

Lifting up his head just enough to see where he was
going, Jake slithered on his belly to the back of the
shack, then rolled down into a small depression that allowed him to move, undetected, several feet away. Here
he was able to let himself down into a gully that was
deep enough to allow him to stand. Once there, he
started running without looking back, until the sound of
gunfire behind him was no more ominous sounding than
corn popping on a stove.

Because he was unarmed, Jake could do nothing but
stay out of sight until the attackers were gone. He
watched from a distance as the three rustlers emptied the
holding pen. He was too far away to really see their
features, so he knew that even if he ran across any of
them in town, he probably wouldn't recognize them.

"Hey, Payson, what about the horses?" he heard one
of the men ask.

"Leave 'em," answered the one called Payson.

"Leave 'em? That's some good horseflesh there!" the
first rustler protested.

"Horses is too easy to identify. We got what we come
after. Let's get out of here."

The last thing the rustlers did before they left was set
fire to the shack.

Jake waited until the rustlers, and the cattle they took

from the holding pen, were well on their way before he came back to the line shack. By then, however, the shack was so consumed with flames that there was nothing he could do about it.

The horses were still in the lean-to. Fortunately they were far enough from the fire so as not to be in any real danger, though they were close enough to be on the verge of panic. They calmed down, however, when Jake showed up and began speaking to them soothingly, showing them that they had not been abandoned.

Jake watched the shack burn. Suddenly there were several gunshots, and Jake, frightened that the rustlers had returned, dove behind a nearby rock. Then, as the muffled gunshots continued to crack and pop, he smiled sheepishly, realizing that what he was hearing was the pistol and rifle ammunition that he and the other cowboys had had with them, cooking off in the flames of the burning line shack.

It was totally dark by the time the fire burned itself completely out. Jake decided to spend the night here so he could go through the ruins the next morning to see if he could salvage anything from the fire. He would have to have daylight to see, and anyway, he figured it would take that long before the burned shack was cooled off enough for him to search.

He spent the night on the ground, wrapped up in one of the horse blankets and warmed by the residual heat of the charred—and, in some places, still glowing—timbers. Early the next morning, as soon as there was enough light to see, Jake started poking through the ashes. He found nothing in the blackened ruins but the rusty hulk of the stove where Ollie had been cooking their supper with the pot of crusty hard beans still in place and a few twisted pieces of metal from the four iron bedsteads. The three bodies were grotesquely charred embers, burned beyond recognition.

The wooden stocks were burned off the rifles, and the handles out of the pistols, but Jake gathered them up nevertheless, thinking that perhaps a good gunsmith could salvage them.

Holding his nose and fighting the revulsion and the urge to vomit, Jake managed to get the three men buried. Then, after saddling his horse, he started back to the main house, bringing along the other three horses on a lead rope. Somehow the riderless horses seemed to sense a loss, for they were completely without spirit during the long ride back, hanging their heads almost as if in mourning for their lost riders.

When Jake reached the main house he turned the horses loose in the corral, then walked up the hill to the big house. He saw his employer, Doyle Hunter, dressed in a dove gray jacket, a dark blue silk vest, and a yellow silk shirt, sitting at a table on the veranda. There were two other elegantly dressed gentlemen with him, and they were being served lunch. Jake recognized the other two diners as Frank Wolcott and George Perry.

Perry was another large ranch owner, and Wolcott, now a rancher as well, claimed to have military experience fighting against the Sioux and the Apache. Jake couldn't speak for his Sioux experience, but he was pretty sure Wolcott had never fought against the Apache.

Jake came up onto the veranda but stopped just at the head of the steps. "Mr. Hunter?" Jake started.

Wolcott was in the midst of telling a story and he looked around, irritated at having been interrupted. Without answering Jake's query, Hunter held up his hand as a signal for him to remain silent, then turned his attention back to Wolcott.

Wolcott finished his tale, eliciting laughter from the other two men. Jake stood by stoically.

"All right, Colby, now, what is it?" Hunter finally asked. Almost at that same moment, Hunter realized that Jake wasn't supposed to be here, and his face twisted in disapproval. "Wait a minute, what are you doing here, anyway? You are supposed to be at one of the line shacks, aren't you?"

"Yes, sir, supposed to be, and I was, until last night."

"You left the line shack last night? Why?"

"Well, sir, I didn't exactly leave the line shack," Jake said. "It was more like the line shack left me."

"The line shack left you? What the hell are you talking about?"

"We were hit by rustlers last night," Jake explained. "Dooley, Troy an' Ollie and I were sitting down to supper. We never saw nor heard them comin'. They opened up on us, an' then they burned the shack down."

"The cattle, man! Did they get any cattle?"

"Yes, sir. They got the ones that were in the holding pen."

"How many?"

"A couple over a hundred," Jake answered.

"A hundred! Did you hear that, gentlemen? One hundred head of cattle."

"You may be interested in knowing that I happened to check the telegraph office before I left this morning," George Perry said. "Cattle closed at seventy-five dollars a head last night."

"Seventy-five dollars a head," Hunter said disgustedly. He looked at Jake. "And the rustlers helped themselves to one hundred head of my cattle while you men just stood by and did nothing? For God's sake, man, why didn't you stop them?"

"There wasn't anything we could do, Mr. Hunter,"
Jake answered.

"There wasn't anything you could do," Hunter par-
roted sarcastically. "Tell me, Colby, why the hell do you
think I pay you men good money to stay in those line
shacks? It's not to sit on your ass, eating my food! It is
to provide sentry duty so you can prevent just such a
thing as this from happening. I thought you were a man
of experience and action, an army scout and Indian
fighter. I was counting on your skills with a gun to prevent things like this from happening. Now, thanks to
your incompetence, I am out seven thousand five hundred dollars. Do you have any idea how much money
that is?"

"Yes, sir, it's a fair amount," Jake answered.

"I daresay it is. It's probably more than you and the
three who were with you will make for your entire, mis-
erable, lives."

"This is exactly the kind of thing we have been talking about, Doyle. This is why we need our own army.
We have to put a stop to this," Perry said.

"Damn!" Hunter said, hitting his palm with his fist.
"All right, George, Frank. Do whatever has to be done.
You can count on my support whenever it comes to a
vote. And you can tell the others that I'm voting for it.
I'm not going to sit around with my thumb up my ass
any longer and let rustlers run roughshod over the land.
By God, this is unbelievable! I mean, they just ride right
in and help themselves without so much as a 'by your
leave.' "

"No, and I don't blame you," Wolcott said. "You
gentlemen just leave it to me. I will take personal charge
of raising the army, sharpshooters who will get the job
done."

"Mr. Hunter, you haven't asked about Ollie, and Troy, and Doolie," Jake said.

Well, where are they, anyway? Afraid to see me, no doubt. I can't say as I blame them."

"They are still back there," Jake said.

"Typical," Hunter said disgustedly. "Keeping watch in case the bandits come back, I suppose. What they are doing is closing the barn door now that the horse is gone."

"No, sir," Jake said. "What they are doing is pushing up daisies. They're dead, all three of them."

"Dead?"

"Yes, sir."

Hunter was quiet for a moment, then he said, "Seventy-five hundred dollars lost, and three men dead. I tell you, boys, if we don't take a stand now, we're going to lose everything we've built out here to the rustlers. We can't afford it, the business can't afford it, and the state can't afford it."

"That's a fact," Wolcott agreed. "The state can't afford it. That's why I think we'll have no trouble getting the governor to grant me a state commission." He turned to Jake. "Did you see the rustlers?"

"Yes, sir, I saw them."

"Were they by any chance wearing a red sash?"

"I beg your pardon?"

"Around their waist," Wolcott said, indicating it with his hand. "Did they have a red sash tied around their bellies?"

Jake shook his head. "No, sir," he said.

"Not that you could see?"

"No, sir, none of them were wearing anything like that."

"No matter, they probably took it off so they wouldn't be recognized," Wolcott said.

"Mr. Hunter, what about the bodies?"

"What's that? What bodies?"

"Ollie, Troy, and Doolie. What are you going to do about them?"

"You said they were pushing up daisies. I assumed you buried them."

"I did, but I figured it was just temporary . . . to keep the wolves away from them. They didn't have coffins, or anything."

"They're cowboys, buried on the range," Hunter replied. "What could be more fitting? We'll leave them where they are."

"Good idea," Perry said.

Jake wondered if Hunter really believed that, or if he just didn't want to be bothered with them. But he said nothing.

"Anything else, Colby?" Hunter finally asked after a moment of silence.

"No, sir," Jake replied. With an almost imperceptible shake of his head, he turned and walked back down the steps.

When he reached the bottom of the steps he turned and looked back up toward the three big ranchers. They were deeply involved in a discussion as to how best to handle the rustlers and small ranchers . . . though Jake was hard-pressed to figure out what role the small ranchers played in all this.

Clearly the thing that most disturbed Hunter was the loss of his cattle. Outside the perfunctory mention of Ollie, Troy, and Dooley, the three cowboys never came up again. Not only did they no longer exist, it was almost as if they had never existed at all.

★ ★ ★

Four

Livermore, Colorado, didn't have much to offer a visitor. It was a one-street town with a few shacks made of whipsawed lumber, the unpainted wood turning gray and splitting, the houses leaning like trees bent by the wind. There was no railroad serving the town, so no signs of the outside world greeted Tom Horn as he arrived. It was a self-contained little community, inbred and festering.

It had been raining for the better part of a week, so the single street was filled with mud and nearly liquefied horse droppings. The horse's hooves made tiny sucking sounds as they were pulled from the muck, and Tom Horn wrinkled his nose against the smell as he rode into town.

He rode slowly, sizing it up with hooded blue eyes, wary as ever of any town he was coming into for the first time. He examined the buildings. There was a rooming house, a livery stable with a smithy's shop to one side, and a general store that said "Drugs, Meats, Goods" on its high false front.

Tom Horn had given up his idea of striking it rich as

a miner, though he had managed to come up with enough color at his diggings to cause an eastern combine to buy out his claim. He went through the money pretty quickly on a drinking, gambling, and whoring spree, and now he was back to earning his living. He had chosen the job he knew best, working for the Pinkerton Detective Agency—tracking, and sometimes killing, men.

He stopped in front of one of the more substantial-looking buildings of the town. It was a saloon, with painted red letters spelling out its name: "Bucket of Blood." He rode up to the hitch rail in front of the saloon, dismounted, pulled the seat of his trousers away from his crotch, then loosened the pistol in his holster.

Across the street from the saloon a small boy, sucking on a red-and-white peppermint stick, peered at him from the general store's front window. A woman's hand came from the shadows of the store to snatch the boy away.

"Who is that man, Mama?" the boy asked. The boy was about ten, towheaded and blue eyed.

"I don't know," the woman answered. The boy got his hair and eyes from her. She might have been pretty at one point in her life, but she was old now—old before her time. The sun and wind in the summer, rain and mud in fall and spring, and cold and snow in the winter had created a back-breaking life that made a twenty-eight-year-old woman look forty. She brushed an errant strand of hair from her face. "You stay away from that window. Whoever he is, it isn't any of our business."

"I betcha he's a gunman," the boy suggested.

The woman laughed. "I'm afraid you've been reading too many of those penny dreadfuls." She looked at the storekeeper. "Honestly, those so-called novels should be taken off the shelves. Still, he is reading, and there is something to be said for that.''

''They are popular books for all the boys Timothy's age,'' the storekeeper agreed.

''But they fill his head with such foolishness. Now, I'd like to look at some patterns if you have any new ones.''

The storekeeper smiled. ''Yes, ma'am, we truly do have some,'' he said. ''The latest fashions from St. Louis arrived by stage just last week.''

Unaware that he had been the subject of conversation, Tom Horn looked up and down the street. A few buildings away a door slammed and a shade came down on the upstairs window of the boardinghouse. A sign creaked in the wind, and flies buzzed loudly around a newly deposited and not yet liquefied pile of horse manure.

The sounds were magnified because despite the conversation in the general store, the street itself was silent. No one moved, and Tom heard no human voice. He knew people were around, though. There were other horses tied in front of the saloon.

He walked over to one of the horses, patted it on the flanks soothingly, then lifted its right hind foot. Scraping away the mud, he examined the shoe, a tie-bar shoe, matching the tracks he had been following. After putting the foot back down, he stepped up onto the porch, then pushed his way into the saloon.

The saloon had more to offer inside than one would suspect by its outside appearance. There was no gilt-edged mirror, but there was a real bar, with large jars of pickled eggs and sausages at each end, and towels, tied to rings, placed every few feet on the customer's side to

provide the patrons with a means of wiping their hands.
Tom used one of the towels to wipe away the mud and
manure he had gotten on his hands from examining the
horse's hoof.

The saloon had an upstairs section at the back. When
Tom glanced up, he could see rooms opening off the
second-floor landing. Even now a heavily painted saloon
girl was taking a cowboy up the stairs with her.

The upstairs area didn't extend all the way to the front
of the building. The main room of the saloon was big,
with exposed rafters below the high, peaked ceiling.
There were nearly a dozen tables full of drinking customers, though there were card games in session at a
couple of them.

Tom bellied up to the bar.

"What'll it be?" the barkeep asked as he moved
down to Tom. He wiped up a spill with a wet, smelly
rag.

"Whiskey," Tom said, putting two bits on the bar.

As the bartender poured the glass, one of the painted
women sidled up to him. There was no humor of life
left in her eyes, and when she saw that Tom wasn't
interested in her, she turned and walked back to sit by
the piano player.

The piano player wore a small, round derby hat, and
Tom chuckled as he looked at it because it reminded
him of the hat Jake Colby always wore when they were
scouting for the army. He wondered where Jake was
now and what he was doing. He felt a momentary nos-
talgia for his days with the army and for his two friends
Al Sieber and Jake Colby.

The piano player, perhaps responding to a request
from the girl who sat beside him, began pounding out a
rendition of "Buffalo Gals," though the music was

practically lost amid the noise of a dozen or more conversations.

One of the men at one of the tables got up and walked over to the bar, carrying his beer with him. There was a star on his shirt. He was about forty, and he eyed Tom with some trepidation.

"I don't see a badge, but you have the look of a lawman about you," the sheriff said.

"I'm working for Pinkerton," Tom answered.

"Same thing. You just passin' through?"

"Not exactly," Tom replied. "I've been following a trail. It led me here."

The sheriff took a drink of his beer as he studied Tom. "Three men?" he asked when he brought the mug down.

"Yes," Tom replied. "They held up a stage just outside of Denver. Do you know them?"

The sheriff shook his head. "Don't know 'em by name," he answered. "But three men rode in this morning that I'd never seen before. They had the look of hunted men about them, but when I checked, I couldn't find any paper on them."

"Far as I know, there aren't any dodgers out," Tom said. "I can describe 'em, though. One big man, with a scar on his face. Another, not quite as big, with red hair and a bushy red mustache . . . though he may have shaved the mustache by now. The third one is small and dark. His name is Eddie Franklin. He's the only one we know by name, because he's the brains of the outfit."

The sheriff nodded and took another drink. "Sounds like the three," he said.

"You have any idea where they might be right now?" Tom asked.

The sheriff raised his eyes toward the top floor. "Seen

'em all three go upstairs a while ago,'' he said.

Tom poured himself another drink, tossed it down, then set the glass on the bar. ''You want in on this?'' he asked the sheriff.

''You plannin' on killin' them?''

''Not unless I have to. They didn't kill anyone, they just held up the stage. I'm goin' to take 'em in, if they'll go without trouble.''

The sheriff shook his head. ''Well, they didn't do anything in my town,'' he said. ''And there's no paper on them. I don't have any jurisdiction.''

Tom knew the sheriff was finding excuses to avoid facing the three men, but it didn't matter. He would rather do it himself anyway.

''All right,'' Tom said. ''I'll handle it. Can I at least count on you to cover my backside?''

The sheriff looked around the saloon and, not seeing anyone he didn't know, nodded. ''Yeah,'' he said. ''You won't get any trouble from down here.''

''Thanks.''

Tom started up the stairs toward the second floor. By now several of the patrons had noticed the conversation between Tom and their sheriff and knew that something was about to happen.

Most of the conversation came to a halt, and the piano player, suddenly realizing that something had changed, stopped playing and looked around to see what was going on. The song came to an end in a few, discordant notes.

The patrons upstairs, made aware by the sudden silence that something must be amiss, paused in their various stages of activity. Some of the more curious stepped out into the hallway to see what was going on. Behind them, the whores also got out of bed and peeked through the doors in curiosity, clutching sheets about them in a vain attempt to preserve some modesty.

"Eddie! Johnny! They're after us!" someone suddenly shouted, and immediately upon the heels of his shout, a gun boomed.

Tom had just reached the top of the stairs at that moment, and the glass ball on the uppermost newel post of the stairway shattered from the outlaw's bullet, spraying out splinters of glass.

Tom returned fire, and the man who shot at him tumbled out into the hallway. This was the big man with the scar on his face. Amid shouts and screams, the other doors slammed as the men and women retreated back to their rooms.

Holding his still-smoking gun, Tom began moving down the hallway. He stopped at the room next to the one that had been occupied by the one who had challenged him, paused for a second, then kicked open the door.

The man inside was waiting for him, and as soon as the door was kicked open, he fired. Tom had jumped to one side immediately after kicking open the door, so the bullets whistled harmlessly through the opening. Dropping to one knee, Tom looked around the door frame. He saw a bushy redheaded man sitting on the bed, holding the pistol out in front of him. The man's eyes were open wide with alarm, and his face was set in a scowl of hate. The whore he had been with was crouched in a corner, screaming in terror.

"Hold it! We don't need to—"

But that was as far as Tom got before the man fired a second time. This bullet also missed, though it whizzed by his ear so close that Tom could feel the wind of its passing.

Tom returned fire, hitting the man in the chest. The outlaw fell forward across the bed, dropping his gun. Tom rushed into the room and kicked the gun across the floor.

"Where is the other one?" he asked the whore.

Terrified, the whore said nothing.

"There were three of them!" Tom said angrily. "Where is the other one?"

The whore pointed to the west wall, indicating that the third man was in the next room.

Eddie Franklin heard the shooting and knew immediately what was happening. What he didn't know was how many deputies were after them.

Damn! He thought. All this for $46, which was the total take from the stage holdup.

Eddie had a moment of panic, wondering what to do. Then, when he heard the shooting in Johnny's room, he decided it was time to leave.

After pulling on his boots and grabbing his hat, Eddie, who was otherwise totally nude, stepped through the upstairs window, crawled out onto the mansard roof, then dropped to the ground. What was left of the $46 was in the room behind him, still in his pants pocket.

"Mama!" Timothy shouted from the front window of the general store. His mother and the storekeeper had already been brought to the front window by the sound of gunfire from across the street. "Look!"

Timothy pointed to the naked man who had jumped down from the second-floor window. In broad daylight, and making no effort to cover his nudity, Eddie Franklin ran around the side of the saloon to the horses out front.

He untied one of them from the hitching rail and climbed into the saddle.

"Get! Get!" Timothy heard the man shout, and the horse bolted down the street at a gallop, the naked man in the saddle leaning forward in an effort to urge even more speed from his mount.

"Oh, my heavens!" Timothy's mother said, putting her hand over her mouth.

The storekeeper laughed out loud. "If that ain't the funniest damned thing I ever did see!" he shouted.

Timothy, too, was laughing.

"He was nekkid, Mama!" Timothy said. "Did you see that? That man was nekkid!"

"Yes, Timothy, I saw it," his mother replied, mortified with embarrassment.

Upstairs, Tom ran to the window at the end of the hall and looked outside, holding his pistol ready in the event he would be given the opportunity to take a shot at Eddie Franklin. When the opportunity didn't present itself, Tom holstered his pistol, then turned and started back down the hall to the head of the stairs. By now several curious onlookers had rushed upstairs and were crowding the hallway and the rooms, gawking at the two dead men. Even the whores stood by in morbid fascination, so intrigued by what they were seeing that they made no effort to cover their nudity. And so interested were the men in the two slain outlaws, they didn't even notice that the women were undressed.

Tom pushed his way down the crowded stairs, saying nothing to anyone. He stepped into the street, looked around for a moment, then picked up two baseball-size rocks and carried them back upstairs. Kneeling in turn beside each of the men he'd killed, without a word he placed a rock under their heads.

"What the hell, mister . . . ? What did you do that for?" someone asked.

Tom Horn didn't answer the question, but when he saw the sheriff he spoke.

"Sheriff, would you see to the buryin' of these two men? And when you're asked, be sure and tell them I offered these fellas the chance to give themselves up. Both of them fired at me first."

"I'll attest to that," the sheriff said. "I seen the way it happened."

"Thanks. Oh, and my name is Horn. Tom Horn."

The sheriff nodded quietly.

Without saying another word to anyone, Tom Horn went back downstairs, then out front, where he mounted his horse and rode away. Behind him the story of the night's exploit was already being told, refined, retold, and refined again. Soon it would become a part of the growing Tom Horn legend.

MEMPHIS, TENNESSEE

The Reverend Carl Jensen was pastor of the Holy Word Church in Memphis, Tennessee. He and his wife, Irene, were childless, so it seemed a natural enough thing for them to become the guardians of fourteen-year-old Laura Place when her mother and father were killed in a train wreck.

Laura's father, John, was Irene's younger brother, an investment broker who had enjoyed a better-than-average income. Thus Carl and Irene's act of Christian kindness in taking in the young orphan girl resulted in their being appointed custodians of a rather generous estate.

But that was six years ago, and by now a new house, new furniture, and more than one unwise investment had totally depleted the girl's inheritance. There was no money left in Laura's trust account, which meant that for the past year she had been a drain rather than an asset to the Jensen family's economic well-being.

The only remaining way to exploit the situation was to wear the responsibility of looking after Laura like stars in their crown, and that they did, with Irene frequently making the point.

"Despite the increased financial burden placed upon our meager income," she told the congregation, "my husband and I feel that Christian charity demands that we continue to provide a home for my poor, motherless niece."

The story played well among the faithful, so well that on two separate occasions the church board rewarded the Reverend Jensen with a generous increase in his salary.

But now Laura was ill. It started yesterday at her "time of the month." She told her aunt that she was having a much heavier flow than normal, including the passing of some clots. It was not a subject with which Irene was comfortable, so she'd passed it off. This morning, however, Laura complained of a general weakness, a severe backache, "bearing-down feelings," and, finally, very sharp abdominal pains.

Irene gave her a tablespoon of molasses with one ounce of ammonia, and that didn't help. When sulphate of magnesia and cinnamon water also failed to alleviate the pain or slow the flow, Irene sent for the doctor. She did so reluctantly, feeling that this was just one more example of how much the girl was costing them.

When the doctor arrived, Irene sent him upstairs to see to Laura, while she busied herself in the parlor, knitting a sweater. She sat there in her rocking chair for several minutes, wondering what could be taking the doctor so long to make a simple examination.

Upstairs, in Laura's bedroom at the end of the hall, the doctor finished his examination, then gave the twenty-year-old young woman something to make her sleep. When he reached the bottom of the stairs he saw Irene sitting placidly in the parlor, knitting the sweater.

"Are you finished with her?" Irene asked.

"Yes."

"It took you long enough. I suppose you'll be charging us an arm and a leg."

"Two dollars, Mrs. Jensen, my usual fee for a house call."

"Send the bill," Irene said. "The reverend will pay you when he can."

"Yes, I'm sure he will," the doctor replied dryly. He had dealt with the Jensens before, and though he knew he would eventually be paid, the process was always painfully slow. "Mrs. Jensen, I feel that there is something I must tell you . . . about your niece's condition."

"What is it?" Irene asked. It wasn't until that moment that she noticed the doctor's serious demeanor. "Oh, my! What is it, Doctor? Heavens, you look as if . . ." She paused in midsentence, then put her hand to her mouth. "Laura? Are you trying to tell me that Laura is seriously ill? That she is going to die?"

The Lord was punishing her, she thought. The Lord was punishing her for having had such unkind thoughts about her niece. Now Laura was going to die, and her death would be a stain on Irene's immortal soul.

The doctor shook his head, then held out his hand.

"No, no, nothing like that," he said quickly.

"Oh, thank goodness," Irene replied. "You had me frightened for a moment."

"Laura is fine," the doctor said. He cleared his throat and took a deep breath before continuing. "But I'm afraid she has lost the baby."

"*She has what?*" Irene gasped. "Did you say she has lost the *baby?*"

"I'm afraid so," the doctor said. He looked at the expression of shock on Irene's face. "She isn't married, is she?"

Mute, Irene shook her head.

"I take it by your reaction to the news that you were unaware of her condition?"

"Totally unaware. Doctor, are you certain?"

"Mrs. Jensen, I have seen my share of spontaneous miscarriages," the doctor replied. "I am quite sure."

"Yes, I . . . I'm sure you are," Irene stammered. She put down the sweater, then got up from the rocking chair and walked to the window, parting the curtains to look outside. "Uh, Dr. Presnell," she said without turning toward him.

"Yes?"

"You won't be saying anything about this to anyone, will you?" Now she turned to look at him. "I mean, it isn't necessary, is it?"

"I won't say anything," Dr. Presnell promised. "But it has been my experience that a young woman who is promiscuous enough to get pregnant out of wedlock once, might well do it again. And if it happens again, there is no reason she couldn't carry it to term. In such a case, it would be impossible to keep it secret."

"You let me worry about that," Irene replied.

Dr. Presnell recovered his hat from the hall tree, then

put in on as he started out. "I left some tincture of opium for the pain, and something to help her sleep," he said. "Just let her rest for a day or two, and she'll be all right."

"Yes, thank you, Doctor," Irene replied mechanically. "I'll see you to the door."

Laura was asleep when Irene stepped into her room. Irene stood at the door and looked at her for a long moment. Despite the fact that Laura was bloodkin, there was very little family resemblance, for Laura was everything Irene was not. Irene was short and dumpy, with mousy brown hair and a round, unattractive face. Her niece, on the other hand, was a beautiful young woman with long, auburn hair, a smooth peaches-and-cream complexion, high cheekbones, and large brown eyes.

"Wake up!" Irene said sharply. "Wake up, you, you harlot!"

Irene's sharp words awakened Laura, though as she was coming from a drug-induced sleep, she was dizzy and disoriented. She looked over toward her aunt.

"Aunt Irene?" she said groggily.

"How could you do such a thing"? Irene asked, the words dripping from her mouth like venom. "Don't you realize that your uncle Carl is a preacher? He has a reputation of morality and decency to uphold."

"What is it, Aunt Irene?" Laura asked, trying to clear the cobwebs from her mind. "Is something wrong? You seem upset."

"Upset? Upset?" Irene shouted. "Of course I am upset! Do you realize what a sin you have committed against the Reverend Jensen? Just what was in your mind, miss? Have you any idea what his congregation will think, what they might do, when they learn that the girl we have raised in Christian love and charity has turned out to be nothing more than a common harlot?''

"A . . . a what? I don't understand.''

"You don't understand the word 'harlot'? Then I'll make it easier for you! You are a whore! How dare you become pregnant out of wedlock while living in the house of a God-fearing man like your uncle!''

Laura gasped. "Pregnant? Oh, my God! Is that what's wrong with me? I'm pregnant?''

"You mean the doctor didn't tell you?''

"No, he didn't say anything. He just told me that I was having a difficult period. Wait a minute!'' Laura sat up in bed, now more confused than ever. "How can I be pregnant if I'm having my period?''

Irene sighed. "You aren't,'' she finally said. "At least, not anymore.''

"But you said . . .''

"I said you were pregnant. You *were*,'' Irene added. "You aren't pregnant now. God has corrected the mistake you made.''

"What do you mean?''

"The heavy flow and the clotting were signs of a miscarriage. God has struck dead the seed of the devil that was growing in your womb. All praise and glory be to His name,'' she said, holding her hands over her head.

"The baby is dead?'' For some strange reason Laura felt a sense of loss, a sadness over the child that she didn't even know she was carrying.

"Yes, thanks be to God, you will not be giving birth to a bastard child. Now, what I want to know is, who is the father?''

Laura didn't answer.

"I asked you, who is the father?''

"What does it matter who the father is, now that the baby is dead?"

"It matters because you didn't get pregnant by yourself. That means someone else knows of your sin and he may tell others."

Laura shook her head. "I'm sure we won't have to worry about that. He won't tell anyone."

"We can't be sure of that, can we? I want to know his name."

Again Laura shook her head, but this time she said nothing.

"I *demand* that you tell me what I want to know," Irene said shrilly.

"I can't. Don't try to force me to tell you. It would serve no useful purpose. All it would do would be to hurt more people unnecessarily."

"I see. So you don't mind hurting me, or the reverend. But you don't want to hurt the one who is the cause of it all. Is that it?"

"Please, Aunt Irene," Laura said again. "What is done is done. I will accept all the guilt."

"How could you do this to us? How could you?" she hissed. "After all we have done for you?"

"I'm sorry," Laura said.

"You're sorry," Irene said. "And you think that will take care of everything? You aren't a child anymore, Laura. A simple sorry will not set right the evil you have done." She glared at her niece for a moment longer, then whirled about and strode angrily from the room.

"How are you, my child?" a man's voice asked soothingly.

Again Laura was asleep, and when she heard her uncle Carl's voice, she woke with a start. Quickly she pulled the cover to her chin and looked up at him with large, frightened eyes.

"There, there, my dear," Carl said. He started to put his hand on her shoulder, but when she cringed he pulled it back. "You have nothing to fear from me," he said.

Laura was quiet.

"Your aunt Irene says that you haven't told her who the father was."

"No, I haven't," Laura replied. There was a beat of silence, then she added, "I . . . I lost the baby."

"Yes, I know, praise be to God."

"I didn't even know," Laura said. "I was pregnant and now the baby is gone, but I didn't even know."

"Yes, yes, well, that's all over now. And I think you are right not to tell who is responsible. It would serve no useful purpose at this point, and it could do irreparable damage to God's church. That is why you must leave."

"You're asking me to leave? But, where will I go? What will I do?"

"It is a big country. There are many places you can go. And, as to what you will do . . . Well, you are a very beautiful woman, my dear, and beautiful women have ways of making money. That was so even in biblical times, for Mary Magdalene was just such a person. I'm sure you know what I'm talking about."

"No, I don't know."

"But of course you know, my dear. After all, it isn't as if you are a virgin. You may as well get paid for what you have been doing. Many women are, you know."

Laura gasped. "My God! You are talking about prostitution! Uncle Carl, are you telling me to become a harlot?"

"I'm just suggesting that prostitution isn't all that different from what you have been doing for these last three years," Carl said. "Ever since that first night, when Satan moved into your soul to allow you to seduce me, you have traded your body and your favors for shelter and food."

Laura gasped. "I seduced *you?* No! No, it wasn't like that at all! You . . . you know I didn't want to do anything! It was *you* who came to my room late at night. It was *you* who made the demands! I had no choice!"

"But of course you had a choice, my dear," Carl replied. "I didn't beat you, did I? I didn't threaten to kill you if you didn't give yourself to me. Did you ever scream out in the night? Did you ever tell your aunt or anyone else about what was going on between us? Did I hold you in this house by force?"

"No, but—"

"No buts, my dear. You could have left at any time. At any time. And it would have been much better for both of us if you had. But, I forgive you."

"You forgive me?"

"Yes. For in a way, it wasn't you, it was Satan himself who took control of your body and soul, and who worked his way with me . . . through you.

"But now I have found the strength to say, 'Get thee behind me, Satan.' This evilness is over. The fornicator has been discovered, and she will be out of this house before any more damage is done."

Suddenly a cold and calculating calmness came over Laura. No longer would she be a victim. No longer would she be frightened of her uncle.

"I will leave, Uncle. But it is going to cost you five hundred dollars."

"Five hundred dollars? Why, that's a fortune, child! You know that I don't have that kind of money."

"Then you had better find some way to get it. I will need that money to get started in my new life, and I'm not leaving without it," she said. "Besides, you owe it to me."

"I owe you nothing! I have fed and clothed you for six years. . . ."

"And fucked me for three," Laura added flatly.

Carl gasped and put his hand to his heart. "My God, girl, listen to you! Do you hear Satan talking through you?"

"Talking *through* me?" Laura said. She smiled, and the smile was totally without mirth. "Don't you understand, you sorry son of a bitch? Satan is talking *for* me."

"Fall on your knees!" Carl said. "Fall on your knees and beg God for forgiveness!"

"I don't need forgiveness," Laura said coldly. "What I need is five hundred dollars, and you will give it to me, or . . . Satan and I will tell Aunt Irene—and the good people of the church—about the little 'secret' you and I have shared for the last three years. Now, which will it be, Uncle? Five hundred dollars and my quiet departure? Or a scandal that will rock Memphis and make the Mississippi River run backward?"

"I'll have the money for you tomorrow," Carl promised.

"Good. You do that, Uncle, and Satan and I will be on the train on our way out of here tomorrow night," she replied.

★ ★ ★

Five

Eddie Franklin was not dressed in standard trail gear. In fact, except for the gray, misshapen, sweat-stained Stetson, he was attired in no particular way that would classify him or identify him as belonging to a certain occupation. However, given that the Stetson and boots were his only items of apparel when he left Livermore, Colorado, he was fortunate to be wearing anything at all.

Over a red flannel shirt he had a brown tweed jacket. His dove gray striped trousers once belonged to a gentleman's formal evening ensemble. Eddie was not wearing them out of any sense of style, but only because when he broke into the secondhand clothing store, they were the only trousers he could find that would fit.

When he jumped out of the window of the saloon he was holding his pistol in his hand, but he had left behind his gunbelt and holster. As a result, he was now forced to carry his pistol stuck in the waistband of his trousers. He knew that he made a thoroughly ridiculous-looking sight, and he wasn't looking forward to the greeting he would get from his friends when he returned to Hole in the Wall.

Eddie, like many other out-of-work cowboys, had taken matters, and a gun, into his own hands to ride a crooked trail. Hole in the Wall was the preferred place of rendezvous for such men: rustlers, horse thieves, and robbers. It was a barren, empty valley approximately fifty miles south of Buffalo and one day's hard ride north of Casper and just east of the grazing lands of the Powder River country.

Hole in the Wall was a basin, hemmed in by rugged mountains and a sheer, thousand-foot-high red wall to the north. There were also numerous caverns and passages where anyone familiar with the place could hide out for days. And because the mountains blocked out the wind, there was always an eerie silence inside, dominated by hot rock and sweet grass in the summer and pristine white snow in the winter.

The main entrance to the valley was a very narrow gorge. This gorge was kept under constant observation by guards, thus providing the men and women who lived inside with as much security as if they were fortified in a medieval castle. This narrow-entrance gorge was the reason the place was called Hole in the Wall.

As Eddie rode north he saw another rider sloping down a ridge, coming toward him and obviously headed for the same place. Eddie stopped and pulled his pistol. If it was someone who didn't know where Hole in the Wall was, he certainly wasn't going to lead him to it.

After watching the approaching rider for a couple of minutes, however, he saw the red sash around the man's belly, so he smiled and put his pistol back into his waistband. The approaching rider was Nate Champion, leader of a group of small ranchers and cowboys. They called themselves the Red Sash Gang because of the red sash they wore. Nate described the Red Sash Gang as a poor man's version of the Wyoming Stock Growers' Association. The members of the Red Sash Gang were friendly to the ex-cowboys and outlaws who lived in Hole in the Wall. They were more than friendly, they were the outlaws' primary market, for most of the cattle rustled from the large ranchers wound up with running brands on one of the smaller ranches in nearby Johnson County.

"With their laws and unfair policies, the big ranchers steal from us, so we steal from them," members of the Red Sash Gang told all who would listen, justifying not only their existence, but also their practice of receiving stolen cattle.

"Why are you dressed so, Eddie?" Nate asked when he came alongside.

"Are you going to a costume ball?"

"By God, I'm lucky to be wearin' anything at all," Eddie replied.

"Why? What happened to you?"

As they rode side by side, Eddie told the story of being surprised by the law while in a whorehouse in Colorado. He added a few embellishments, making it an entire posse instead of just one man and throwing in a gunfight in which he believed he at least "winged a couple." By the time he was finished with the story, Nate was whooping with laughter and Eddie, gratified to have someone to talk to after his long, solitary escape, laughed with him.

"Wait till they hear that tale inside," Nate said. "That'll keep the fellas laughing for days."

"What are you doing up here, anyway, Nate? You joining with us?"

"No," Nate replied. "I'm still trying to make a go of it with my ranch."

Eddie snorted. "You don't really think the big cattlemen are going to let any of you small ranchers survive, do you?"

"I know they're going to try and put us out of business," Nate said. "But I'll be damned if I'm going to let them do it. That's why I'm in here. I'm looking to get a good buy on a few more head."

"Ha!" Eddie laughed. "Well, I reckon you'll get about as good a buy in here as you're going to find anywhere."

Suddenly Nate held up his hand as a signal for them to stop.

"What is it?" Eddie asked.

"I just saw a flash of light up there," Nate said. "They've seen us."

"Yep," Eddie replied. "Come on, we'll go on in. They'll be watchin' us pretty close now, until they figure out who we are."

The two man sat erect in their saddles, riding slowly but resolutely toward the opening of the gorge. This was the prescribed ritual for anyone who was going inside. Even now, concealed rifles were trained on them, and it always made Eddie feel a little on edge, knowing that his survival depended upon a nervous guard and an itchy finger. What made him even more anxious was the realization that the guards who watched the entrance were normally selected from the newest, youngest, and most unstable of the group.

Not until one of the guards showed himself, standing up and holding his rifle down around his knees, did

Eddie and Nate relax. By the time they reached the far end of the gorge, nearly a dozen people had come out to watch them ride in, for Hole in the Wall was so isolated that the arrival of anyone from the outside was an exciting break in their routine.

"That's some outfit you're wearin' there, Eddie!" someone called, and the others, noticing his strange garb, began to laugh.

"Wait till he tells you the story of how he come by it," Nate said. "It's the funniest damn thing I ever heard."

A young woman with mousy brown hair and a round, rather plain-looking face came out of the crowd. Eddie recognized her as Johnny Howard's girlfriend, and he tried to avoid looking into her eyes. He didn't want to have to tell her what happened, but she was determined to get his attention, and finally he knew that he could put her off no longer. He looked at her.

"Howdy, Lucy," he said quietly.

"Where is he, Eddie?" she asked. "Where's Johnny Howard?"

Eddie took off his hat and stared at it for a long moment.

"Eddie?" Lucy asked, her voice rising in concern. "Where is he?"

"I'm sorry, Lucy," he said. "Johnny got hisself killed."

Lucy put her hand over her mouth, then let out a long, heartrending scream.

"Lucy, I'm sorry," Eddie said. "There wasn't nothing I could do."

Shaking her head no, Lucy turned, then ran away, sobbing uncontrollably. Two more women hurried to her side to comfort her.

A tall man with a fleshy, prominent nose, dark brown hair, a thick mustache and flashing black eyes came out to meet Eddie and Nate. This was Joe Curry, and while there was no such thing as a mayor of Hole in the Wall, if there had been, Joe would have been the mayor.

"I see that Bert isn't with you, either," Joe said. "Was he killed, too?"

Eddie nodded.

"You three boys tore out of here, bound and determined you were going to make your fortune down in Colorado. It didn't turn out that way, did it?"

Eddie shook his head. " 'Fraid not," he replied quietly.

"Uh-huh," Joe said. He sighed. "Well, next time you're in Buffalo, you'd better tell Bert's sister what happened."

"Yeah, I guess I'd better."

Nate cleared his throat. "Now I feel like a fool, talking about how funny everything was," he said. "Didn't stop to think they was two good men killed."

"Hell, Nate, don't worry about it," Joe replied. "If Johnny and Bert was here, they'd be wantin' to hear a good story."

That night, after a good meal, Eddie, who had changed into more suitable clothes, told the story of his ill-fated venture. He embellished Bert's and Johnny's roles, insisting that their early warning and "holding off the posse" had allowed him to escape with his life, if not with his clothes.

"You know the name of the lawman who was chasing you?" Joe asked.

"Yes, I heard it spoke," Eddie said. "But I'd never heard of him before, so it didn't mean anything to me. But I'll say this for him. He's a damned determined kind of a man. He got onto our trail and hung on it like a bird hound.''

"What was his name?'' Joe asked.

"Tom Horn.''

"Did you say Tom Horn?'' Nate said, reacting.

"Yes. Why? Have you heard of him?'' Eddie asked.

"I should smile, I've heard of him,'' Nate said. He looked at Joe. "Joe, you mean you haven't ever heard of him?''

"Can't say as I have,'' Joe admitted.

"Well, hell, he's about the best scout the U.S. Army ever had, is all,'' Nate said. "I've read about him in·the newspapers. He was the one who brought Geronimo in. He's also supposed ·to be one crackerjack rider and roper. To say nothing of being a deadly shot.''

"I can testify as to how good a shot he is,'' Eddie said. "And tracker,'' he added.

"And you say this all happened down in Colorado?'' Joe asked.

"Yes.''

Joe leaned over the roasting spit and carved off a piece of meat from the haunch that was dripping juices onto the fire.

"Well, all I can say is, I hope the son of a bitch stays in Colorado and keeps the hell out of Wyoming,'' Joe said as he blew on the meat to cool it, then took a big bite.

Although Eddie Franklin had looked over his shoulder all the way back to Wyoming and Hole in the Wall, he need not have worried about Tom Horn. Even before Eddie left Livermore, Colorado, events were already unfolding in Kansas that would take Tom Horn off Eddie's trail and start him in pursuit of another.

In Topeka, Kansas, two men, one named Angus Pike and the other Deke Craven, robbed and murdered a Pacific Railroad Express agent and his wife, then took turns raping their fourteen-year-old daughter. When they were finished they left behind an enraged community and the soul-scared shell of a once vibrant young girl.

The railroad hired Pinkerton Detective Agency to find the men and bring them to justice. The two men had fled the state, but they couldn't outrun Western Union messages, which traveled with the speed of lightning, and when the two were spotted in Colorado a telegram put Tom Horn on their trail.

As Tom rode across the high desert country, he could hear the metal bit jangling against the horse's teeth. Hooves clattered on the hard rock, and the leather saddle creaked beneath his weight. Tom pulled his horse to a stop, then dismounted, unhooked his canteen, and took a swallow of water. He poured some water into his hat and held it in front of his horse. The horse drank thirstily, then nudged Tom for more.

"Sorry. I know it isn't much," Tom said to his horse. "But for now, it will have to do."

Tom walked for a while. He couldn't give his horse any more water, but he could relieve him of the burden of carrying any extra weight.

Just before nightfall he came across the monastery that had been his destination. Sangre de Cristo had been built by the Spanish one hundred years earlier and was still being used for its original purpose. Except for the members of the religious order who lived in the monastery, no one, Indian or white, lived within fifty miles of the place, and as far as anyone could tell, no one had ever lived here. That begged the question as to why the monastery had been built in this location in the first place, and even more curious, why did the religious order continue to occupy it?

Tom had asked that question of Father Santos when he was here before, and Santos had replied enigmatically: "The answer is a mystery, and the mystery is the answer."

Angus Pike and Deke Craven were wanted criminals with long records. As a result, their faces were on Wanted posters that were plastered over half a dozen states. Nearly everywhere they went someone recognized them, and if they didn't have the courage to confront the two men themselves, they were at least able to keep the law posted on the men's whereabouts.

A bartender recognized them in Orchard, Colorado. He overheard them talking about the town of Carr, where Pike had a brother. That was the information that was telegraphed to Tom Horn, who immediately headed southeast from Carr. It was his plan to get to Sangre de Cristo before Pike and Craven did. He had no doubt but that they would show up there. Anyone leaving the railroad right-of-way and cutting across the desert country to Carr would have to stop at the monastery, for there was no other source of food or water within several miles in either direction.

Tom reached Sangre de Cristo just before dark. The monastery was surrounded by high stone walls and secured by a heavy oak gate. When Tom pulled on a rope attached to a short section of log, the makeshift knocker banged hard against the large, heavy gates, creating a booming thunder that resonated through the entire monastery. A moment later a small window slid open and a brown-hooded face appeared in the opening.

"Who are you?" the face asked nervously.

"My name is Tom Horn."

"What do you want?"

"I want food, water, and shelter for the night."

"I'm sorry. We can grant no entry."

"But, Brother, I am out of water. You can't turn me away," Tom said.

"I am truly sorry," the monk said. "God go with you." The little window slammed shut.

Tom had been here before and had never been denied entry. In fact, he knew the gatekeeper personally, a man named Brother Mathias. Brother Mathias had a weakness for hoarhound candy, and Tom sometimes brought the confection to him. Therefore he knew from the very beginning of their conversation, when Brother Mathias asked who he was, that something was wrong. Brother Mathias was trying to send Tom a message.

Angus Pike and Deke Craven were standing just inside the gate. Craven was peering through the crack between the timbers of the gate.

"What's he doin'?" Pike asked.

"He's ridin' off," Craven answered.

Pike chuckled, then put away his pistol. He looked at the short, overweight monk. "You done that real good, Padre," he said. "I don't think he suspects a thing."

"I am not a priest," Brother Mathias answered. "Therefore it is not proper to address me as Padre."

"Yeah, well, brother, father, padre, reverend, pastor, what the hell difference does it make? All you religious guys are called somethin'. Come on, let's go see if the cook has our supper finished. I'm starvin'."

The three men walked back across the little courtyard, which, because of the irrigation and loving care bestowed upon it by the brothers of the order, was lush with flowers, fruit trees, and a vegetable garden. There were a dozen or more monks in the yard, each one occupied by some specific task.

The building they entered was surprisingly cool, kept that way by the hanging ollas that, while sacrificing some of the precious water by evaporation, more than repaid the investment by lowering the temperature by several degrees.

"Who was at the gate?" Father Santos asked.

"A stranger, Father. I do not know who he was," Brother Mathias replied.

"And you denied him sanctuary?"

"I had no choice, Father," Brother Mathias said, rolling his eyes toward Pike and Craven.

"You sent him away?" Father Santos asked Pike and Craven.

Pike was a big ugly man with yellow eyes, a drooping eyelid, and a puffy scar passing through the eyelid and coming to a hook under his nose.

Craven was much smaller, with a ferretlike face and skin heavily pocked from the scars of some childhood disease.

"He wasn't no ordinary visitor," Pike said. "His name was Tom Horn. I've heard of him. He's not exactly someone we want around right now."

"I see," Father Santos said. "Still, to turn someone away is unthinkable. We have always obeyed our Christian imperative to offer water, food, and shelter to those who ask it of us."

"Yeah, well, you're showin' all that by takin' care of us," Pike answered. "Now, what about that food? How long does it take your cook to fix a little supper?"

"Forgive me for not mentioning it the moment you came in," Father Santos said. "The cook has informed me that your supper is ready."

"Well, now, that's more like it! Why didn't you say somethin'?"

"What is this?" Pike asked a moment later when a bowl of beans was set on the table before them.

"This is your supper."

"This is it? Beans? What about that Christian kindness you were talkin' about? You didn't offer us no meat," Pike growled.

Father Santos shook his head. "I'm sorry. In this order we do not eat meat. This is our regular fare. We cannot offer you what we do not have."

"It ain't that bad, Angus," Craven said, lifting a spoon to his mouth. "It ain't bad at all, and it sure beats jerky."

Tom waited until it was dark before he returned to the monastery. Leaving his horse hobbled, he slipped up to one of the side walls, then, using chinks and holes in the stone facade to provide foot and handholds, and the night to provide cover, he climbed up, slipped over the top, and dropped to the ground inside.

Most of the buildings inside the monastery were dark, for candles and oil for lamps were precious commodities to be used sparingly. Here and there, however, a flickering light managed to escape, and a full, bright moon kept it from being too dark. The chapel, dormitory, stable, storage, and grain buildings gleamed like white blossoms in the soft, silver light.

The night was alive with the long, high-pitched trills and low violalike thrums of the frogs. For counterpoint there were crickets, the long, mournful howl of coyotes, and, from the stable, a braying mule and a whickering horse.

With his gun in hand, Tom moved toward the chapel,

staying in the shadows along the wall. He found a window and looked inside. There he saw Pike and Craven, whom he recognized from their pictures on the Wanted posters. He also saw Father Santos. Pike and Craven were pointing their pistols at Father Santos, who was clutching a chalice and cross to his chest.

"Please," he heard Father Santos's pleading voice. "You cannot take the chalice and the cross. They are sacred relics, given to the service of God by the king of Spain more than one hundred years ago. Ten abbots before me have kept them safe. I will not be the one who loses them."

"They're made out of gold, ain't they?" Pike asked.

"Yes."

"Then I'm takin' 'em."

"You will have to kill me first," Father Santos insisted.

"Well, hell, preacher man, killin' you ain't no problem," Pike said, cocking his pistol.

"Boys, my name is Tom Horn!" Tom shouted. He was outside the chapel, looking through the window. This was certainly not the most advantageous position from which to challenge them, but he had no choice. Pike was about to kill Father Santos. "Put your guns down and come outside!"

"What the hell! Where did he come from?" Pike shouted. He snuffed out a candle by his side, plunging the chapel into darkness so that Tom could no longer see anyone inside. But because he was outside and lighted by the brightness of the moon, he was very visible to both Pike and Craven. Both fired at him.

Tom felt a hammer blow to his shoulder. He returned fire, using the flame pattern of one of the outlaws' guns as his target. He heard someone groan, then fall. A mo-

ment later he heard a crash of glass from the other side
of the building and realized that the other outlaw had
jumped through the window. Hurrying around the building, Tom saw a man running toward the stable.

"Hold it right there!" he called. "I've got a bead on
you!"

Whoever was running turned and fired, and Tom
heard the bullet graze off the building behind him. He
fired back, and the runner dropped his pistol, then put
his hands on his chest. Tom saw his adversary fall before, to his surprise, he found himself growing very
dizzy.

"Mr Horn! Mr. Horn, are you all right?" Father Santos called, coming from the chapel.

"No, I'm not. I feel . . ." Tom felt himself starting to
fall . . . then everything went black.

Deke Craven was the outlaw Tom had shot in the dark
room. Angus Pike was the one who tried to get away,
only to be shot down outside. Both Pike and Craven died
of their wounds during the night.

The next morning the brothers had the two outlaws'
bodies lying out in front of the chapel, and they watched
with stoic curiosity as Tom, who was now so feverish
with his wound that he could barely walk, very metic-
ulously placed a rock under the head of each. He stood
there for a moment, looking down at them, hoping that
their deaths would, somehow, comfort the mother and
the young girl they had so brutally raped.

Then he saw an amazing thing. Even though these
were the same two outlaws who had been in the process
of stealing their most precious artifacts, the brothers of
Sangre de Cristo prayed for their eternal souls, then bur-

ied them, if not in the consecrated graveyard, then at least on the grounds.

It was two more weeks before Tom, his shoulder patched and now nearly mended, was ready to leave the monastery. During the two weeks he spent there he found much to admire in the way the monks lived their lives of quiet service and selfless devotion. He contrasted that with his own life of danger and violence. He spoke to Father Santos about what he was feeling and thinking.

"The thing is, Father, I haven't always been a good man," he admitted. "I've drunk a lot, whored a lot, and I've killed. Mostly, I've only killed those who needed killin'."

"It is not for us to judge who needs killing," Father Santos said. "All are God's children. Do you think He loves some more and others less?"

"Don't reckon I ever thought of it that way," Tom replied. "At least, not before now. Those two galoots I killed were as evil as anyone who ever lived, yet the brothers prayed for their souls and mourned over their deaths like they were one of their own."

"In that we *all* children of God, they *were* our brothers," Father Santos said. "That made them, as you say, one of our own."

"Yeah, well, I have to tell you, I was powerfully impressed by that," Tom said. "So, I've been wondering, what if I gave up the life I been livin' and started livin' like the brothers?"

"Praise be to God. I'm sure the brothers of Sangre de Cristo would be very pleased to know that they have set an example by which a man could change his life," Father Santos replied. "For it is by touching lives like yours that we are able to reach the outside world."

"No," Tom said, rubbing his chin. "I don't think you

understand what I'm gettin' at, Father. What I'm sayin' is, I'd like to be one of the folks livin' here. I'd like to become a . . . what do you call 'em? Monks? Brothers?''

Father Santos was quiet for a long moment, then he put his hand on Tom's shoulder. ''Son, you don't know how it pleases me to hear you make such a declaration. But I'm afraid you haven't actually thought it through. Of course you are grateful to the brothers for treating your wounds, and you have found much to admire in them. That is to be expected, and it is a good and noble thing that you want to be one of them. However, before you can *become* one of them, perhaps you should spend some time *being* like them.''

''Being like them? What do you mean?''

''When you leave here you must try, to the best of your ability, to live a godly and righteous life,'' Father Santos said. ''Do that for four or five years, then come back to the monastery and we will gladly receive you as one of us.''

Tom stroked his mustache. ''What you're tellin' me is, I have to live a life just like these fellas, no drinkin', no whorin', none of that, for four or five years before I can join up with you?''

''Yes.''

''Well now, it's easy enough for these fellas to do that,'' Tom said. ''They're in here, where there ain't no drinkin' and whorin' to be had. But I'm goin' to be out there, where it's everywhere.''

''Facing daily temptation, yes, I know,'' Father Santos said.

''I don't think I can do it,'' Tom said.

''We all fall short of God's expectations of us,'' Father Santos said. ''But we are never excluded from His love. Do the best you can.''

"All right," Tom said. He sighed. "I reckon the first thing I ought to do is get out of the job of killin' people . . . even them that needs killin'."

On the afternoon of the day before he left, Tom Horn composed a letter to send to the Pinkerton office in Denver. In the letter he tendered his resignation.

"You have a fine organization, but I have no more stomach for it," he said in the letter. "Please take me off your role of active agents, as I intend to seek employment elsewhere."

★★★

Six

Jake Colby checked the return address on the letter that had been sent to him at the ranch and compared it with the address on the building in front of him. When he saw that the addresses matched and, indeed, the painted sign identified this as the office of "Jay Northington, Attorney at Law," he dismounted and tied his horse off at the hitching rail out front. He reread the letter.

Dear Mr. Colby,

My name is Jay Northington, and I am an attorney at law, practicing in Casper, Wyoming. If, at your convenience, you would be so kind as to visit me at my office in Casper, we can conduct some business that will be to our mutual benefit. I look forward to meeting with you, soon.

Yours Sincerely,
Jay Northington
Attorney at Law

Jake had no idea what necessary business the lawyer was talking about, but he was able to get permission from the ranch foreman to ride into town and find out.

When he stepped inside, the rather smallish but nattily dressed man who was sitting at a rolltop desk looked up.

"May I help you, sir?" he asked.

"Are you the lawyer?" Jake asked.

"Oh, good heavens, no, sir, I am not a member of the bar," the man replied with a nervous laugh. "I am Mr. Thorndike, Mr. Northington's legal clerk."

"Northington, yes, that's the name. I need to see him."

"Have you an appointment?"

"Well, I've got this letter. He asked me to come see him."

Thorndike removed his wire-rim glasses and polished them, then put them back on and took the letter from Jake and glanced through it.

"Ah, yes, sir, of course."

"Of course what?" Jake asked, still confused by the whole thing.

"If you'll just wait here a moment, sir, I shall inform Mr. Northington of your presence."

"Yeah, but what I want to know is, what the hell is this all ab—?" That was as far as Jake got with his shouted question before Thorndike disappeared through a door in the back of the room.

Left alone in the outer office, Jake looked at the letter again, as if by reading it one more time, he could ascertain what Northington wanted with him. It didn't help, so he turned his attention to examining the lawyer's office. On the wall, a ticking Regulator clock measured the time. Beside the clock was a stuffed moose head and, beside that, a painting of a train going through a mountain pass at night, with every window of every car unrealistically lighted. A United States flag stood in a stand at one corner of the wall, and the Wyoming State flag was at another.

"Mr. Colby?" a new voice said.

Jake looked toward the speaker and saw a man of medium height, with thinning ash blond hair and a ruddy complexion. Like Thorndike, he was wearing a suit, but even though Jake didn't know clothes, he could tell that this suit was of much better quality than the one worn by Thorndike. In addition, the suit was accented by a gold watch chain that stretched across the man's chest. "I'm Jay Northington, attorney at law," the man said. He pulled open a little gate in the railing that separated the reception room from the clerk's area. "Won't you come into my office?"

"What's this all about, Mr. Northington?" Jake asked. "As far as I know, I'm not in any kind of trouble, so I don't see why I need a lawyer."

"Please," Northington said, holding out his hand in invitation. "If you will be patient for just a moment, it will all be explained to you."

Jake was about to speak again, then he accepted the lawyer's invitation to patience. Actually, curiosity had already brought him this far, so there was no way he wasn't going to see it out to the end. He shrugged once, then followed Northington into his office.

"Have a seat, Mr. Colby," Northington invited him.

Jake sat in a chair alongside Northington's desk as Northington pulled a folded paper from one of the several cubbyholes. "Ah, here it is," he said, unfolding the paper. He called over his shoulder to his clerk.

"Mr. Thorndike, would you please come in here to witness the reading of the will?"

"Yes, sir," Thorndike answered, coming into Northington's office in response to the call.

"Reading of the will? What will?" Jake asked.

"The last will and testament of Oliver Henderson."

"Ollie?" Jake snorted. "Hell, Ollie didn't have a pot to piss in, nor a window to throw it out of. What was he doing with a will?"

"Oh, but you are wrong, Mr. Colby," Northington said. "True, Mr. Henderson wasn't a wealthy man, but he was a prudent one. Last year, it seems, he took out a life insurance policy, naming his estate as the beneficiary. Then he made out a will to disburse the estate."

"I'll be damned," Jake said.

"It is a very short will," Northington went on. "But perfectly legal." He cleared his throat, then read aloud: "I, Oliver Henderson, being of sound mind and body, leave all my money to be divided equally amongst my three pards: Jake Colby, Troy Gibson, and Dooley Jones. If one of them should precede me in death, the money will be divided equally among whoever is still alive."

The lawyer laid down the paper, then looked at Jake. "You are the only one still alive," he said. "Therefore, the entire amount goes to you."

"How much is it?" Jake asked, absolutely shocked by the information.

"After I deduct my fee, you will receive a bank draft for four thousand four hundred and twelve dollars and seventeen cents."

"Well, I'll be damned," Jake said. "Who would've ever thought that? I wonder why Ollie did such a thing?"

"I can only tell you what he told me when he came in to have the will drafted," Northington said. "He had no relatives, or at least none of which he was aware, and he didn't want to, to quote him: 'Leave this world without so much as a scratch mark to show that I was here.' I think he just wanted to make certain someone would remember him.''

"There's not much of a chance I'll ever forget him," Jake said. "Not now."

Northington pulled another piece of paper from his desk. This was a bank draft for the amount he had mentioned. There was also a receipt attached to it.

"If you would be so kind, Mr. Colby, as to sign this receipt, I'll turn this bank draft over to you."

"All right," Jake said, signing the document.

Northington handed him the check. "There you are, Mr. Colby. You are now a man of means," he said.

"Thank you," Jake said, taking the money. He looked at it for a moment, then looked up at Northington. "Mr. Northington, I wonder if I could hire you to do something for me?"

"Of course," Northington answered. "What do you have in mind?"

"I would like for you to find a piece of land I could buy with this money," he said.

"Residential, commercial, farmland? What?"

"Rangeland," Jake said. "A place with water and grass where I can run a few head of cattle."

"I'll be glad to look around for you."

"Don't worry about whether or not it has a house or barn or anything," Jake said. "Right now, all I'm interested in is the land. The buildings and the stock will come later."

"And if I find such a place?"

"Buy it," Jake said. "And when you fill out the papers, call it the OH Ranch."

"OH?"

Jake smiled. "For Ollie Henderson," he said. "That way he'll be remembered for as long as the ranch lasts. And that's going to be for as long as I live," he added emphatically.

When Jake Colby told Doyle Hunter that he was planning on buying some land and starting a small ranch, Hunter didn't appreciate the idea.

"I'm short of men as it is," Hunter said. "What with Hank, Dooley, and Troy gettin' themselves killed."

"Don't worry about that, I'll be glad to continue to work for you, Mr. Hunter," Doyle said. "At least part-time, until I get on my feet."

"No, I'm afraid that won't be possible," Hunter replied. "I've signed an agreement with the other members of the Wyoming Stock Growers' Association. We will not hire any cowboys who own their own ranch."

"Why not?"

"Why not? Because people like you have only one way to build up their herd, that's why. And that's by stealing."

"I'm not a cattle rustler, Mr. Hunter."

"I'm sure you're not. Not now," Hunter replied. "But many a man who started out with good intentions has wound up throwing a long rope. And face it, Colby. There is absolutely no way a small rancher can make it."

"Why not? There are a lot of ranches in Wyoming. Some of them must be paying off."

"Do you have any idea what you are going to be up against? Blizzards in the winter, droughts in the summer, fluctuating cattle prices at the market . . . All of that combines to make the profit margin very small."

"If the cost of running the ranch is kept very low,

then the amount of profit I have to make will also be low,'' Jake insisted.

''Uh-huh. And how do you intend to keep the cost of running your ranch so low?''

Jake took off his small derby hat and began turning it in his hand, examining it closely as he did so. ''For one thing, I won't have a payroll to worry about. I'm going to run the ranch myself. I also intend to keep my stock investment low by rounding up all the mavericks I can find.''

''There's a fine line between rounding up mavericks and out-and-out rustling,'' Hunter said.

''Why, that's not true,'' Jake said. ''What's more, Mr. Hunter, you know it! Wasn't my main job last year roundin' up mavericks and puttin' your brand on 'em?''

''That was different,'' Hunter insisted. ''Chances are that many if not most of those mavericks were mine in the first place.''

''Not all of them came from the Rocking H, Mr. Hunter. You'll remember that you sent Ollie and me out into the breaks, looking for unbranded calves. And I know for a fact that those weren't yours.''

''I didn't do anything wrong,'' Hunter said.

''No, sir, and I never said you did,'' Jake replied. ''Unbranded mavericks out on the range are the property of whoever gets their brand on them first. That's common law. But what I did for you I can do for myself. I intend to get my brand on as many of them as I can. As long as it's legal to put your own brand on range mavericks, I aim to take advantage of it.''

Hunter smiled, though it was a smile without mirth. ''Ah yes,'' he said mysteriously. ''As long as it is legal.''

*   *   *

At the Cheyenne Social Club that very evening, George Perry, Frank Wolcott, and a third man were having dinner. The third man was Dave Porter, a deputy sheriff from Laramie County. It was obvious that the three men were engaged in an intense and sometimes acrimonious meeting, but as they were speaking in hisses and whispers, no one who wasn't at the table could follow their conversation.

"I thought there wasn't going to be any killing," Perry hissed in a way that showed his disapproval of the fact.

"I'm sorry about that, Mr. Perry," Porter answered. "But you asked me to hire someone who couldn't be traced back to the WSGA, and that meant I had to make a deal with men who were already in prison. When you get involved with that kind of person, you have to be ready for the consequences."

"Yes, but they were specifically told, no killing," Perry repeated. He looked over at Wolcott, who thus far had been quiet. "You know what that makes us, don't you, Frank? That makes us accessories to murder!"

"Calm down, George, we're no such thing," Wolcott soothed. "Like you said, we specifically let it be known that we didn't want any killing—legally, that let's us out of the killing. What they did out there at that line shack, they did on their own."

"Besides, it's too late to do anything about it now," Porter reminded them. "If anyone goes after those three men for murder, they are going to testify in court that we are the ones who hired them to steal Hunter's cattle."

"And that will make us accessories to cattle rustling," Wolcott pointed out.

"Yes, but it's not the same thing. We didn't steal cattle to line our own pockets," Perry said, justifying his participation. "In fact, we didn't make a penny from it. It was only a ploy, designed to prod Hunter into coming over into our camp."

"Do you think the reason for robbery makes any difference to the law?" Wolcott asked. "Regardless of how noble a purpose there was for the robbery, a robbery did take place. And because we were a part of it . . . whether we took any money from it or not, we are now cattle thieves, pure and simple."

"All right, technically we may be cattle thieves," Perry agreed. "I can live with that, given that I know in my heart why I did it. But I certainly did not intend for anyone to be killed, and I don't know whether I can live with that or not." He looked at the deputy sheriff. "Tell me, Porter, why did they think it was necessary to kill Hunter's riders?"

"The way it was told to me," Porter answered, "is that when they got to the holding pen where the cattle were being kept, they saw that the line shack was full of Hunter's men. They didn't expect anyone to be there, but when there was, they figured they had better get rid of all the witnesses."

"Actually, George, it's better for us this way," Wolcott said. "Suppose Payson and his boys left witnesses who could testify, and suppose, based on those witnesses' testimony, Payson and his men were caught? Do you believe for one minute that Payson wouldn't tell who hired them?"

"Mr. Wolcott is right, Mr. Perry," Porter said. "What happened is all for the best."

"Which brings up a question. Where are Payson and his men now?" Wolcott asked.

"You don't have to worry about them," Porter said. "They are down in Colorado somewhere." He smiled.

"And the best thing is, they didn't cost us a penny. They paid themselves by selling the stolen beeves."

"Come on, George," Wolcott said. "Don't worry so much. We got exactly what we wanted, and it didn't cost us anything. You can't really ask for more than that, can you?"

Perry let out a long, slow sigh. "I suppose you're right," he finally agreed. "But I never would have gone along with this if I had thought some innocent men were going to be killed."

"It is a sad fact of life that some innocent men are always killed in wars," Wolcott said easily. "And whether you realize it or not, George Perry, we are involved in a war here." He suddenly smiled. "Besides, our plan worked, didn't it? Hunter is now solidly in our camp, isn't he?"

Perry nodded. "Yes," he said. "The robbery finally brought him around. Whatever the Wyoming Stock Growers' Association decides to do, we can count on Doyle Hunter for support."

Wolcott held up his glass. "Gentlemen, the maverick law goes up for the executive signature tomorrow, and when I spoke to the governor this morning he assured me that he would sign it. The opening salvos of this war have been fired, and I am pleased to say that we are the ones who fired them."

THREE WEEKS LATER

Jake dismounted in front of one of the more substantial buildings on the long, manure-filled main street of Buffalo, Wyoming. A sign over the door read:

U.S. POST OFFICE
BUFFALO SALOON
JIM AVERILL, PROP.
"Enemy to injustice,
Friend to the small rancher."

"Hello, cowboy, welcome to the Hog Ranch," a
someone said when Jake stepped through the front door.
The person who greeted him was a heavily painted,
large-boned woman wearing a bright print dress.

Confused by the welcome, Jake paused for a second.
"I thought this was Jim Averill's place."

"It is, it is," the woman assured him, laughing at his
confusion. "Jim runs the post office and the stock pens
out back. I run the saloon . . . and the women," she
added with a ribald smile. "My name is Ella. Ella Watson. Would you like a drink, honey?"

"Yes, thank you, Ella, I don't mind if I do," Jake
replied, stepping up to the bar.

Although there was a bartender on duty, Ella went
around behind the bar to pour the drink herself. "In case
you didn't catch my drift, drinks aren't the only thing I
supply," she said seductively as she slid the glass across
the top of the bar.

"Oh, uh, thank you, but I, uh . . ."

"Oh, heavens, honey, I'm not tryin' to sell myself,"
Ella said, laughing. "I've got half a dozen girls here who
work for me. I'm sure we can find someone more to
your liking." She backed away from the bar, then turned
sideways and thrust a hip out provocatively. "On the
other hand, I might just be able to teach you a trick or
two myself," she added with a ribald grin.

"Ella, for chrissake, will you leave the man alone?"
The voice came from a man who had just entered the

room. "Can't you see that he isn't interested in you?"

"Well, you can't blame a girl for trying, can you, Jim? I mean, he is a handsome critter . . . even if he is wearing a silly-looking hat."

Smiling, and taking off his hat, Jake turned toward the person who had just come in. He saw a man of medium build, with friendly eyes, a full mustache, and a receding hairline. The man was smoking a cigar and wearing a suit complete with a silk vest. "I'm Jim Averill," the man said, introducing himself. "And Ella is right, that *is* a rather silly-looking hat."

"So I've been told," Jake replied, sticking out his hand for a handshake. "I'm Jake Colby."

"Ah yes, Mr. Colby. I got a letter from Mr. Northington, your lawyer in Casper. I believe you wanted to buy enough land to start a small ranch?"

"Yes, sir."

Averill smiled. "Well, I think you are going to be very pleased. I've found just the place for you. Three sections of land, with a year-around water supply, good grass, and, more important, bordered by free range, which gives you plenty of room to expand. Also, at no extra cost, there's already a house and barn. No bunkhouse for cowboys, but then, I don't reckon you'll be runnin' an outfit for a while. From what I hear, you're going to do it pretty much on your own."

"That's right."

"What about cattle? Do you need some to get started?"

"I sure do. I plan to go out looking for mavericks, and I'm going to brand as many of them as I can, but I'll need a few head of mature stock as well."

"I'll supply that for you, too," Averill promised.

"We try to anticipate everything you could possibly need here."

"Remember, that's 'everything,' " Ella added breathily.

Jake chuckled. "Yes," he said. "I'll remember."

"You said you were going to hunt mavericks," Averill said. "Well, I don't want to put a damper on things, but have you heard of the maverick law?"

"The maverick law? No, what is it?"

"It's a new law that just went into effect. If you ask me, it's just another way the big ranchers have of running roughshod over the ranchers and farmers in the state," Averill answered contemptuously. "It says that all unbranded cattle are the property of the Wyoming Stock Growers' Association."

"All unbranded cattle?"

"Yes, even your own. In other words, the WSGA could hire a detective and send him out onto your ranch and claim your own cattle that you haven't branded yet. In theory, I suppose they could even send you a bill for the calves you do brand."

"How could such a law be passed?"

"Quite easily," Jim answered with a snort. "When you consider that the WSGA has the governor and state legislature in their hip pocket. I reckon they can do just about anything they want to do."

Jake stroked his chin. "So *that's* what he meant," he said.

"That's what who meant?"

"Doyle Hunter."

"The Rocking H?"

"Yes, I used to ride for him. I told him I was going to put my brand on mavericks for as long as it was legal and he replied, 'As long as it is legal,' as if he knew something I didn't know. I thought he was just blowing off steam . . . but now I see that he had this law in mind, even then.''

"The law is patently unfair," Jim said. "I wrote a letter to the editor of the *Cheyenne Daily Mail*, expressing my opinion of it. And I've already heard from several honest people in the state who had no idea such a law had been passed. That's the only way they got it through, you know. They sneaked it through the legislature and across the governor's desk without the people of Wyoming realizing what was going on. Now that I've told them about it in my letter, though, I have no doubt but that the law will eventually be repealed.''

"Yeah, well, as far as I'm concerned, I've already repealed it," Jake said resolutely. "I'm going to brand every maverick I can find, just like I planned. And if I have to take on the entire Wyoming Stock Growers' Association all by myself, I'll do it.''

"You don't have to be by yourself, unless you choose to be," Jim said.

"What do you mean?''

"Have you ever heard of the Red Sash Gang?" Averill asked.

"Yes, I've heard of them.''

"What have you heard of them?''

"That they are a group of cattle rustlers who identify themselves by wearing red sashes,'' Jake said.

Averill shook his head. "The big cattlemen would have you think that they are nothin' but rustlers, but it's not that way at all. Don't get me wrong, I'm not saying there isn't a long rope thrown now and then . . . and I'm pretty sure they've all bought a stolen cow or two. But what they really are is a group of small ranchers and cowboys banded together for mutual benefit.'' He chuckled. "You might say the Red Sash Gang is no different from the Wyoming Stock Growers' Association, only the Red Sash boys don't have the money and the power the WSGA has. What they *do* have is a good leader, a man named Nate Champion, and a lot of good men who are loyal to each other. If you're going to be a small rancher in Johnson County, you could do a lot worse than join up with those boys."

"Thanks, I might do that," Jake agreed.

Seven

"Nanny Laura, look at me! Look at me!" five-year-old Bernie Rodl called.

Laura Place was in the backyard of the Rodl home, a huge edifice done in the style known locally as "Brewery Baronial." Martin Rodl was the head of Rodl Brewery, one of the biggest beer breweries in the city. He was also the father of two small children, and Laura was in the employ of the Rodl family as their children's "nanny," a term she had never even heard until she accepted the position with the Rodl family.

Bernie was at the top of a rather low sliding board, and he put both hands up in the air as he started down the slide, thus precipitating his call.

"Oh, Bernie, that's very brave of you!" Laura called back enthusiastically as she tied three-year-old Magda's shoes.

"Wheee!" Bernie squealed as he slid down the board.

"Well, the children seem to be having fun," a man's voice said.

"Papa, Papa, did you see me slide down the board with my hands up?" Bernie called out in delight when he saw his father.

"I sure did."

"Daddy, I found a flower," Magda said, running toward him and holding out the wilted bloom she had been carrying. "Nanny Laura said I could give it to Mommy."

"I'm sure Mama will love it," Martin said. He picked her up, gave her a hug, then set her back down. "She's ready to leave now. Suppose the two of you run into the house and tell her good-bye?"

Both children started toward the house on a run, but Laura called out to them.

"No, no! You know your mama doesn't want you to be running through the house! Now, slow down and walk like the little lady and little gentleman I know you are."

"Yes, Nanny Laura," they replied, immediately slowing to a walk.

Laura followed the children inside. Their mother, Gretchen Rodl, was standing in the foyer, giving detailed instructions to the liveryman on what she wanted done with her luggage. She was about to leave for Milwaukee to be with her sister for the birth of her sister's first child.

Gretchen was a big-boned woman, very tall, with hair the color of winter grass. She had an oversize nose and small, close-set eyes. Going along with her physical unattractiveness was a very unpleasant, overbearing personality. She was ill-tempered with all of her servants, aloof with her children, and particularly domineering toward her husband.

Martin Rodl was just the opposite. He always had a pleasant word for those who worked for him and a smile for his children, and he never challenged, or argued with, his wife. He was also a much better-looking man than Gretchen was a woman. Laura had not the slightest idea what attraction there could have been between husband and wife. She did know, however, that whatever might have been there originally was gone now. Thus it was that though she'd turned him away the first few times he'd come to her, she had finally given in, and Martin Rodl, who was one of the wealthiest men in St. Louis, had become her lover. She had been having an affair with him now for quite some time.

"Mommy, look, I brung you a flower," Magda said, presenting her mother with the drooping, wilted bloom.

"For heaven's sake, Magda, don't bring that weed into the house. Laura, you know I don't approve of that. You should have taken it away from her."

"Yes, ma'am," Laura said, noticing the look of hurt and rejection on the child's face. How could anyone be so cruel?

"I'll be back in three weeks. You children be good, and mind Nanny Laura."

"Yes, ma'am," the children answered as one.

Gretchen offered her cheek to Martin, and dutifully he kissed it. "Take care," he said.

"Good-bye, Martin. Good-bye, Laura." Gretchen had the same voice inflection for both. It was quite obvious that three weeks' separation from her husband, or her children, for that matter, was not going work much of a hardship on her.

The day after Gretchen left for Milwaukee the housekeeper took the cars to St. Charles to spend the night with her mother. The cook and her husband, the yardman, lived not in the main house, but in a small servants' house at the rear of the property. The butler and the liveryman lived in an apartment over the carriage house, which meant that the only ones left in the main house were Laura, the two children, and, of course, the children's father.

Laura had known for the last two weeks that the housekeeper would be gone tonight, and secretly she had made plans for the evening. She got the children into bed earlier than usual, then she had the cook prepare Martin's favorite meal: lamb chops and roasted potatoes. When Martin arrived home from the brewery, Laura greeted him just inside the front door, wearing a daringly low-cut "evening toilette" she had bought at Famous-Barr just for this occasion. Martin's quick intake of breath and the little red lights that came on in the bottoms of his eyes showed her that the gown was working its desired effect.

"Where is Mrs. Day?" Martin asked, referring to the housekeeper.

"She is spending the night in St. Charles," Laura replied.

"And the butler?"

"I told Mr. Forbis I would serve you tonight. There's no one here but you, me, and the children. And the children are in bed."

Martin smiled at her. "Why, if I didn't know better, I'd say you had something planned."

"If you knew better," Laura replied, "you would *know* that I had something planned."

"And just what would that be, I wonder?" He put his hand gently on the back of her neck and pulled her to him. They kissed, then she pulled away from him coquettishly.

"Not yet," she said. "I had the cook prepare your favorite meal. Let's eat."

"We can always eat," Martin said, reaching for her again.

"Please, Martin, tonight, couldn't it just be as if . . . ?" She let the sentence hang.

"As if?"

"As if . . . we had a right to do this," Laura explained. "As if we were married, and as if the children upstairs were *our* children, and . . ." Again she let the sentence hang, preferring that to totally exposing her soul to him. Was it so wrong to want a family and nice things?

Martin laughed easily. "Of course, my dear, if it makes you happy. And how were our dear children today?"

"They were fine," Laura answered. "Only they missed their father, and I missed my . . ." She paused before she could say the word "husband."

"Well, we are all together now, aren't we?" Martin replied. "Come, let us see what we have for dinner."

They ate dinner leisurely, sitting not at opposite ends of the long table, as did Martin and Gretchen, but together at the same end, the small distance between them lighted by a single candle. The china, silver, and crystal gleamed in the still flame of the candle, and Laura gave in to the fantasy that—for tonight, at least—she *was* Mrs. Martin Rodl and the mistress of this house.

Afterward, when they went upstairs, Laura started down the hall toward her own room, but Martin pulled her back.

"No, not tonight," he said. "Tonight we use my room."

"Oh, Martin, no," Laura said. "I wouldn't want to go in there, in . . . her . . . bed."

Martin laughed. "Silly girl. Do you think Gretchen and I share the same bed?"

Laura was surprised by the response. "Yes, of course," she answered. "You mean, you don't?"

Martin shook his head. "We don't even share the same bedroom," he said. "Come, let me show you."

After leading Laura down the hallway, he opened the double doors at the far end. Gretchen's room was enormous, four or five times larger than Laura's room. It was furnished with massive, carved oak furniture, a dresser, armoire, and chest. The most dominating feature, though, was a great four-postered, canopied bed. The walls were decorated with large photographs of stern-looking men and women, and to Laura it looked as if, at that very moment, they were all looking disapprovingly at her.

"Here it is," Martin said.

"Her room is very . . . big," Laura replied. Big was the only word she could find for it. There was nothing about it that was particularly attractive, nothing that was personal, and nothing that was in the least feminine. But then, Gretchen was a woman without frills.

"You've never been in here?" Martin asked.

"No. I've no reason to ever come in here," Laura answered. "Where is your room?"

"Through that door," Martin said. "Which, you will notice," he added, "can be conveniently locked from this side. That is to prevent any nocturnal visitations unless they are solicited. And they never are."

Martin led Laura across the bedroom to the other door, then pulled it open. It revealed another room, about one-third as large as Gretchen's room.

"As you can see, however," Martin continued, "I do have another door that opens onto the hallway. That means she can't actually make me a prisoner in my own bedroom. And, of course, it allows me the opportunity to make a few visits where, fortunately, I am not rejected."

"I have often wondered how you could sneak away without her knowing about it," Laura said.

Martin reached for her again, pulling her to him for another kiss. This time she didn't resist him, and when he began undoing the catches and ties of the gown she had worn especially for this evening, she helped him, so that within a moment she was standing before him naked.

Before Martin, Laura had known only one other man sexually, and that had been her aunt's husband. She had responded to him because she'd had no choice. But in responding to him, she had made a fascinating discovery. Men, who had the advantage over women in every other endeavor, were at a distinct disadvantage when it came to sex. Laura learned that with only the slightest effort she could arouse passions, excite needs, and enflame desires. Then, by acceding to or denying those passions, needs, and desires, she could exercise a great deal of control over a man. With her uncle she learned to enjoy that power, if not the sex itself.

She refined her art of seduction with Martin as he grunted and ground and thrust into her. She orchestrated her body movements to accommodate him, using those things she had learned—a tease here, a concession there—until he was totally subservient to her will. Then his moment came, and she felt his body begin to jerk in convulsive jolts, before, finally, he spent himself in her, in satisfied, orgasmic shudders.

How men groveled so for this moment, she thought. She wondered what they felt, what sort of pleasure there was for them in the sex act. She knew it must be something extraordinary, and secretly she sometimes wished she could feel it, too. But if sex wasn't meant to be physically satisfying for a woman, it wasn't without its pleasures. Here she was, little more than a poor servant girl, yet she could bring a wealthy and important man like Martin Rodl to the point of total surrender. It was a feeling of exhilarating power.

WYOMING

As Jake rode in the shadow of the Big Horn Mountains, he found himself comparing this wild and beautiful Wyoming country to the Ozark Mountains of Missouri, where he was raised. Though he believed his part of Missouri was equally beautiful and, indeed, would have considered himself disloyal if he'd thought otherwise, equal beauty did not mean equal grandeur, and there was a great deal of grandeur to enjoy in this rugged, wide landscape.

Here, in the Powder River Basin with its deep, grassy valleys and heavily timbered slopes, he had bought three sections of land to call his own. The OH Ranch was marked by growths of pine and spruce, interspersed with thickets of aspen. He was pleased to see that there was also a great deal of game here, and he had already found bits and pieces of ancient arrowheads, proof that game had always been abundant.

Although only three sections of this land were his, they were bordered on two sides by open range, with grasses and water that could be used by anyone who wished to use it.

"A fella really doesn't need to own that many acres," Ollie had told him one day when they were talking about every cowboy's dream of owning his own spread. "All you really need is enough acres for the house and out-buildings, a corral, and a source of water. What with the open range law, your cattle are free to graze wherever they can find the pickin's."

Someone else had owned the ranch before Jake, and he had built a small house and barn. But the previous winter had been particularly brutal. All across Wyoming thousands of head of cattle had been killed by the heavy snows, and while the large ranchers suffered, many of the smaller ranchers were ruined, including the previous owner of the ranch that now belonged to Jake. Jake wasn't particularly happy about taking advantage of someone else's misfortune, but he had gotten a good price on the land and he was determined to make the best of it.

It was a wonderful, exhilarating feeling, and last night he'd eaten his meal of bacon and biscuits alongside an open campfire while he'd smelled the woodsmoke and watched the changing shadows about him. As he'd listened to the crack of elk horns on a dead branch up the canyon, and the whisper of wind in the tips of the spruce, he'd known that this was the culmination of his lifelong dream. Despite the difficulties that lay ahead of him, he was determined to make a go of his ranch.

Before Jake went to sleep last night, he had even allowed himself the luxury of dreaming ahead, to a day in the distant future when he would be the grand old man of a successful ranch, with a wife and children to help him make the ranch a home.

He needed to round up mavericks to get started, and that he was going to do, maverick law or no maverick law. But it was now midafternoon of his second day of hunting for mavericks, and so far he had found none.

It was curious, though. When he was running down mavericks for Doyle Hunter and the Rocking H, it seemed as if he could find them up every draw and in every canyon. Why couldn't he find any now?

When he reached a new network of draws for him to search, however, his hope was renewed. From outward appearances these particular canyons were dry and hot and choked with dust. He knew from experience, however, that many of them would have rocky stream beds where water ran year around, and it was in there, around those water sources, that he would most likely find what he was looking for.

Then, as he searched the ground at the entrance to one of the canyons, he felt a surge of excitement. Here were the unmistakable signs of a cattle trail threaded through the maze of more narrow deer trails, zigzagging through the brush and up the slopes.

Jake pushed his horse through knee-high clumps of sun-bleached grass. Here the air smelled of dry sage, green pine, and hot soil. He rode through one of the draws to a grassy glade where a thin ribbon of water, sparkling in the sunshine, broke musically over smooth, glistening rocks. Jake dismounted, then unsaddled his horse and let it drink its fill. He tied it to a tree, giving it enough room to graze, then he filled his canteen and, hooking it over his shoulder, started on foot up one of the trails to see if he could find any cattle.

Jake had gone no more than a mile when he heard it—the bawling of calves and the lowing of cows. When he reached a bend in the draw, he was close enough to hear unshod hooves clattering on the rocks, and he knew that he had found a rather sizable number. He moved up behind a rock to have a look and counted over sixty animals all together, some twenty-five to thirty of which were calves. How many of the calves were unbranded—and, indeed, if any of the cows were unbranded—he had no idea. But he was sure that he wouldn't come away empty-handed.

When Jake returned to the place where he had tied his horse, he was startled to see another horse there, tied to the same tree. Quickly he pulled his pistol and looked around, finally spotting the rider in a squatting position on a flat rock overlooking the stream. The rider's back was to Jake, and Jake saw that the man was wearing a red sash around his waist.

Jake searched the area very carefully to make certain no one else was around, then, when he was sure that there wasn't, he put his gun back into his holster loosely and started down toward the stream, walking very quietly.

"Good afternoon," he said when he was no more than twenty yards away. He was gratified to see that his approach had been unnoticed, for his words seemed to startle the man, who jumped. Quickly, though, he regained control of himself, and he stood and turned toward Jake.

"Afternoon," the man replied. He was small and dark, though with the look of wiry strength.

"Something I can help you with?" Jake asked.

"You make it sound like maybe I was trespassin' or somthin'."

"Wouldn't exactly call it trespassing," Jake replied. "But you don't generally see a man coming into another man's campsite without being invited."

"Sorry. Didn't see no campfire, nor the makin's of one. Didn't take it for a campsite. Thought maybe you'd just stopped to let your horse water and graze while you took a walk your own self to water the lilies."

"Mister, if I have to take a piss, I don't need to walk somewhere else to do it. I'm not so goddamned shy I won't pee in front of my own horse," Jake answered.

The stranger laughed. "I reckon you got me there. Listen, don't want to cause you no trouble. I'll just mosey on if my bein' here's a bother to you."

"No, that's all right," Jake said, satisfied now that the man represented no immediate danger to him. He stuck out his hand. "The name is Colby. Jake Colby."

"Eddie Franklin."

"Eddie Franklin?"

Eddie was curious by Jake's reaction to his name. Although there were no Wanted posters out on him in Wyoming, there were in Colorado, Nebraska, and Nevada, and he wondered if Jake might be a lawman.

"You heard of me?" Eddie asked.

Jake's face was a study of concentration for a moment, then it broke into a big smile. "As a matter of fact, I have," he said. "You ever know a fella name of Ollie Henderson?"

"Ollie Henderson? Hell yes, I know him. How is ole Ollie gettin' along these days, anyhow?"

"You mean you haven't heard?"

"Heard somethin' about Ollie? No, can't say as I have."

"Hate to be the one to tell you this, but Ollie's dead."

"Dead? How? Throwed? Stampeded? Get some bad whiskey? What?"

"He was killed by cattle rustlers," Jake said.

"Damn. Tryin' to save someone else's cattle, too, no

doubt," Eddie said. He sighed. "Hope he got a decent burial. He was a good man."

Jake recalled burying Ollie's charred body. "I buried him myself, and said a few words over him," he said.

Eddie nodded. "I reckon that's good enough. A cowboy can't ask much more than that he's got a good friend to say words over 'im after he's gone."

"I see you're wearin' a red sash," Jake said. "You a small rancher?"

"Nope, just a cowboy," Eddie replied. "Why? Have you heard of the Red Sash Gang?"

"Oh, yes, I've heard of it."

"What have you heard?"

"Depends pretty much on who I heard it from," Jake replied. "From Mr. Hunter, and the others back at the Rocking H Ranch, I heard that the Red Sash Gang was a bunch of cutthroat murderers and cattle thieves."

"I reckon we've done our share of that," Eddie admitted. "What else have you heard?"

"Jim Averill speaks well of the Red Sash Gang. He says it's composed of small ranchers and cowboys who are just trying to make a living."

"Jim Averill is a good man," Eddie said.

Jake smiled. "He struck me as such. Listen, you want to join camp with me tonight?"

"Don't mind if I do," Eddie replied. "I killed a rabbit a while back. I could cook 'im for our supper, but I'm runnin' short on salt, and I don't have any coffee at all."

"That's all right, I've got some of both," Jake offered. "That'll be my contribution to our supper."

"Good enough," Eddie said enthusiastically.

Jake started laying a fire while Eddie skinned and cleaned the rabbit he had shot.

"How'd you and Ollie get together?" Jake asked.

"Me'n Ollie hooked up first down in Colorado, workin' for Hogjowl Lambert on the HL Ranch," Eddie answered. "Then we come up here to work at the Rocking H. What about you? Where do you know Ollie from?"

"He was still at the Rocking H when I came there," Jake answered.

"You work for Doyle Hunter, do you?"

"Not any more," Jake replied. "I quit." By now he had enough wood gathered for the fire, and he set to lighting it.

"Good for you. Don't know how anyone can work for that no-'count son of a bitch." Eddie peeled the green bark off a small tree branch, then used it to spit the rabbit. He put the cleaned stick up on a couple of forked limbs, then sat back while the meat began to cook.

By the time they finished their supper, darkness had set in and the two men, strangers only hours earlier, were as comfortable together as if they had shared the trail for many years. Jake drew up his saddle for a backrest and made himself comfortable before the fire, watching the glow of the embers and the licking flames. Tiny, orange-shining sparks rode columns of heat high into the night sky, there to blend with the thousands of stars that had spread their array above them.

Jake had spent many nights like this, as a scout for the army, as a hunter for the railroad, and as a cowboy for hire. But tonight he was doing so as his own man, and he felt freer than ever before in his life.

"Ollie ever tell you how I come to leave the Rockin' H?" Eddie asked, pulling the makings from his shirt pocket and rolling himself a cigarette. He held out his pouch toward Jake, but Jake declined and saw the little look of relief on Eddie's face when he did so. Out on the range, tobacco was more dear than coffee to those who used it.

"As I recall, he said it had something to do with Doyle Hunter cheatin' you out of some money,"

Eddie finished rolling the cigarette, then stuck the tube in his mouth and lit it with a burning brand. "That's what he did all right. If you're in the mood to listen, I'll spin you a story about it," he offered.

Jake knew that storytelling around campfires was an art form, requiring as much talent and providing as much entertainment as the art of singing, or dancing, or play-acting. And though he had just met Eddie, he had an idea that Eddie was very proficient in the art.

Jake took off his hat and put it on the ground in front of him. "I'm all ears," he said.

Eddie looked at Jake's hat, and though Jake could tell that he wanted to make some comment about it, he said nothing. Instead he began telling his story.

"Well, sir, it was two years ago," Eddie started. "It seems the good folks down in Casper had a cowboy dance and picnic planned to sort of kick off the spring roundup. For three of us Rocking H cowboys, that was really welcome, 'cause me and Jimmy Goodhill and Ollie Henderson had spent the winter out in one of Doyle Hunter's line shacks. It had been a long time since we'd seen a pretty girl . . . hell, it had been a long time since we'd seen any kind of a girl at all. And near 'bout as long since any of us had had anything to drink.

"The boys was already whoopin' it up pretty good in the bunkhouse that night, gettin' a little rambunctious with one another, but it was all in good fun. We was shoutin' back 'n' forth 'bout what all we was goin' to do at the dance, how many drinks we'd drink, how many girls we'd dance with, an' when we got into town, ever'thing was goin' pretty much the way it was supposed to.

"We was all havin' a good time, an' the next thing you know, I was little drunk and Jimmy Goodhill was a little drunk." Eddie chuckled. "Actually, I guess we was both a lot drunk. Anyhow, we both went to dance with the same girl at the same time, and got into a little tiff about whose girl she was, anyway. Which when you get right down to it didn't make no sense a'tall, 'cause she was one of Ella's whores. Now, I got nothin' against whores, you understand, but what I mean is, she wasn't my girl and she wasn't Jimmy's girl, she was anybody's girl.

"But, bein' as we was both drunk an' all, we didn't see it quite like that at the time. So, we commenced to have a big fight. By the way, did you ever know Jimmy?"

"No, I don't believe I ever met him," Jake replied.

"Well, he was a big son of a bitch. A good man, but big as a barn and strong as an ox." Eddie grew silent for a moment. "A big man like that . . . you don't never expect to see him die from anythin' short of a bullet or bein' run over by a train or somethin', but they say he took sick an' died last year. Got the pneumony and up an' died, just like that." Eddie snapped his fingers, then took a couple of puffs from his cigarette before continuing his story.

"Well, like I say, he was a big son of a bitch and there was no way I could handle him on my own, so I grabbed ahold of the first thing I could grab ahold of and . . . 'crash!' " Eddie made the sound. "I brung it down right on top of Jimmy's head. Well, Jimmy, he went out like a candle, and the thing I hit him with was busted into pieces. Turns out what I hit him with was a glass pitcher that Mr. Hunter had loaned to the folks that was havin' the dance and picnic. And here's where the bad part comes in. Hunter claimed the pitcher come from England or France or some such place as that. He said the thing was worth three hundred dollars, which just happened to be exactly what he owed me for the winter's work I'd just done for him. The son of a bitch said he was goin' to hold back the money to pay for the pitcher I just broke.

"Well, sir, there ain't no way you goin' to ever make me believe that pitcher was worth what Hunter said it was. I mean, if it was, what the hell was it doin' at a place like that in the first place? And in the second place, it's not like I done it on purpose. Hell, I was tryin' to bust Jimmy's head, not the goddamned pitcher."

Jake laughed.

"Well, the outcome of it all was, Hunter didn't pay me what he owed me, so I quit, and I ain't punched a Rocking H cow since."

Eddie was silent for a moment, then he chuckled and added, "Well, that ain't quite true. Truth to tell, I've punched quite a few Rocking H cows since. But I ain't punched none of 'em *for* him." The chuckle changed to a laugh.

"You mean you've branded a few of his mavericks?"

"Mavericks, steers, heifers, yearlings, I've took my money and then some out in hide," Eddie said. "Rocking H cow hide," he added.

"Rustling?"

"Like I told you before, I've rustled a few head," Eddie admitted. He squinted through the cigarette smoke at Jake. "Never killed any honest cowboys, though. So if it was rustlers that killed Ollie it wasn't me.''

''It was rustlers all right,'' Jake said.

''How do you know?''

''I was there, in the line shack, when they hit us. They just started shootin'. Then, when they thought they had all of us killed off, they burned the shack and took the head we had penned up.''

''There are some bad apples, even among us honest rustlers,'' Eddie replied. ''How'd you get away?''

''I managed to crawl through the floor, then I got away from underneath. They never saw me.''

Eddie flipped away the remains of his cigarette butt, then looked at Jake and smiled, his teeth glowing orange in the firelight. ''Well, I'm glad you got away. Else I wouldn't have found myself a new friend. Now, tell me about that hat.''

''This hat?'' Jake asked, picking it up.

''That hat. How'd you come by it? I mean, you have to admit, it's not like any other hat a fella is likely to find out here.''

''This is called a bowler,'' he said. Several people had commented about Jake's hat over the years, and he had always put them off. But there was something about tonight—about two men meeting in the middle of the wild country and establishing an immediate friendship—that made Jake willing to share.

''My ma died when I was eight,'' Jake said. ''So there was just my pa and me. Pa owned a store in Kansas City, a haberdashery, known for its hats. He always used to tell me that the store was going to be mine someday. But when I was eighteen there was a panic, and there wasn't enough money left to spend on unnecessary items, such as men's hats and fine clothes. Pa had to borrow from the bank to keep his store open, but conditions got worse. On top of that, Pa had a bad heart. Then the bank took first the store and then his house away from him.

"Pa went down real fast after that. He felt like he had failed me. Truth is, I never wanted to run a haberdashery store anyway, only I couldn't tell him that."

Jake was quiet for a moment. "Pa cried on his death-bed," he said. "I'd never seen him cry before. Even when things were at their worst, I'd never seen him cry. He pointed to this hat, which had once been the most expensive item in his store, and told me it was the only thing he had left in the world to leave me.

"I told him it was the grandest hat in the world, and I would never get rid of it. I've had this hat for fifteen years," he said. "And if it came to a choice between losing the land I just bought, or losing this hat . . . I'd give up the land."

"By God," Eddie said, his voice thick with emotion. "If anyone ever tries to take that hat from you and I'm around, I'll shoot the son of a bitch dead, I promise you."

Jake chuckled, then handed the hat to Eddie. "Would you like to try it on?"

"You don't mind?"

"No, go ahead."

Eddie put the hat on, tilted it first one way, then the other, then, with a laugh, took it off and handed it back to Jake.

"I think it looks better on you," he said. Then, chang-ing the subject, he asked: "By the way, what are you plannin' to do with the cattle you found up this draw?"

"You know about those?"

"Was followin' the sign in here when I found your horse tied to the tree. Figured there was someone scoutin' 'em out on foot, so I just waited. How many in there?''

"Fifty or sixty. Maybe half of 'em unbranded calves."

"You got a place to sell 'em?"

"Sell them? No, I'm going to keep them. I figure these calves, and what few head of cattle I could buy from Jim Averill, would be the start of my herd."

"Jim Averill is a good man, but why buy cattle from him when they're right here for the taking?"

"I don't want to start my ranch with rustled cattle. Besides, I've already made the deal with Averill."

"Jake, where do you think Averill gets his cows?" He pointed to himself. "From people like me, that's where."

"Maybe so, but I'd be buyin' 'em, not stealin' 'em," Jake replied. "A small point, I'll admit."

"Yeah, so small a point that when the big ranchers get into the lynching mood, they don't make any difference between the rustler who steals the cattle and the small rancher who buys them," Eddie replied. "Just thought I'd point that out."

Jake put his hand to his neck almost subconsciously. "Thanks," he said. "I'll keep that in mind."

"Anyhow, when you get right down to it, with this new maverick law even the unbranded calves would be considered rustled cows, if you took 'em."

"I don't plan to pay any attention to the maverick law," Jake said.

"Maybe you don't, but it's for damn sure that the Wyoming Stock Growers' Association will. And so will the state law. That means you're going to be called a rustler, whether you think you're in the right or not. And

the way I look at it, if you're going to have the name
. . . you may as well have the game.''

"I know you won't understand this, Eddie. But *I'll*
know the difference,'' Jake said.

"You don't plan on tryin' to stop me tomorrow, do
you?'' Eddie asked. "If I take them other cows, I
mean.''

Jake chuckled. "I got enough of a problem dealin'
with my own conscience,'' he said. "I don't aim to deal
with yours, too.''

Eddie smiled. "Well then,'' he said. "What do you
say that tomorrow mornin' you an' me do some cow
business? You take the calves, I'll take the others.''

"Seems fine by me,'' Jake agreed.

"By the way, what's the name of your ranch?''

"I'm callin' it the OH.''

"The OH?''

"After Ollie Henderson,'' Jake explained.

"You got a brand yet?''

"OH, I guess,'' Jake answered.

"Let me show you something,'' Eddie said. He took
a stick and made a mark on the ground.

"What's that?'' Jake asked.

"It's the letter *H,* with a rocker under it.''

"The Rocking H brand,'' Jake replied.

"Now look at this,'' Eddie suggested. He turned the
rocker under the H into a complete circle, so that the
brand now looked like an H with a circle around it.
"OH,'' he said, pointing to the mark. "The Circle H.
Your brand.''

"That brand could cause me a lot of trouble,'' Jake
said, pointing to it.

Eddie chuckled. "Maybe. But it could cause Doyle

Hunter a lot more trouble,'' he said. ''If you got the guts to use it.''

Jake stared at the mark on the ground, and as he did so, he recalled Doyle Hunter's total lack of concern over the three men with him at the line shack, getting killed. He also recalled the look of arrogance on Hunter's face as he gloated over the successful passage of the maverick bill.

''The Circle H,'' he said. He laughed. ''Yeah, I like that.''

Jake and Eddie were just breaking camp the next morning when suddenly a large group of riders came upon them. Two of the riders moved away from the others and rode over toward Jake and Eddie. Eddie saw that Jake took off his red sash before they approached, doing it in such a way as to not be noticed.

One of the two riders was white haired and had a bushy white mustache. The other was clean shaven, with a drawn, pockmarked face. Both had hard, piercing eyes, and both were wearing stars on their vest.

''What are you two men doing here?'' the white-haired rider asked.

''This is open range, isn't it?'' Jake replied.

''Yes.''

''Then what does it matter what we're doing here?''

''Don't get smart with me, sonny,'' snapped the white-haired rider. He pointed to the star he was wearing. ''My name is Tucker. I'm a private detective, working for the Wyoming Stock Growers' Association. That gives me the right to ask as many questions as I want, and if I don't like the answers I get, I am empowered by the governor to arrest you.''

''The governor? I thought you said you were a private

detective for the WSGA," Eddie said. "What does the governor have to do with them?"

"Everything," Tucker replied. "He's granted us the same powers as state lawmen. So when I'm talking to you boys, you can just figure you are talking to a state lawman. Now, I'm goin' to ask you one more time. What are you doin' here?"

"We're hunting," Eddie said.

"Hunting what?"

"Deer, elk, wild turkey. Whatever we can find," he answered.

Tucker stroked his mustache, then nodded. "I don't believe you," he said. "Not for one minute. I think you boys are out here to brand mavericks, and that's the same thing as rustling cattle."

"Do you see any cattle here?" Jake asked.

"No, and it's lucky for you we don't. I'm going to let you go, this time. But if I ever run across you again and you have as much as one cow, branded or unbranded, I'm going to hang you where I find you."

At that moment another rider joined Tucker and his companion.

"Come on," called the other rider. "We found fifty or sixty head holed up in the draw ahead."

"Bring 'em in," Tucker ordered. He looked back at Jake and Eddie. " 'Don't suppose you boys knew anything about them cows?"

Jake shook his head. "Like we said, we were hunting deer and elk."

Tucker looked at the two men for a moment longer, then, without so much as another word, the three men turned and rode off.

"Damn," Jake said. "That's why I haven't found any mavericks. The big ranchers are out roundin' them all up themselves. They're doing exactly what they say we can't do.''

"How's your conscience now?'' Eddie asked.

"I've got a feelin' it's not goin' to bother me quite as much as I thought it would,'' Jake replied.

"Then you think you and me can do some business?'' Eddie asked.

"I'm sure we can.''

★★★

Eight

Ella Watson had come to St. Louis for the express purpose of hiring someone to work for her at the Hog Ranch. Two of her girls had gotten married, and Jim had suggested that perhaps this would be a good time to get in someone who was new and fresh. Ella agreed but was determined not to hire just anyone.

"If we are really going to do this," she said, "the girl needs more than just looks and a willingness to lie with anyone with the price for her services. I want to bring someone out here who has a little class."

"Well, you can rob the finishing schools as far as I'm concerned," Jim had told her. "But don't be surprised if you can't find anyone like that. A girl with class isn't likely to go into our kind of business." When he saw the pout on Ella's face, he laughed. "Present company excepted, of course."

Maybe class wasn't exactly the word to describe what she was looking for, but Ella knew that she would recognize it when she saw it. And so far, she had not seen it in the Gateway City. Maybe she could find someone in Denver.

Having given up on St. Louis, Ella was now in a hired cab, turning west onto Market, which was the street side of Union Station. The hollow clopping of prancing hooves made a staccato beat on the brick pavement as the driver maneuvered the carriage through the traffic, then brought it to a stop under the Union Station porte cochere.

"Union Station, ma'am," the driver announced.

"Thank you," Ella said, paying her fair, then allowing him to help her down.

Inside the station the marble floor of the grand hall teemed with humanity: men and women moving to or from trains, children laughing or crying, and redcaps scurrying about under the burden of passengers' luggage. A train was just pulling into the station now, and as it arrived, Ella could feel the floor rumbling underfoot.

She checked her baggage through to Denver, then went to find an empty seat in the waiting room. That was easier said than done, because the waiting room was very crowded, and not until another train was called did any seats open up.

Ella finally found a bench that was placed back to back with another bench. The second bench was occupied by a very pretty young woman and an expensively dressed, somewhat older man. Ella's proximity to the couple made her privy to what turned out to be a very personal conversation.

"But where will you go, Laura?" the man asked. "What will you do?"

"I don't know," the woman answered. "Kansas City, Denver, San Francisco. Anywhere to get away from here. And I'll do whatever I must to get by."

"Do you know anyone in those cities?"

"No."

"Then why go?"

"I can't stay here. Especially now that I know you will never marry me."

"Did I ever tell you that I would marry you?"

"No, but you . . . you gave me reason to believe that you would."

"I'm sorry if you feel I gave you such an impression. I thought you understood that you were my mistress, and that you would never be anything more. Gretchen understood our relationship, and she approved of it. If she could, why couldn't you?"

"That is the cruelest blow of all," Laura said. "All this time I thought what we had together was private. I had no idea that Gretchen knew. That you actually shared with her the intimate details of what we did together."

"It was the arrangement by which I agreed to marry her," the man explained. "By becoming Gretchen's husband, giving her children, and taking the Rodl family name, the brewery would remain in the family, and the name would be the same. As payment for those services I was to be provided with a generous stipend, and though divorce is out of the question, I would be free to live my own life. That means I could have a mistress if I wanted. The funny thing is, I never wanted one until I met you. Before you, no woman was ever more than a momentary diversion. But you . . . you are my life."

"Oh, don't say such things to me," Laura said emphatically. "How can you live such a farce?"

"I can live it easily," he answered. "And you could, too, if you would just let yourself. Don't you see, Laura?

You and I can be together as much as we want, without fear of discovery. All you have to do is accept the terms.''

"The terms being that your wife supports both of us? No, thank you. I can't do it, and I don't know how you can. She may be your wife, but you are a kept man."

"I admit that I am, and I make no apologies for it. I have grown used to the good life, and as long as the money and my social position are guaranteed, I will do whatever Gretchen asks of me. You can stay with me and share in my good fortune . . . or you can stand on principle and leave. The choice is yours."

"I have made my choice."

The man said nothing for a moment, then he spoke very quietly. "Then allow me to wish you the best of luck," he said. Slowly he turned and walked away.

Ella listened to Laura sob quietly for several moments before she leaned across the back of the bench to speak to the young woman.

"So, I will ask the same question your man friend asked. Where will you go? What will you do?" she asked.

Astonished that someone had spoken to her, Laura looked up as she dabbed at the tears in her eyes. "I beg your pardon, were you talking to me?"

"Yes," Ella said. "I was eavesdropping, and I heard the conversation between you and your gentleman friend. Every word," she added pointedly.

"Madam, you . . . you had no right," Laura said.

"Yes, I know, and I apologize, but I couldn't very well put my hands over my ears, now, could I? Besides, I believe I have a solution to your problem."

The gall of Ella's approach was so startling to Laura that she stopped crying.

"You have a solution?"

"Yes."

"What makes you think I have a problem?"

"Wouldn't you say that having an intimate relation-ship with a man who is married to someone else . . . and who won't seek a bill of divorcement to marry you, would be a problem?" Ella said.

"I wouldn't say anything," Laura answered. "In fact, I find it difficult to believe that I'm even talking to you." She blew her nose.

"But you are interested in my proposal. Am I right? Or at least curious?" Ella persisted.

"Perhaps astounded by your audacity would be a more apt way of putting it," she suggested.

Ella put her hand across the back of the bench, offer-ing it to Laura. "Ella is my name. Ella Watson. I heard the man call you Laura." Ella's hand hung over the back of the bench. "Are you going to shake my hand, or am I just going to leave it hanging out here like a dog with a wounded paw?"

Despite herself, Laura laughed. "Laura Place," she said, taking Ella's hand.

"I am right in assuming that you are leaving St. Louis, aren't I?" Ella asked.

"Yes."

"Not that it is any of my business, but where are you going?"

"Why would the fact that it isn't any of your business stop you? It hasn't before now," Laura answered. "But if you must know, I have no idea where I'm going. I'm just going."

"To get away from your gentleman friend?"

"Under the circumstances, I'm not sure I could call

him either a gentleman or my friend," Laura said. "But yes, I'm going to get away from him."

"Are you going back to your family?"

Laura shook her head. "I have no family. Look, Miss Watson . . ."

Ella held up her hand and shook her head. "Please, not Miss Watson. Call me Ella."

"Ella, why are you asking me all these questions?"

"Because I am interviewing you for a job," Ella replied. "That is, if you want it."

"Where is this job?"

"In Wyoming."

"Wyoming? That's . . . that's way out west somewhere, isn't it?"

"It's five days from here, by train and coach," Ella replied.

"Isn't that wild country? I mean, with Indians and desperadoes and so forth?"

"We don't have any Indian problems, though we do have our share of desperadoes. And it is wild, but it is also beautiful. And exciting, Laura. More exciting than anything you have ever dreamed of. Come with me. You'll never regret it."

"Yes, you said that. What I don't know is what kind of work you're offering."

"You would work for me at the Hog Ranch."

"The Hog Ranch? Heavens, I don't know anything about hogs."

Ella laughed. "It's a saloon," she said. "That's just what it's called. It doesn't really have anything to do with hogs."

"A saloon? I don't know anything about liquor, either."

"Well, people do come there to drink," Ella said.

"But mostly it is a place where people come to relax and have a good time. It is a social club."

"Not only do I not know anything about liquor, I don't drink."

"That's too bad. You are missing one of life's pleasures," Ella replied. "But, it doesn't matter whether you drink or not. All that is required of you is that you socialize with the men who come there. They like to drink in places where there are pretty women, and they like to keep company with them."

"And you would hire me just to keep company with the men?"

"Yes."

"I'm not exactly sure what you mean by 'keeping company.'"

"Whatever arrangements you want to make with the men patrons, other than sit with them while they are drinking, is strictly up to you. But if the man goes upstairs with you, I get forty percent of what you get."

"My God," Laura gasped. "You're talking about whoring, aren't you?"

"Yes, dear, I am," Ella said easily. "Though those of us in the avocation prefer to use the term 'soiled dove.' It has a gentler sound, I think, than whore."

"Those of us in the avocation? You mean you? You are a, uh, soiled dove?"

"Of course. I wouldn't ask any of my girls to do anything I won't do myself."

"How many . . . girls, do you have?"

"Three now. I did have five, but two of them got married."

"Married?"

"That's the biggest problem someone like me faces. We bring our girls out there and the next thing you know they fall in love with someone and off they go to get married.''

''I didn't think a man would marry a girl like that.''

''Honey, the men so outnumber the women out there that any woman from fourteen to seventy-four can get married anytime she wants. Now, what do you say? Are you interested in the job?''

''Could I ask you a question?''

''Of course you may.''

''Would you approach just any woman with this proposition? What made you think I would be interested in such a thing?''

''I just took a chance,'' Ella said. ''It was obvious from the tone of the conversation between you and your friend that you aren't a virgin.''

''I can see that I must be more guarded in my conversation,'' Laura said.

''Then that first . . . big step, has already been taken,'' Ella said. ''The next step, if you should decide to take it, is a very small one.''

Laura felt her head spinning, and she recalled the conversation she had had with her uncle just before she'd left Memphis. . . .

''It is a big country. There are many places you can go. And as to what you will do . . . Well, you are a very beautiful woman, my dear, and even in biblical times, beautiful women had ways of making money. You will find a way. I'm sure you know what I'm talking about.''

''No, I don't know.''

''Of course you do. After all, it isn't as if you are a virgin. You may as well get paid for what you have been doing. Many women are, you know.''

''My God! You are talking about prostitution. Uncle Carl, are you telling me to become a harlot?'' . . .

"Thirty percent," Laura said.

"I beg your pardon?" Ella replied.

"I'll whore for you, Ella Watson," Laura said resolutely. "But I'll only give you thirty percent of what I take in."

Ella laughed out loud, then took Laura's hand in hers and shook it again. "You've got yourself a deal, girlie," she said. "And I've got a feeling that, even getting only thirty percent, I'm going to make more money from you than from all the other girls combined."

Theresa, Wyoming, was much too small for street lamps. The lights the stagecoach passengers had seen from a distance as the coach clung to the precarious switchback down the side of the mountain had come from the handful of buildings in the town. There was a hotel and restaurant, a general store, a saloon, and a livery stable that also served as the stage station. In addition to the five commercial buildings there were, perhaps, a dozen houses.

Ella and Laura were on the stage now, because Casper was as far as they could come by train. In Casper it was necessary for them to leave the train and travel some distance north, by stagecoach, to reach Buffalo. Now, after half a day's run from Casper, the stage was putting in to Theresa for the night.

The coach clattered into town, the light from its twin kerosene side lamps illuminating the dusty street. Finally it drew to a stop in front of the livery stable, and the lantern hanging on the sign to illuminate it also dimly lit the inside of the coach. Laura had been sleeping, and when the coach stopped, it awakened her.

Hostlers hurried out of the stable and began unharnessing the team to lead them off for food and water.

The driver and guard climbed down and stretched tiredly just outside the coach.

"Where are we?" Laura asked, rubbing her eyes.

"We're in Theresa," Ella answered. "We'll spend the night here. Are you hungry?"

"Yes, I am, a little," Laura replied.

"Good. The man who owns the saloon is a friend of mine. His kitchen cooks a pretty good steak. Also, we can get a room there that's a lot nicer and cheaper than we can at the hotel."

"All right," Laura said. "Whatever you say."

There were six passengers in the stagecoach, and as they got out, the other four, two men and two women, started toward the hotel.

"Have a nice night," Laura called to them. "We'll see you tomorrow."

"Good night to you, miss," one of the men called back.

"Horace!" His wife said sharply, and the man turned his head back to the front, looking away from Laura and Ella.

The woman's action puzzled Laura, as had the behavior of all of them during the trip. Although she had made several attempts to engage them in friendly conversation, they had answered each time in monosyllables, making it obvious that they didn't want to talk.

"I wish I knew what I said to make them angry," Laura said.

"To make who angry, dear?"

"The other passengers. They've hardly spoken to me for this entire day."

Ella laughed. "Oh, honey, you're going to have to get used to that. I'm afraid it comes with being a whore."

"But . . . I'm not a whore yet. And anyway, how do they know?"

Ella brushed her hair back from her face and chuckled. "Well, they see a pretty girl with me, and they just put two and two together."

"Do you know those people?"

"I don't know them, but I'm afraid they know me," Ella said. "It seems that a lot of people out here know me . . . or at least know about me. I'll admit, it bothers you at first . . . but you'll get used to it soon enough."

Inside the North Star Saloon, the piano player was grinding out the song "Little Joe the Wrangler." One of the bar girls was leaning on the back of the piano, singing along off-key, but she was the only one who was paying attention to the music. At all the other tables and along the bar, the cowboys and assorted other patrons were engaged in so many loud, animated conversations that the piano and singer were barely audible.

"Ella!" someone squealed, and the greeting was repeated by another, until within a short time there were three bar girls gathered around Ella and Laura.

"Girls, this is Laura Place," Ella said, introducing Laura to the others. "Laura, all three of these girls have worked for me at one time or another. There are too many for me to introduce, I'll let them introduce themselves to you."

One by one the girls introduced themselves, then asked Laura where she was from and how long she had been "on the line."

"I beg your pardon?" Laura replied. "On the line?"

"My God, Ella, you didn't snag a virgin, did you?" one of them asked. The others laughed at her remark.

"Let's just say she is new to the business," Ella replied. "Very new," she added pointedly.

"You girls aren't being paid to entertain other women," a man said, coming over to join them. Although he was scolding them, it wasn't a harsh scold, and one of the girls playfully stuck her tongue out at him as she returned to the bar to move among the men.

"How's it going, Ella?" the man asked.

"Fine, Billy, fine," Ella answered. "This is Laura Place. I'm taking her up to Buffalo to work for me."

Billy appeared to be in his fifties. Except for a line of hair above each ear, he was bald. He had a round, red face and gray eyes enlarged by the thick-lensed glasses he was wearing.

"Laura, it's another full day's stage ride up to Buffalo," Billy said. "If you don't want to go that far to work for this hard woman, you are welcome to stay here and work for me."

"Thanks," Laura said. "But I started out with Ella, so I guess I'll stay with her."

"What do you think, Billy?" Ella said. "You can't buy loyalty like that, you know. It has to come from inside."

"I suppose it does," Billy replied. "Listen, I want you to tell Jim Averill something for me."

"Sure, I'll be glad to."

Billy looked around to make certain he wasn't being overheard. "There's talk," he said. "The Wyoming Stock Growers' Association is hiring detectives to crack down on the rustlers and the small ranchers."

"What's that to Jim? He's neither one."

"That may be," Billy said. "But from what I hear, he's on their list. They think he's dealing in stolen cattle."

"Hell, Billy, you know how things are up in Johnson County," Ella said. "You can have a bill of sale and it doesn't mean anything. What with the WSGA on one side and the Red Sash Gang on the other, who knows what a cow's pedigree is?'' She laughed. ''Lord knows if they ever start checking people's pedigrees as close as they do a cow's, there are going to be an awful lot of people branded as bastards up there.''

Ella and Billy laughed out loud, then Billy grew serious again. ''You mind what I say, you hear? I don't like what's going on, and I want you folks to be careful up there.'' He nodded toward a table. ''Now, you two ladies go back there and have a seat. I'll send your supper out, no charge. And when you're ready to go to bed you can have the first room on the right at the top of the stairs. That way you can come down to catch the stage tomorrow without disturbing anyone.''

''I don't care what anyone says, Billy, you're a good man,'' Ella teased.

They were eating supper when three men, who had been at the bar, came toward their table. They stopped about halfway between the bar and the table, and one of them came forward several more feet. His eyes were yellowish brown, his skin was sallow, and his face was gaunt, almost as if the skin lay right next to the bone of his skull. His two top teeth were missing. He had a scraggly beard, not as if he were purposely growing one, but as if he had been too lazy to shave for the last several days. He was one of the ugliest men Laura had ever seen, was in fact frightening in his ugliness. He raised a bony hand and pointed his finger at Ella.

''You're the one that runs the Hog Ranch, ain't you? That saloon and whorehouse up in Buffalo?'' he asked.

''I am,'' Ella answered. She was not exactly short with them, but her answer was perfunctory enough that it offered no hint of invitation for any further attention.

"This here one of your new girls?"

"We are traveling together," Ella replied.

"She's a looker," the man said. He ran a hand through his oily black hair, as if by that action he could make himself more presentable. He nodded toward the other two. "Me'n my two pards was talkin' over there, an' we 'bout decided she's the purtiest whore any of us ever seen."

"We appreciate your comment," Ella said. "But as you can see, we are having our supper."

"Tell you what. You let me'n my two pards have first crack at her an' we'll pay double whatever you're goin' to charge them rustlers up in Johnson County."

Laura gasped quietly. Was this what it was going to be like for her? She was not a virgin, and she knew that she was going to be expected to sell herself to men. But she wasn't quite ready . . . and she wasn't sure she could ever be ready to go with someone like this.

"You come up to Buffalo in a couple of weeks," Ella offered. "We'll see if we can accommodate you."

Laura looked over at Ella as if pleading with her to never force her to accommodate anyone like this.

"Naw, it has to be right now." He grabbed himself suggestively. "Me an' my pards is horny, and we're wantin' a little poke tonight, if you understand what I'm talkin' about."

"Oh, I understand you," Ella said. "The question is, do you understand me? The answer is no."

"What do you mean, no? She's a whore, ain't she? That means she's got to go with whatever man has enough money to pay for it, and by God, the three of us have the money. We done a little favor for the Wyoming Stock Growers' Association, so we got lots of money. Right, boys?''

''Right,'' the other two replied.

''And the way we look at it, there ain't nothin' better to spend it on than a women. Most especial if she's as good-lookin' a woman as this here'n.''

''I'm sure there are plenty of women working here who would be glad to have you spend money on them,'' Ella answered.

''We don't want them. We want this one.''

''Sorry, gentlemen, but she is not for sale. Not here, and not today, and if you persist with this attitude, not ever, to you.''

''Well now, by God, maybe we'll just take what we want,'' the leader of the group said. ''What do you say, boys? I mean, it ain't rape if you pay for it.''

''What? Ella, no! Don't let them!'' Laura said, fear causing her words to emerge as a choked cry.

''Girly, you ain't countin' on her to protect you, are you?''

''Is there no one here who will help us?'' Ella called.

The music and the conversation stopped as the saloon patrons all looked over toward the evolving drama.

''Mr. Payson, why don't you and your friends leave those ladies alone?'' Billy called to them. ''You heard what they said. They don't want anything to do with you.''

Payson, who was the leader of the group, turned toward the saloon keeper and held out his left hand, pointing his long bony finger at him. His right hand caressed the handle of his holstered pistol as if he were telling Billy to stay in his place if he didn't want any trouble.

''They're whores,'' Payson said. ''They ain't got the

right to tell us they don't want nothin' to do with us, as long as we're willin' to pay for it.''

''I don't see it that way,'' another voice said. ''Seems to me like they can do business with whoever they want to. And they don't want to do business with you.''

Payson looked toward the man who had spoken. ''Stay out of this, friend. This here ain't none of your business,'' he hissed.

''That's your second mistake,'' the man said. ''I'm not your friend. Your first mistake was to bother these ladies. And if they are willin' to accept my help, I aim to make it my business.''

''Yes, please, help us!'' Ella said.

''There you go,'' the man said. ''She just made it my business.'' Although he smiled at Ella's invitation, the smile didn't reach his eyes. Instead his eyes continued to hold the three men in a steady, powerful, unwavering gaze.

''Mister, you just won't go away, will you?'' Payson said. He and the other two turned to confront this man who had the audacity to challenge them. Payson's hand was already over his gun, and the other two moved their hands into position as well.

The challenger stood perfectly still, as unintimidated by the posturing movement of the three as if they were merely passing the time of day. ''I'm staying. You're leaving,'' the man said.

''There are three of us here, mister,'' Payson pointed out. ''And I don't mind tellin' you, we ain't strangers to the gun. Now, who the hell are you, that you are so ready to die for a couple of whores?''

''The name is Tom Horn,'' the man said easily.

The three men blanched visibly.

"Payson?" said one of the three, his voice thin and strained.

Payson licked his lips nervously, then nodded to the other two. "Let's go, boys," he finally said. "Looks to me like some folks can't tell when other folks is just funnin'."

Slowly, and without ever presenting their backs to Tom Horn, Payson and the two men with him moved toward the front door, then outside, into the night. The deathly silence inside the saloon continued until, a moment later, all could hear the sound of the three horses galloping away.

That action seemed to release all the pent-up tension, and there was a sudden explosion of sound as the men and women began laughing and talking in the excited way of those who have either just cheated death or have just witnessed it. And though neither was the case this time, there was as sudden a release of tension as if it had been one or the other.

Tom walked over to Ella and Laura's table. "Are you ladies all right?" he asked.

"We're fine, thanks to you," Ella said. "Are you really Tom Horn?"

"Yes, ma'am, that's my handle."

"Well, I've heard of you, Tom Horn, but I've never met you. I'm mighty glad tonight was the night that the situation was remedied."

Tom smiled at them, and Laura couldn't help but notice the difference between the smile now and the smile he had given those three men earlier. This smile was warm and genuine. The other had been cold and terrifying.

Then, without any further exchange, Tom Horn turned away from their table and walked back to the bar, where half a dozen men were waiting to buy him a drink.

"God in heaven," Laura said under her breath as he walked away. "I've never seen anything like that. Those men were ready to kill each other."

"No, they wouldn't have killed each other," Ella said, correcting her. "Tom Horn would have killed them."

"One man against three?"

"He isn't just one man. He is Tom Horn."

"Yes, obviously that name means something," Laura said. "To those men, and to you, though, exactly what, I don't know."

"It means sudden death for anyone who crosses him."

"But he seemed so gentle just now."

"So many of them are like that. It's what makes them so fascinating."

"So many of *them?* Them who?"

"Professional gunmen," Ella said easily. "Men who make their living by killing other men."

Laura looked at Tom Horn, who was now standing at the bar, drinking and laughing with those who had gathered around him as if they were guests in the drawing room of the Rodl House back in St. Louis.

Looking at him now, she was hard-pressed to believe what Ella said about him. But the eyes he had shown Payson and the other two men were windows to hell. Intuitively Laura knew that this was a man to whom killing came easily. She felt a shiver pass through her, then remembered something that her father used to say to her, when she was a very young girl, whenever she shivered.

"Someone has just stepped on your grave," he would say.

★ ★ ★

Nine

When Laura first opened her eyes she lay with her head on the pillow for a moment or two, wondering where she could be. A very bright sun, streaming in through the window, illuminated the room. The walls were covered with a floxed wallpaper that featured a design of baskets of blue flowers.

Then she remembered. This was her first morning to awaken in Buffalo, and this was the room Ella had told her would be hers.

"Mary! Mary, you get those clothes hung up on the line, do you hear me?"

"Yes, Mama, I'm doing it now," a young girl's voice answered.

The voices were coming from outside, drifting into the room on the soft breeze that filled the muslin curtains at the slightly raised window and lifted them, cloudlike, over the carpeted floor.

Laura heard the little girl singing a cheery morning song, and she raised her head to look outside. When she did so she discovered that she was looking down onto an alley. The little girl, whose voice she had heard, was busy hanging a wash on the line in the backyard of the house just across the alley behind this building.

Laura sat up, wondering what time it was. From the position of the sun, she knew that it must be fairly far into the morning, but she and Ella had arrived late last night and the trip was long and tiring. Also the town, which had been so noisy last night, was very quiet this morning, making it conducive to sleeping late.

"We'll talk tomorrow," Ella had told her last night just before they went to bed. "I'll explain everything to you then. Tonight, you just rest."

Laura dressed, then went out into the hallway. When she did so, she saw a very stout, very plain-looking woman folding towels and sheets and stacking them on shelves in a hall closet. She had never seen so many towels before, and she wondered how one place could use so many.

Another door opened, and a pretty young woman came strolling toward the closet. Laura looked at the young woman in some surprise, because not only was she pretty, she was also totally naked!

"Margie, I ran out of towels last night," said the naked girl. She had long, luxuriant black hair, and she brushed her hand through it to push the strands away from her face.

"They were here all along, Julie," the older woman answered. "I brought them in from the line and folded them; I just hadn't gotten around to putting them in the rooms yet. You could've come got them anytime you wanted them."

"I don't want to come get them, I want them in my room," Julie said. "I thought we had an understanding, a division of labor, so to speak. We fuck, you keep us supplied with clean towels.''

Laura gasped silently at hearing such frank language spoken so easily.

''I'm just one person,'' Margie said, walking away in a huff.

Julie turned to Laura, who had been watching everything in fascinated curiosity. ''I tell you, sometimes that woman can be pure mean-spirited,'' she said. She smiled warmly and stuck out her hand. ''You must be Laura, the new girl.''

''Yes,'' Laura answered.

''I'm Julie,'' the girl said. Laura shook Julie's hand, trying to act as if there were nothing unusual in shaking hands with a naked woman. ''Last night, after you got in, Ella told us about you.''

''How many of you are there?'' Laura asked.

''There were five of us, but two girls left. So now there are only three . . . well, four, counting Ella, and five, counting you. You probably won't see any of the others till tonight. Most of 'em sleep all day and don't come out until night. I'd be asleep, too, but I had a visitor who came in early this morning.''

''A visitor?''

''A customer.''

''Oh, yes, of course,'' Laura said.

''Julie? Julie, I must be going,'' called a man's voice from the room with the open door. A man followed the voice, stepping out into the hallway. He was wearing a strange-looking hat, with a small round crown and a small brim. And he was wearing absolutely nothing else. Laura stared at him with her mouth agape.

''Margie, did you get my clothes washed?'' the naked

man asked, showing no more concern than Julie had over being naked in front of Laura.

"Yes," Margie answered, and she pointed to a table upon which lay his freshly laundered underwear, shirt, and pants.

"Thanks," the man mumbled. As he ambled by Laura, he tipped his hat. "Mornin', ma'am," he said politely.

Laura was stunned. She had never seen anyone as ruggedly handsome as this man was: tan, tall, and angular, with wide shoulders, a deep chest, narrow hips, and flat buttocks.

As she had known only Carl Jensen and Martin Rodl, they were also the only men she had ever seen naked, and neither of them had looked at all like this man. Were all cowboys like this one?

She watched, as if mesmerized, as the handsome young man picked up his clothes, then went back into the room from which he had come.

"Careful," Julie said with a quiet laugh. "I've seen that expression in girls' faces before. It almost always leads to more trouble than it's worth."

"What . . . what are you talking about?"

"If you let them get to you, the next thing you know, it stops being a job and you start taking it personal. When that happens you may as well call it quits, because, honey, you'll never be worth a damn after that."

The young cowboy, who by now had finished dressing, reemerged from the room. Flashing a smile and a wave, he trooped loudly down the stairs.

"That was Jake Colby," Julie said. "I expect you'll be seeing him pretty soon."

"No, I won't," Laura said. "I mean, if he is yours . . ."

Julie laughed. "Honey, you didn't listen to a thing I said, did you? None of them are mine . . . and they are all mine. That's the only way you can make it in this particular avocation."

Jim Averill met Jake Colby downstairs. "I've got your cattle for you," Averill said. "Come on outside and have a look."

"All right," Jake said.

He followed Jim out the side door and across an open area to a large cattle pen. There were two or three hundred head of cattle milling about in the pen, several near the large watering tank and several more near the feeding trough. There was a strong odor coming from the pens. The odor would, no doubt, be objectionable to some people, but not to Jake. He found it exciting because of the potential it represented.

"Over there, in that holding pen," Jim pointed out. "There are forty head, already branded with your brand."

Jake looked at Jim. "Already branded? How so?"

"I figured if I sold them to you, I may as well brand them for you as well," he replied.

Jake climbed onto the fence and looked at the cattle he had just bought. These weren't mavericks, they were mature animals, thirty-eight cows and two bulls.

"I think you'll agree with me that there are some fine-looking animals here," Jim said, climbing onto the fence to stand alongside Jake. "Especially considering that you're getting them for ten dollars a head."

One of the cows wandered over to the fence, then stopped very close to Jake. It was so close, in fact, that Jake was able to put out his hand to actually touch the circled H brand. As he ran his fingers across the wound he could feel that the top three-quarters of the circle that enclosed the letter *H* was freshly applied. The rest of the brand, the H and the quarter-circle arc just under the H, were old scars. He pulled his hand away, then looked directly at Jim.

"These are—"

"You ever heard the expression 'Don't look a gift horse in the mouth'?" Jim asked, interrupting him.

"Yeah, I've heard it."

"There's another expression we have out here," Jim said. "It is, 'Don't look too closely at the brand of any cattle you might buy at twenty percent of the market value.'"

Jake nodded. "I was just going to say these are fine-looking brands," he said.

Jim chuckled, then stuck his cigar back into his mouth. "Come on into the house. I'll feed you breakfast, then get a bill of sale made up."

"Thanks," Jake said. "By the way, who is she?"

"Who is she? Who is who?"

"You know who. The new girl Ella brought back."

Jim chuckled. "You like her, do you?"

"She may very well be the prettiest woman I've ever seen," Jake said. "Makes a fella wonder how someone like her would ever wind up in the business."

"Who knows why she came here?" Jim replied. "The girls who do are generally running away from something back home. I never ask. I figure if they've run away from some problem, they don't need me bringing it up again."

"Sounds reasonable to me," Jake agreed.

By the end of the day Jake had all the cattle driven back to the Circle H Ranch. He drove them through into a small canyon that was on his ranch. The canyon was closed in on three sides The far end had been fenced shut, as had this end, though for now the gate was open to allow Jake to push his animals through. Once they were inside, Jake closed the gate, then climbed onto the fence and looked out into his private little valley as the cows he'd just brought began moving around, testing the grazing and finding the water. These forty animals joined the twenty-five head that Eddie had sold him and the ten mavericks he had managed to round up himself, giving him a total of seventy-five. He estimated that his land and the adjacent rangeland would easily support five thousand head of cattle. A quick calculation told him that five thousand head at $75 a head would bring $375,000.

"Over a third of a million dollars!" Jake said aloud. "When I get that many head, I will be a rich man! I'm going to do it, too. Sure as God made little green apples, I'm going to do it!"

Back at the Hog Ranch, Ella had called Laura down to the kitchen. Here, sitting across the table from each other and drinking coffee, they were having the talk she had promised.

"I've looked over your clothes," Ella said. "I'm afraid you're going to have to have all new outfits."

"Why is that? I have very nice clothes. All the latest fashions from St. Louis."

"Yes, dear, and they are wonderful if you are going to a concert or a play, or to some society lady's afternoon tea," Ella replied. "But the clothes you wear here will have to be more, uh . . . ."

"Seductive?" Laura asked.

Ella chuckled. "I was going to say showy, but seductive is good. Here," she said. She laid a handful of brass coins on the table in front of Laura. "Take these down to the seamstress's shop and have Mrs. Teasdale pick out the clothes you'll need. She's outfitted all my girls, she'll know what to do."

Laura picked up the brass coins and looked at them in curiosity. On one side was the bas-relief bust of a woman. On the other side were the words "Redeemable for one dollar at the Hog Ranch."

"What is this?" Laura asked. "What are these things?"

"Money," Ella answered easily.

"Money? Are you serious?"

"Sure," she said. "These brass checks are good as gold here. They buy drinks, food, and a girl's time. And because of that, they have value. They are passed as legal tender all over town." Ella laughed. "I heard tell they've even turned up in the church offering plates."

"All right," Laura said. "If you say so." She scooped up the coins, then left to go shopping.

It had been dark when she'd arrived in Buffalo last night, so this was her first view of Buffalo. The town was small. Any two blocks in Memphis or St. Louis would contain more people and businesses, she thought. Still, there was an excitement about the place that she had not experienced in either of the cities she had lived before.

She walked by a photo gallery. "Photographs taken by expert artist," read a sign in the window.

Laura stopped to look at a few of the pictures, then, with a gasp, noticed that there were at least three rows of photographs of dead men, lying in stiff, awkward angles. Sometimes the eyes were open, sometimes they

were shut. Sometimes they were only half-open, and
sometimes one would be open and one shut. But in every
case their faces were twisted in an expression of final
agony.

A sign below the pictures read "Citizens of Johnson
County, be vigilant! The big ranchers and the Wyoming
Stock Growers' Association have hired assassins to sys-
tematically murder innocent small ranchers and cowboys."

Laura shuddered, then turned away and walked
quickly down the street to the seamstress's shop.

The musical tinkle of a tiny bell attached to the door
announced Laura's presence when she went inside.

Laura saw a dress dummy just about her size, and she
stepped back to get a perspective of it. The dummy was
wearing a very pretty green dress with gold faille upon
the bodice. Such a dress would highlight her auburn hair
and bring out her eyes, and that very comment was made
from behind her.

When she turned, she was looking into the eyes of a
pleasant-looking, middle-aged woman. The woman was
smiling at her.

"I beg your pardon?"

"I said that dress would really make your hair and
eyes look pretty. You must be Ella's new girl."

"Yes. Are you Mrs. Teasdale?"

"That I am, dear," Mrs. Teasdale said. She tilted her
head to one side to study Laura. "Oh, yes, this will be
great fun," she said. "You are such a pretty thing that
I am going to enjoy fixing you up."

"Thank you," Laura said, pleased to hear a friendly
voice from someone who wasn't passing judgment on
her new profession.

THE CAPITOL BUILDING, CHEYENNE

Tom Horn sat quietly in an anteroom off the reception area of the Board of Livestock Commissioners Office Building for the state of Wyoming. He was waiting to keep his appointment with someone, though exactly whom he was to meet had not yet been told to him. He had been brought here by a letter he'd received from an old friend who was still with the Pinkerton Detective Agency.

> Dear Tom,
>
> I know you have quit the Pinkerton Agency because you said you have no more stomach for such as we do. But what I'm figuring now is that you have about had your fill of the peaceful life and are ready, once more, for an interesting job. If such is the case, get yourself to Cheyenne, Wyoming, and speak with a Mr. William Irvine. He is a wealthy cattleman and a member of the Wyoming Stock Growers' Association. He has a job that would be just down your line, and it would pay very well, too.

Tom located Irvine and showed him the letter, asking him if he knew anything about it. Irvine answered that he did, then asked if Tom would wait in the adjoining room for a few minutes.

"I want you to meet with a very important person," he said.

"Who?"

Irvine shook his head. "I'd rather not say, not until I get the two of you together in the same room."

Irvine had offered no further clues as to who the very important person was, and Tom Horn, burning with curiosity, was waiting to see who it was. He had a rope's end that he had braided, and now, as he waited, he took out the little piece and began unraveling it so he could rebraid it. It was a nervous habit he had, to keep his hands busy and help him to pass the time when he was forced to wait. In the profession he had most recently begun, he was sometimes required to wait for long periods of time.

Outside the room he could hear the hollow sound of boots striking marble as the state employees of the livestock commissioners hurried to and fro on their business.

Then, suddenly, and without anyone knocking to announce entry, the door opened and Tom looked up to see Irvine standing there.

"Did you get that important fella I'm supposed to meet with?" Tom asked.

Irvine looked all around the room, as if making certain that no one else was there, then he stepped into the room and spoke back, over his shoulder, to someone who was behind him but still out of sight.

"You can come in, sir," Irvine said. "It's all right."

A well-dressed and exceptionally prosperous-looking man stepped into the room. Irvine took another look around just outside the door, then closed it behind them. The well-dressed man looked quite nervous.

"Excellency, this is Tom Horn. Mr. Horn, this is Governor Richards."

Tom stood up, then walked over toward the governor. He put the rope's end away, then rubbed his palm on his pants before he extended his hand. "Governor, you say! Well, it's a real honor to meet you, Governor," he said, shaking the governor's hand. "Don't know as I ever actually met anyone as important as a governor before.''

"Mr. Horn," Governor Richards replied, "I've heard a lot about you."

"Yeah, well, you know what they say about that. Don't believe a word of it," Tom quipped.

"If I can't believe any of it, Mr. Horn, then I am wasting my time here," the governor replied, showing no sense of humor. "You *are* good with guns, are you not? I mean, that is what they say."

"Yes, sir, I reckon I am pretty good with them," Tom replied. "I've made my living with them for several years now . . . as an army scout, deputy sheriff, U.S. marshal, Pinkerton agent, and, uh, a few other things."

"I also heard that you underwent a conversion of sorts . . . that you got religion and decided not to use your guns anymore. Yet you obviously have continued to do so. Tell me, Mr. Horn, how do you accommodate one fact with the other?"

"Have you ever heard of the Sangre de Cristo monastery?" Tom asked.

"Yes," the governor replied. "It's in Colorado, isn't it?"

"It is, sir. And the men there—they call themselves brothers—they are like no one you've ever seen." Tom's eyes were shining in admiration. "They saved my life by nursing me back to health after I was shot up in a little fracas. But that's not what I'm talking about. What I'm talking about is the fact that they are the finest, most noble men you would ever want to meet. I thought, for a while, that I would like to be just like them, and I tried to join up. But the old padre there knew better than to let me do it. He told me to wait four years

. . . and if I still felt like it, to come on back and they'd take me in.''

"And?" the governor asked.

Tom smiled sheepishly. "Truth is, Governor, it didn't take four days for me to know I could never be like them. So, I got me a three-day drunk and a two-day whore to put all of it behind me. Since then I have been earning my money the only way I know."

"Uh, Mr. Horn has been doing some work for the Wyoming Stock Growers' Association, Governor," Irvine put in.

"Yes," the governor replied. "I've heard of your work. That is why I'm here."

Tom shook his head. "Sorry, Governor, but I'm not interested in becoming a lawman for the state," he said. "I have found the private detective business to be more to my liking."

"And more profitable?" the governor asked.

Tom nodded. "Yes, sir," he answered without backing away from the challenge. "And more profitable."

"Mr. Horn, I am the governor of Wyoming, that is true," Richards said. "But I also own a rather substantial ranch up in Big Horn County, and like many of the other ranchers in the state, I have been plagued by the virtual army of thieves and rustlers who are running roughshod over our state. So it is as a rancher, and not as a governor, that I want to talk to you."

"So what you're saying is, if I do any work for you, it will be as a private detective?"

"Yes, and for a private citizen," the governor replied.

"All right," Tom agreed. "I can handle that."

"Tell me, Mr. Horn, if I decide—as a private citizen—to hire your services, what kind of service might I expect?"

"Guaranteed service, Governor."

"Guaranteed?"

"I will drive every rustler out of Big Horn County. If I don't, I will take no pay whatever, other than a three-hundred-and-fifty-dollar advance, which I shall require to buy two horses and a pack outfit."

"And if you are successful?" the governor asked. "What kind of compensation are you looking for?"

"If I do the job to your satisfaction, Governor, I want five thousand dollars."

"Five thousand dollars?" the governor asked, obviously startled by the amount. "Isn't that a little steep, Mr. Horn?"

"I don't think it's too steep," Tom replied. "You see, Governor, if everything else fails, I have a system which never does. And for five thousand dollars, I place no limit on the amount of men I have to get rid of."

"Get rid of? You mean, run out of the county?"

"Out of the county, out of the state," Tom said. "There are some who will take the warning and pull up stakes and leave, and you'll never have any more trouble with them. But there are others—and these are generally the ones giving you the most trouble—that can't be run out of the state."

"What do you do with those?"

"With men like that, Governor, there's only one thing you can do," Tom said. "And that's get rid of them permanent."

"What do you mean by—"

Tom held up his hand. "You're the governor of the state, Governor Richards," he interrupted. "There are some things it would be best that you not know. For both your protection and mine."

Governor Richards cleared his throat. "Uh, yes, to be

sure," he said. He turned and walked away, then stood there for several seconds as if trying to decide what to do.

Tom stood up. "Governor, I get the sense that while you might want me to work for you, it wouldn't be wise for you to tell me so yourself. And that's probably a good thing for both of us. I presume that I've told you about all you wanted to know, so I'll be going on. I shall be glad to hear from you, or from someone who has your interests at heart, anytime you think I can be of service."

The governor neither responded to Tom's comment nor looked around.

"Good day to you, sir."

"Good day, Mr. Horn," the governor said, still not looking around.

"Mr. Horn, will you wait for me outside?" Irvine asked.

"Sure, I'd be glad to," Tom Horn replied.

After Tom left, Irvine spoke to the governor. "What do you think?" he asked.

"I think Mr. Horn has the right attitude about keeping me out of it," Richards replied.

"I understand," Irvine replied. He cleared his throat. "Now, Governor, about this other thing. Wolcott is still pushing for a state commission. He wants you to appoint him a colonel in the Wyoming militia."

Richards shook his head. "No," he said. "I'm not going to do that."

"But, Governor, the WSGA has already raised over one hundred thousand dollars! We've bought horses, wagons, supplies, and we've got over forty men, trained sharpshooters, armed and ready to go. You were aware of this, I know you were. We have kept you well informed. You could have stopped us at any time with but a word, if you didn't approve."

"I could have, and I have not. Neither am I stopping you now," Richards said, holding up his hand. He turned to face Irvine and let a small smile play across his lips. "Tell Wolcott he can call himself captain, major, colonel, anything he wants. I don't intend to confirm it . . . but neither will I deny it."

Irvine smiled. "Yes, sir, I understand," he said. He rubbed his hands together. "Governor, we've done some good work here today. I predict that cattle rustling is soon going to be as much a part of our past as the buffalo."

When Irvine stepped out into the reception area, he saw Tom Horn engrossed by a picture he was viewing through a stereoscope.

"Mr. Horn?"

"Have you ever looked through one of these things?" Tom asked. "This here is of the Grand Canyon. I've been there, and it looks just like this. I mean, you can almost feel yourself fallin' into the damn thing. How do they do that? How do they make these pictures seem so real?"

"I don't know . . . it has something to do with looking at two pictures with two eyes, so that when you put them together it gives them depth."

"What will they think of next?" Tom said, lowering the device.

"Meet me at the bank at one o'clock this afternoon," Irvine said. "I will give you the three hundred and fifty dollars then."

Tom put the device back on the shelf from which he

had taken it, and he rubbed his hands together. ''Tell the governor he won't be sorry,'' he said.

Irvine cleared his throat. ''We'll keep him out of it,'' he said. ''I'd rather his name not be mentioned again.''

''I understand,'' Tom said. ''I'll see you at one.''

Irvine watched Tom Horn walk away, wondering if he had made a mistake. Was Tom Horn really able to do what he claimed? And if he could do it . . . was that really what they wanted? He sighed. Maybe Wolcott and his private army would be successful. If so, they wouldn't even need Tom Horn's particular brand of service.

★★★

Ten

When someone knocked on the door to Laura's room, she took a deep breath before she opened it. Julie and Sally, and one of the other girls who had befriended her, had told her that they would walk down with her.

"If you have someone with you when you go into the parlor the first time, it isn't as hard," Julie suggested.

"That's the truth," Sally said. "I remember the first time I went down to meet all the men. I was scared to death. I don't think I could have done it if Julie hadn't been with me."

"And now you have two of us," Julie said, smiling at her. She reached out to hook her arm through Laura's. "Come on," she invited. "I won't let anyone eat you."

Sally laughed, then got on the other side, so that with Laura in the middle, they descended the stairway into the parlor of the Hog Ranch.

Several men were already in the parlor, drinking and talking and laughing with each other and with the other women who had gone down before them. The men were ranchers and cowboys, and some of them, Julie had hinted, were actually outlaws.

There was nothing in Laura's experience that had prepared her for this type of man . . . certainly no one in her uncle's church in Memphis or anyone connected with the Rodl Brewery in St. Louis. These men were nearly all young and so full of restless energy that they reminded her of a skittish team of horses, waiting to bolt. There was a rakishness about them that both excited and frightened Laura. All of them were wearing guns and knives, boots and chaps, and hats. They had the interesting habit of doffing their hats when they first came in contact with one of the girls, but once conversation was enjoined, the hats would go back on their heads.

Also—and this she found particularly interesting—nearly all of them were wearing a bright red sash tied around the waist. When Laura asked about it, Julie explained that the sash was a symbol of membership in "sort of a cattlemen's club."

Although all the other girls were moving easily around the room and flirting outrageously with the men, Laura was much more reticent. Overwhelmed, if not actually frightened by it all, she went over to the piano and moved into the corner behind it, as if seeking protection from the walls. She smiled shyly whenever someone spoke to her, but she made absolutely no effort to mingle with the crowd. Instead she preferred to watch from her safe position, studying the interaction of these strange men and loose women.

She almost laughed in spite of herself, for "loose" was the word she had always heard in connection with women who made their living through prostitution. And now *she* was a loose woman, in intent if not yet in fact. But she didn't feel loose. She felt just the opposite. She felt as tightly wound as a pocket watch.

"Honey," Ella said after Laura had stood in the same

corner for nearly an hour, refusing to mix in with the others, "I didn't bring you all the way out here from St. Louis just to hold those two walls together. They have stayed up quite nicely for some time now all by themselves."

Those who were close enough to overhear Ella laughed, and Laura felt her cheeks burn in embarrassment.

"I'm sorry," Laura said.

"I know that breaking in is going to be difficult for you. So I'm not going to say anything else to you about it. But you are going to have to come out and mingle with the others sometime. I just want you to be thinking about it, that's all."

"What about mingling with me?" a man's voice asked, and Laura looked beyond Ella to see Jake Colby, the man she had seen with Julie that morning. When she thought of just how much of him she actually had seen, she blushed again.

"This is Laura Place, Jake. It's her first night, so I'm not going to try to rush her into anything."

"All right, what if we just go up to your room and have a drink and talk?" Jake suggested. "I'll pay the same thing as if I were enjoying your . . . uh, services, but you don't have to do anything," he added quickly, to counter any objection Ella might have.

"What about that, Laura?" Ella asked. "If you are uncomfortable down here with this crowd, going upstairs with Jake might be an easy way for you to at least get to know one of our customers. And this crazy galoot has offered to pay you the same for it," she added with a big smile.

Laura nodded. "All right," she said. "I'll go with him."

Smiling, Jake reached out to take Laura's hand in his.

"Hey, look at Jake!" Eddie Franklin called from his position over on the sofa. Julie was sitting on Eddie's lap, running her fingers through his dark hair. "Leave it to ole Jake to get the newest and prettiest girl here!"

"Hey!" Julie protested, hitting him playfully on the head and shoulders. "I thought you told me I was the prettiest."

Eddie put his arms around her, as much to keep her from hitting him as to express affection. "You are, darlin', you are! You just ain't the newest," he said, trying to assuage her feelings, while Julie and the others laughed at his discomfort.

Laura took Jake upstairs, then into her room. When the door was closed behind them the piano music and the laughter and the boisterous voices from below faded quickly into the background. The effect was sudden and dramatic. It was as if they had been magically transported to another time and place so that they were, truly, alone.

But with this came an awkward awareness of just how alone they actually were. There was a long moment of heavy silence. Finally Jake spoke.

"So, uh, where are you from?" he asked.

"St. Louis," Laura replied. "Before that, Memphis."

"St. Louis is a nice town," Jake said. "Never been to Memphis, though."

"It's nice, too," Laura said. Despite the conditions under which she'd left Memphis, she did have pleasant memories of the city when her parents were still alive.

There was another long moment of silence.

"Is this your first time out west?" Jake asked.

"Yes."

"Do you like it out here?"

Suddenly Laura laughed out loud.

"What is it? What's so funny?" Jake asked, surprised by her laughter.

"Nothing. You. Me," she said. "You brought me up here to talk, and you are trying so hard to find something to talk about. But we both know that's not really what you want, is it?"

"I'll admit that it's not what I want to do. But it is what I said I would do," Jake said. "And I am a man of my word."

"I'm sure you are," Laura said.

The two were quiet for another moment; then, with a resigned sigh, Laura began to loosen the fastenings on her dress.

"Wait a minute. What are you doing there?" Jake asked.

"This is really rather silly, you know. After all, I'm not a virgin, and being a whore, or loose woman, or soiled dove, or whatever it is called, is why I came out here. And if I don't do it tonight, now, with you, I don't know if I will ever find the courage to do it."

"Are you saying that you intend to go to bed with me?" Jake asked.

Laura stopped in the middle of removing her clothes and stared at Jake for a long, penetrating moment. "I haven't misunderstood, have I? This *is* what you want?"

"Oh, my, yes! Of course it's what I really want," Jake replied. "But I don't want to force you into anything. I mean, not after I promised that I wouldn't. So, are you sure you want to do this?"

Laura thought of the scene just outside her room this morning, when Jake had ambled nude down the hall. Then a strange thing happened. She began to feel anew the tingling warmth she had experienced when she'd seen him this morning. And though being with a man wasn't new to her . . . this strange sense of anticipation she was feeling was totally outside her realm of experience.

"Yes," she said, meaning the word more than she thought she would. "I'm sure."

Laura leaned over and extinguished the lantern, but the moon outside was high and so full and bright that even without the lamp, the room was still illuminated by a soft, silver light. It cast everything in subtle shadows of silver and black, allowing them to see each other as they began to remove their clothes.

When she was naked, Laura slipped quickly, and somewhat modestly, into bed. Her modesty did not preclude her desire, though, for as she waited for Jake to finish undressing and get into bed, she felt as if her blood were turning to hot tea.

What was happening to her? She had never felt anything like this before.

Jake climbed into bed, then put his arms around her and pulled her to him. "You've been on my mind ever since I saw you this morning," he whispered to her. "I've never seen anyone as beautiful as you. I've never wanted anyone as much as I want you."

Without protest, Laura gave herself to him, expecting it to be as it always was, expecting to be in control—of the situation, of him, and of herself. But that wasn't how it was. Always before, the act of lovemaking had been an exercise in power and control. It was, in fact, this power and control that had enabled her to bear the unwelcome visitations forced upon her by her uncle. It was also how she was able to derive some degree of personal satisfaction from her relationship with Martin Rodl. But there had never been anything that she could, even remotely, call fulfillment. Indeed, she was absolutely convinced that sex was intended to be satisfying for the man only.

But she didn't believe that now.

After many minutes of the most pleasurable sensations she had ever known, Laura was so suddenly and unexpectedly propelled to a new and extremely heightened sensation that the experience frightened her. Then, from somewhere deep inside, she felt a warm delight that grew in intensity until it exploded in a burst of all-encompassing rapture. The event so overwhelmed her that it caused her body to tremble. Nothing she had ever done, or even imagined, could have prepared her for this moment. She had no idea there could be a pleasure so sweet, an ecstasy so complete, a rapture so overpowering! Was this what men felt? Did Jake feel this as well? And if so, did he feel it as intensely as she?

Jake's frenzied and gasping conclusion told her that he did, and at that precise moment if he had asked her to go to China with him, she would have.

Over the next several weeks there were other men besides Jake. And now that Laura knew pleasure was possible for a woman as well as a man, she schooled herself to accept it. This made her time with them bearable for her and even more pleasurable for them. But not with any of them did she attain the pinnacle of sensation that she had reached with Jake Colby.

For his part, Jake quickly became a regular, coming in to see her at least once a week throughout the entire winter. At first Julie and the other girls teased Laura. Then, when it became obvious that Laura was getting serious, Ella warned her about getting too involved.

"Remember, hon," Ella told her. "What you are experiencing with Jake Colby isn't a courtship. You are a prostitute, and Jake pays you every time he comes to see you. And he knows that any other man who has the price of your services has just as much right to your body as he does. Eventually that can't help but start to eat at him, and when it does, he is going to resent who you are, what you do, and you. Maybe not now, maybe not tomorrow, but someday. These things never work out.''

''But when you came to St. Louis to hire me, didn't you say that it was because a couple of your other girls had fallen in love and gotten married?''

Ella shook her head. ''No, child, I didn't say they fell in love,'' she said. ''I just said they got married. They found someone who offered them a way out of this business before it was too late, and they took it.''

''Then why is what I am doing any different? I mean, if Jake offers to marry me, are you saying that I shouldn't?''

''Honey, as far as I'm concerned, if Jake Colby offers to marry you and you want to use that as your ticket out of here, take it,'' Ella suggested. ''Oddly enough, those marriages do have a way of working out, perhaps because both sides come into it with their eyes open and no expectations of love. All I'm trying to tell you to do is to hang on to your heart.''

Although Laura listened to Ella, she didn't pay much attention to the advice. She was sure that none of the other girls had ever faced quite the same dilemma. Then Julie confessed that she was in love with Eddie Franklin, but she would never let him or anyone else know, because she was positive that Eddie would never settle down.

''And if he believed I was having such thoughts about

him, he might even stop coming to see me altogether,''
Julie concluded. ''So please don't tell anyone what I just
said.''

''Don't worry, your secret is safe with me,'' Laura
promised. Julie's confession told Laura that there was at
least one other person who could feel the same way. She
was glad, then, that this business was not so debilitating
that the inevitable outcome was to become totally jaded.

At first Jake would come in on Saturdays like everyone else. But nearly everyone else came in on Saturday
as well, so it was an exceptionally busy day for the Hog
Ranch. And even though Jake could pay for Laura's
services for the entire night, the ''night'' didn't start until eleven o'clock. That meant he had to share Laura with
everyone else until eleven, and on Saturday night that
could be a considerable number.

Thursday, by contrast, was the lightest night of the
week. Laura told Jake that if he could rearrange his
schedule so as to come in on Thursdays, he would have
her all to himself from the moment he arrived. And because Jake was now his own boss, the change was easily
made.

As Laura fell deeper and deeper in love with Jake,
she began to count the days of the week between their
visits. During the week in between his visits she would
pass the time, when not actually working, by planning
elaborate dinners, which she would have ready for Jake
when he arrived on Thursday night. She also started doing extra little things for him, such as darning socks,
replacing missing buttons, and sewing tears in his shirts
and trousers.

For his part, Jake brought Laura little gifts, and quietly, because they didn't want Ella to know their plans,

they began talking about getting married, planning to take the step "sometime next year."

Jake shared his dream with Laura, the one that had occupied his thoughts for many years now. They would get married and start a family, then build up a herd and raise sons at the same time. Then, when his sons were old enough to help, the herd would be big enough to ship to market.

As Laura shared her secrets with Julie, so too did Jake need someone to talk to. That someone was Eddie Franklin. And although Eddie was Jake's closest friend, it was with some trepidation that he confided in him that he was in love with a whore.

"Ah, don't let it worry you none that Laura is a whore," Eddie Franklin said. "If I was the settlin' down type, I could settle down with Julie, same as if I'd met her in church. And I don't have no doubt but that Nate Champion will wind up marryin' Sally someday. When you get right down to it, I'll bet you half the wives in the West are whores. I've always held that whores was good people, and it's the cowboys' breedin' with whores that's made the westerner such a hearty soul."

Jake laughed. "Eddie, that kind of wisdom should be written in a book."

"Hell, don't think I ain't never thought of writin' me a book," Eddie replied. "I've lived a life that would make a story, and that's a fact."

This particular conversation was occurring just after Eddie had delivered another twenty head of cattle to Jake. Jake and Eddie moved the new cows into his little valley, then Jake closed the gate behind them.

"Pretty good-looking animals," Jake noted as the

new cows hurried off to join the rest of his small but growing herd.

"I've got my eye on another ten or fifteen head," Eddie said. "They're backed off into a draw . . . been there a couple of weeks now. Like as not they'll just die in there, or go wild, if somebody don't take 'em out. If you want them, I can make you a real good price on them."

Jake shook his head. "No thanks. I've got a hundred head now. And four good seed bulls. That ought to give me a pretty good start. I don't reckon I'll be needin' any more."

"That's a shame," Eddie replied. "You've been a pretty good customer. But as long as I've got Nate Champion and Jim Averill to sell my cows to, I reckon there will still be a need for my peculiar brand of services."

"Yeah, unless your 'peculiar brand of services' winds up getting you, and all the rest of us, strung up to some cottonwood tree somewhere," Jake cautioned him with a nervous laugh.

"Listen, if they hung everyone who got their start in this business by rustling cattle, there wouldn't be enough trees west of the Mississippi to handle the rope. And there wouldn't be a rancher left," Eddie insisted. "I told you I used to work for the Rocking H. Would you like to know what my job was for the first two years?"

"What?"

"I would go down into Texas and drive cattle back up to Wyoming to stock the Rocking H range," Eddie said. "Onliest thing is . . . it wasn't bought cattle, it was stole cattle." He laughed. "That's where I learned the profession I am not practicing."

"Really?" Jake asked, surprised at the information.

"Yeah. That's what makes this whole 'war against rustlers' so goddamned hypocritical. I'd be willin' to bet that ninety percent of the cows in Wyoming are descended from rustled Texas stock. Hell, there ain't none of us up here in Johnson County doin' a damn thing that all of them big ranchers hadn't already done. But now that they've all got theirs, they're aimin' to hang on to it by keepin' the rest of us down. Hell, this ain't just my say-so. Ole Jim Averill hisself has written a couple of articles in some of the big newspapers sayin' that same thing."

"I knew Jim had written a couple of letters to the editor about the maverick law," Jake said. "I didn't know he'd written any articles. He seems to be a pretty articulate man."

"Articulate? What's that?"

"It means he is a well-spoken man," Jake explained.

"Oh. Yeah, well, he's that all right, and educated, too. He went to one of them fancy schools back east, did you know that? Cornell, I think it was. Anyhow, he not only knows the big cattlemen for what they are, he lets everyone else know, too, by his articles and letters, and by the things he says to people who come to the Hog Ranch. If you ask me, that's why everyone hates him so much."

"He'd better be careful and not get them too angry at him," Jake said. "The Wyoming Stock Growers' Association is a pretty powerful group, especially with the governor and the legislature behind them. There's not much telling what they may do next."

"Whatever they decide to do, don't forget that they're going to have us Red Sashes to contend with," Eddie answered. "I expect they'll think twice before they try anything."

* * *

On the next morning after the twenty cows were delivered to Jake, Eddie Franklin was sitting on the hole of the privy behind his tiny one-room shack. Attending to his morning constitutional, he could hear the flies that were buzzing noisily around the growing pile of "night soil" beneath him. Adding to this morning concert was the wind whistling through the cracks between the boards and the far-off screech of a hawk.

As Eddie sat there attending to his business, he was reading the *Johnson County News,* chuckling occasionally over the jokes he found in the "Humor of the Day" column.

" ' "Wasn't the late missionary a tender-hearted fellow?" the bishop asked at the good reverend's funeral,' " Eddie said, reading aloud. " ' "Yes," the cannibal replied, picking his teeth. "Him was very tender." ' Haw haw! That's a good one!" Eddie laughed.

Suddenly the door to the outhouse was jerked open and Eddie looked up in surprise. "What the hell?" he gasped. "Who the hell are you? What do you want?"

Because the intruder was silhouetted against the bright sky, Eddie couldn't see any of his features. He could see, however, that the man was holding a gun, and the gun was pointed right at him.

"Eddie Franklin," the man hissed, "I am a cattle detective hired by the Wyoming Stock Growers' Association to hunt your kind down. Your cattle-rustling days are over."

"All right, arrest me, take me in, I dare you," Eddie challenged defiantly. "Because I warn you, if I go to court for cattle rustling, I'm going to tell the truth about everything I know. And I don't think the people who are paying you to hunt me down are going to want to hear the truth!''

''I'm afraid you don't understand,'' the intruder said in a soft, gentle voice. ''I'm not taking you to court. I *am* the court.''

Suddenly the truth dawned on Eddie, and he felt a quick-building panic. ''Oh, sweet Jesus! You're going to kill me, aren't you?''

''You brought it on yourself, Eddie Franklin.''

With the absolute realization that he was going to die, the panic subsided, to be replaced by a peace. He recalled something he'd heard in church once years ago. Something about a ''peace that surpasseth all understanding.'' That was what he was feeling now.

''Will you at least let me pull up my pants?'' Eddie asked calmly. ''I mean, I don't want it to be told in ever' whorehouse an' saloon in Wyoming that Eddie Franklin was shot while he was taking a shit.''

Suddenly the intruder chuckled, then he stepped back away from the door of the privy. ''You make me laugh,'' he said. ''I don't want to kill anyone who makes me laugh.'' He waved his pistol in a dismissing fashion. ''Come on, get out of here,'' he invited him. ''Have you got a horse?''

''Of course I've got a horse. I'd be a damn poor rustler without one.''

Again the intruder laughed. ''Get him saddled, and ride on out of here. Go to California or some such place. Get all the way out of Wyoming and don't come back.''

Eddie breathed a sigh of relief over his reprieve. ''Thanks,'' he said, buttoning his trousers and starting toward the lean-to that was about twenty yards away from the privy. Not having a barn, he kept his horse in the lean-to. ''And don't you worry none about ole Eddie

Franklin comin' back to Wyoming. Been wantin' to see California, anyway. I figure I'll just head out that way. You won't be hearing from me again.''

Eddie neither heard the shot fired nor felt the bullet. Dying almost instantly, he fell forward, facedown, with blood and brain tissue oozing onto the ground through the large wound in the back of his head.

The man who shot him walked over and looked down at him, then used his foot to turn him over. Although Eddie's eyes were wide open, they were already glazed with death.

"Sorry, but I couldn't let you go, Eddie Franklin," the assailant said, speaking to Eddie's corpse. "The best thing I could do for you was to kill you when you didn't know it was comin'. I hope it gave you some comfort."

Quietly the assailant knelt and placed a rock, which he had brought for just this purpose, under Eddie Franklin's head.

Eleven

DENVER

The depot in Denver had several tracks under a great covered shed. The shed, which smelled of coal dust, smoke, steam, and teeming humanity, was a symphony of sound: steel rolling on steel, clanging bells, chugging pistons, rattling cars, shouted orders, and the cacophony of scores of conversations.

Frank Wolcott, who was wearing the uniform of an army colonel, returned the salutes of a couple of cavalry privates who had just detrained and were heading toward the main building. The two soldiers passed George Perry, who was coming from the main building out into the car shed.

"Should you be doing that?" Perry asked Wolcott when he reached him.

"Doing what?"

"Saluting soldiers as if you were a real colonel?"

"I am a real colonel!" Wolcott snapped. "I am a colonel in the Wyoming militia."

"That's not the army."

"During the Great War, do you think officers of the various state militias weren't treated as if they were in the real army? I'll have you know, by God, that Custer himself was a general in the Michigan militia."

"Yes, but we're not exactly at war."

"The hell we're not," Wolcott replied. "That's what this is all about, and don't you forget it. You lose sight of the fact that this is a war, and the rustlers and the small ranchers are going to get the better of us."

"Whatever you say," Perry said, wishing now that he had never brought up the issue in the first place.

"Did you find the stationmaster?" Wolcott asked. "What did you find out about the train?"

"The last word they got is that the train from Texas is on time. It will be here in half an hour," Perry said.

Wolcott pulled out his pocket watch, snapped open the case, and examined it, then put it back. "All right," he said. "We'll wait right here."

Half an hour later the train they were waiting for, its bell clanging, rolled in slowly. The engineer was hanging out of the cab window, concentrating on the track end ahead, as escaping steam curled up around him and glowing embers dripped onto the track bed from the now banked firebox.

With a hiss of its Westinghouse air brakes and the squeal of steel on steel, the train came to a halt bare inches before contacting the end-of-track barrier.

Wolcott and Perry moved up to stand alongside the train, close enough to hear not only the hiss of escaping steam, but the snap and pop of cooling bearings and fittings.

From a vestibule that was several cars down the train, a tall, steely-eyed man stepped onto the platform and looked around. This was Frank Canton, former sheriff of Johnson County and now chief of detectives for the Wyoming Stock Growers' Association. Canton, who was originally from Texas, had a deserved reputation of being quick and deadly with his gun. He had been sent back to his native Texas by the wealthy ranchers to recruit old friends and acquaintances who were equally skilled with guns. These Texas gunmen were to be the core the cattlemen's private army, and to support this army, one hundred members of the Wyoming Stock Growers' Association had pledged $1,000 each.

Canton, standing tall and erect, looked up and down the platform, searching for a familiar face.

"Look at the son of a bitch standing there like he was king of the world," Wolcott snarled. "I can't wait to see the men he brought us. God help us, he probably emptied every jail in Texas."

Perry chuckled. "As big as Texas is, that would sure be a lot of jails," he suggested.

Wolcott glared at him.

There was bad blood between Wolcott and Canton because Wolcott had assumed that his position as head of the army would also put him over all of the detectives, including Canton. But Canton went to the executive committee of the WSGA to tell them that if they put Wolcott over the detectives, he would quit. Not wanting to lose Canton, who was their only proven gunfighter, the committee told Wolcott that he would have no authority over Canton or his detectives.

When Perry saw that Wolcott was going to make no move to contact Canton, he called out and raised his hand.

"Mr. Canton! We're down here!"

"Ah, there you are," Canton said. Perry started toward Canton, and reluctantly Wolcott followed along.

"Been waiting long?" Canton asked.

"Not too long," Perry replied. "We checked the train schedule, and here you are, right on time."

"Good," Canton said. He looked at Wolcott. "Well, Wolcott, I've got your army."

"Where are they?" Wolcott asked. "Bring them out here so I can get a look at them."

Canton stood there long enough to let Wolcott know that he didn't intend to jump to his orders; then, when his point was clearly made, he disappeared back into the train. A few moments later he reappeared, followed by a body of men.

"Oh, look at them," Perry said enthusiastically. "You were wrong, Colonel Wolcott. They are a good-looking bunch of men, well able, I would say, to take care of themselves."

Twenty-two tall, well-proportioned men got off the car, each carrying a rifle and wearing a holstered revolver. Many had knives as well, and a few were wearing bandoliers of ammunition.

"Here they are," Canton said. "Pound for pound, they are as good a bunch of fighting men as you will find anywhere in the world."

"Is that so? Do any of them actually have any fighting experience?" Wolcott asked. "I mean, other than barroom brawls."

"All of them have been under fire at one time or another," Canton insisted. "Some have served as Texas Rangers, some as sheriffs, or deputy sheriffs, and some as deputy U.S. marshals. They are all crack shots, and they aren't afraid of a fracas."

"I'd like to say a few words to them," Wolcott said.

"Be my guest," Canton invited, stepping back and

holding his arm out toward the armed men.

Wolcott looked over the assembly. Though he wouldn't let Canton know it, he had to agree that these were exactly the kind of men he had hoped they would be able to recruit. They were clear-eyed men with strong features and good physiques. In fact, they were the best-looking bunch of men he had ever seen assembled in any one group.

Others in the depot, however, saw only a group of armed and ferocious-looking men. Several people who were passing by, going to or away from the trains, would, upon finding themselves in proximity to such a group, get anxious looks on their faces, then turn and move away quickly.

Wolcott cleared his throat. "Men, I am Colonel Wolcott. I will be your commander during the expedition before you. You have been brought together to take part in an operation that is unique in the annals of law enforcement. Indeed, it should be considered as a military operation, and you should think of yourselves as soldiers in an army rather than as deputy law officers."

"Look here, mister . . . ," one of the men started to say.

"You will address me as ''Colonel.' ''

"What's that?"

"I am a colonel and you will address me as such," Wolcott insisted. "If we are going to be successful in our venture, then we must have military discipline."

"Canton didn't say nothin' 'bout bein' in no army."

Wolcott looked over at Canton. Canton was making no effort to hide the bemused expression he had on his face as he watched Wolcott try to deal with this group of headstrong men.

"What exactly *did* Mr. Canton say?" Wolcott asked.

"He told us we was comin' up here to clear out a bunch of rustlers that you boys couldn't handle by yourselves."

"And he said we'd be gettin' paid pretty good for it," another added.

Wolcott sighed. The men would have to be disciplined, of that he was sure. But the Denver depot was not the place to do it. Instead he decided to address the issue of their pay.

"Indeed, you will be paid well," he said. "You will receive wages of five dollars per day, plus all expenses. In addition"—he held up his finger to make the point—"there will be a bonus of fifty dollars paid for every rustler killed."

"To the person who kills him?"

Wolcott shook his head. "Not just to the person who kills him. The bonus is paid to everyone, regardless of who kills the rustler. So if there are ten rustlers killed . . . every man of you will receive five hundred dollars."

"Yahoo!" someone shouted, and his shout was echoed by all the others.

"And as a matter of prudence, we have also taken out a three-thousand-dollar life insurance policy on each one of you. So those of you who have family will have the peace of mind of knowing that they will be looked after in the event you are killed."

"Frank," Perry said.

"It's *Colonel* Wolcott," Frank said, determined to make certain that the men understood he was senior to everyone now present.

"Very well, *Colonel* Wolcott. These two men want to talk to you."

"What two men?" Wolcott asked, looking around.

"Those two," Perry said, pointing out a couple of

police officers. Canton was already there with them.

"This is Colonel Wolcott," Canton told the policemen when Perry and Wolcott arrived.

"Yes, gentlemen, I am in charge here," Frank said. "What can I do for you?"

"Colonel Wolcott, I am Sergeant O'Mally of the Denver Police Department," replied the bigger of the two policemen. He pointed to the Texans. "Would you be for tellin' me what in the name of all that's holy you are about here?"

Wolcott cleared his throat. "These are members of the Wyoming militia," he replied.

"Wyoming, is it?"

"Yes."

"Sure, an' if it's Wyoming militia they are, what are they doin' in Denver? The passengers are a wee frightened, and they are beginning to complain."

"We are just passing through, Sergeant. These men will all be on the next train headed for Cheyenne."

"Aye, they will be, an' that's for sure. But not armed like that," O'Mally said. " 'Tis the law here that before a body can board a public conveyance leaving this depot, he has to check through his guns. Will your men be for doin' that, now?"

"No, that is quite unacceptable. I explained to you that this is a military unit, and I will not ask these men to give up their arms," Wolcott said.

"Then, I'll not be for lettin' them get on."

"Excuse me, gentlemen," Canton said. "Perhaps I can offer a solution. Sergeant O'Mally, what if we had a private car, attached to the train?"

"It won't do," O'Mally replied. "For sure'n they would still have access to the rest of the train."

"I forgot to mention that we also have four freight

cars loaded with supplies . . . which we bought from the Denver merchants, I might add. Suppose we connected the freight cars to the end of the train, then attached our private Pullman at the end of the freight cars. That would provide some separation from the rest of the passengers.''

''The situation would still be same. Whether the car 'tis separated or not, you would be attached to the train,'' O'Mally insisted.

''Very well,'' Canton said. ''We'll just keep the men here until the governor of Wyoming clears it with the governor of Colorado. But I have to tell you, these men are mostly from Texas, and Texas men tend to get a little rowdy if you try to keep them in one place for too long. I'm not sure we can keep them confined to the depot, though we'll do our best.''

''No,'' O'Mally said, shaking his head forcefully. ''You'll not be for keepin' them here in the depot. Not armed the way they are.''

''What is the alternative?'' Canton asked. ''That you take them to jail? How are you going to do that? There are only two of you, and neither of you is armed. And I don't think these men would go willingly.''

''Aye, it would seem that you have me there,'' O'Mally said. He took off his dome-shaped hat and ran his hand through his red hair. Finally he sighed in resignation. ''All right, get your cars connected and have them on the next possible train to Cheyenne. Just be promisin' me that you will keep them out of trouble until the train pulls out.''

''Don't worry, we'll take care of them,'' Wolcott promised.

With one final glance toward the heavily armed men, the two police officers left.

"What do you mean, you'll have the governor of Wyoming contact the governor of Colorado?" Wolcott asked after the two policemen were gone. "Have you gone crazy? You know the governor wants to be left out of this."

"I know," Canton replied. "But I also knew that these two policemen didn't want a bunch of heavily armed men hanging around the depot any longer than they had to. I ran a bluff on them, and it worked."

"What if it hadn't?"

Canton chuckled. "Well, *Colonel*," he said, coming down so hard on the word "colonel" that he made a mockery of it, "if it hadn't worked, I guess we would have been forced to kill them."

Perry gasped, then stared at Canton for a long moment. He wasn't sure if Canton was teasing or not.

When the train reached Cheyenne, the special attachment of freight cars and the Pullman were shunted over into the switchyard. There, three stock cars filled with horses, a baggage car, and a caboose were added to make a new train. Here, too, they were met by Doyle Hunter and nineteen other members of the Wyoming Stock Growers' Association, all armed and ready to join with the group.

There was a carnival-like atmosphere on the grounds of the Cheyenne railroad station. Literally hundreds of townspeople had poured out into the switchyard to congregate alongside the private train. Vendors were moving through the crowd, hawking their goods. An itinerant preacher had climbed onto an overturned box and, holding the Bible open with his left hand, struck it repeatedly with his right as he shouted an unintelligible sermon to the crowd. In addition to sounds of the vendors, the preacher, the laughter and conversation of the crowd, the chug of locomotives, clattering hooves, and the occasional neighing of a horse, there was also the music of the fireman's band playing martial airs.

"What is all this?" Canton asked in exasperation, throwing out his hand to take in the circus that was spread before him. "Why are there so many people here?"

"What did you expect?" Wolcott asked. "We are an army going to war, and like any army going to war, we are marching off with the good wishes of our citizens."

"But how did they know we were coming?"

"I told the newspapers," Wolcott said. "I'm sure they have printed it in several editions, by now."

"You *told* the newspapers?" Canton shouted in an exasperated tone of voice. "Why did you do that? Don't you think our chances for success will be much greater if we are able to surprise the rustlers?"

"That might be the way you do it with your detectives, Mr. Canton. But we are an *army,* by God. And, as an army, we don't have to skulk through the dark for anyone. I told the newspapers because I think the people of Wyoming have a right to know that there are men who are willing to put their lives on the line for them."

"That's bullshit, Wolcott, and you know it," Canton replied. "There's not a man here who is putting his life on the line for the citizens of Wyoming. They are putting their lives on the line for the money we promised them. Even the wealthy cattlemen who are sponsoring this aren't doing it for the citizens of Wyoming . . . they are doing it for themselves."

"Whatever the motive, I know from experience that an army needs the morale lift it can get from a rousing send-off," Wolcott said. "I do not, for one minute, regret that I let it be known what we are about.''

At that moment two men approached Wolcott. One, Wolcott recognized as David McCloud, city editor for the local *Cheyenne Sun*. David smiled and shook Wolcott's hand.

''Well, Colonel Wolcott, I thank you again for the information you provided me. As you can see, my story was quite well received. All these people are here to see you off and wish you well.''

''Yes, thank you, Mr. McCloud,'' Wolcott replied. ''You did a good job.''

Shaking his head in disgust, Canton walked away from them, leaving Wolcott to deal with the newspaperman himself.

''Now, I have a favor to ask of you,'' McCloud said.

''What is that?''

''This is my friend Vernon Peterson. He is a correspondent for the *Chicago Herald*. He and I would like to accompany your expedition against the rustlers.''

Wolcott shook his head. ''No, I'm afraid that would be impossible. This could be quite dangerous.''

''We are fully prepared for that danger,'' McCloud said. ''Haven't newspapermen faced such dangers before, during the war?''

''Yes,'' Wolcott agreed.

''Why would you consider us any less willing to face these dangers than our brothers have been before us?'' McCloud wanted to know.

''And consider this,'' Peterson added. ''Any story I write for the *Chicago Herald* will, no doubt, be picked up by the Associated Press and reprinted in papers all across America. This is a way for you to see to it that your side of this story reaches the public.''

Wolcott stroked his chin for a long moment, then he

nodded. "All right," he said. "The two of you may go. But you are responsible for your own safety. I can't be bothered with you."

"Don't worry about us," McCloud said. "We'll take care of ourselves."

Arrangements had already been made with the Union Pacific to supply an engine and train crew for the army's private train. Just as Wolcott concluded his conversation with McCloud and Peterson, the engineer and conductor approached.

"The train is assembled, Mr. Wolcott," the conductor informed him. "Have you any specific instructions?"

"Yes. I would like to get under way as quickly as we can get everyone boarded," Wolcott said. "Hurry up. Put us at Casper and we will do the rest."

★★★

Twelve

Ragged gray clouds hung low in the cold April sky, threatening rain but, so far, not delivering on their promise. The four black horses that had drawn the hearse into the graveyard stood by in well-trained stateliness as Eddie Franklin's coffin was taken from the back of the black-and-glass coach. Half a dozen wagons and buckboards had followed the hearse into the graveyard, and the thirty or so people who had used these conveyances now climbed down and walked over to stand by the open grave.

Several women were present, including the sisters and wives of other members of the Red Sash Gang, as well as all the whores from the Hog Ranch. But only Julie was dressed in widow's weeds, complete with a black veil.

With a look toward the sky, as if mouthing a silent prayer for the rain to hold off, Father Gaylord McKenzie, rector of All Saints Episcopal Church, began the graveside rites.

"Man, that is born of a woman, hath but a short time to live, and is full of misery. He cometh up, and is cut down, like a flower: he fleeth as it were a shadow, and never continueth in one stay.''

Julie sobbed aloud, and Laura, who was standing next to her, put her arm around her.

''Yet, O Lord God most holy, O Lord most mighty, O holy and most merciful Savior, deliver us not into the bitter pains of eternal death.''

The rector looked at Julie and nodded. After lifting the veil and wiping away the tears, Julie, who had been chosen for the task, leaned down and picked up a handful of dirt. She dropped it onto the pine box that was Eddie's coffin.

''For as much as it hath pleased Almighty God in his wise providence to take out of this world the soul of our deceased brother, Eddie Franklin, we therefore commit his body to the ground; earth to earth, ashes to ashes, dust to dust; looking for the general Resurrection in the last day, and the life of the world to come, through our Lord Jesus Christ; at whose second coming in glorious majesty to judge the world, the earth and the sea shall give up their dead; and the corruptible bodies of those who sleep in him shall be changed, and made like unto his own glorious body; according to the mighty working whereby he is able to subdue all things unto himself.''

The graveside service completed, the mourners began returning to their wagons and buckboards for the drive back into town, while behind them they could hear the sound of dirt being shoveled, as the gravedigger began closing the grave.

Back at the Hog Ranch, Jim Averill and Ella Watson held a wake for Eddie, and in attendance were Jake, Nate Champion, Joe Curry, and several of Eddie's small rancher, cowboy, and outlaw friends. Julie was taking

Eddie's death particularly hard, and even though she had no direct relationship with him, the others, even Ella, were treating her as if she really had been Eddie's wife.

Jake was sitting on the sofa between Julie and Laura, providing both of them with what comfort he could. He wasn't surprised to see that Laura was taking it nearly as badly as Julie. After all, Eddie had been his closest friend, and Julie was Laura's closest friend. What Jake didn't realize, though, was that it wasn't as much Eddie's death that bothered her as what his murder represented. To Laura, it represented a real and immediate threat to Jake and to her own happiness.

"You know what I can't help but think?" Laura asked.

"What's that?" Jake replied.

"I can't help but think that it could have been you we buried today."

"I suppose it could be anybody," Jake admitted. "John Rollins was killed not long ago, and he was one of the straightest men I've ever known."

Laura put her head on Jake's shoulder. "Promise me," she said.

"Promise you what?"

"That you won't let anything happen to you."

Jake chuckled. "I don't plan to," he said.

"If it did . . . if you were to be killed, like Eddie, I couldn't go on. I wouldn't stay here . . . not one more minute would I stay here."

Jake put his arm around Laura. Seeing them together that way seemed to make Julie even more aware of her own loss, and she began sobbing anew. Jake, realizing intuitively what Julie was thinking, put his arm around her as well.

"Well, if you ask me, it's an outrage," Jim Averill

said. His voice was angry and loud enough to cut through a dozen or more conversations, thus getting everyone's attention. "The big ranchers are so far above the law now that they can pay to have anyone killed they want, without any fear of reprisal."

"It's like they were paying someone to shoot wolves, or other such varmints," Nate Champion suggested. He took a drink, then wiped his mouth with the back of his hand. "Only we ain't varmints, by God, we're men!" Sally, who was sitting next to him, wiped her tears away and nodded in the affirmative.

"Jim, don't you have some friends down in Cheyenne who could look into this?" one of the cowboys asked.

Jim shook his head. "I'm afraid not. I'm as much a pariah to these fellas now as you boys are. I've taken your side in the letters and articles I've written, and now they are convinced that every cow I own had somebody else's brand before it had mine."

"Now, where in the world did they get such an idea?" Nate asked sarcastically, and everyone laughed.

Jim held up his hand. "All right, all right, I'll admit, I don't question you boys all that closely when you bring stock in to sell. So I guess that does sort of put us all in the same boat. But I don't mind telling you, this boat has a leak, and it is sinking fast. The big ranchers are coming after us, and they're coming hard. There's no telling where this is all going to end . . . but I don't think it's going to end well."

"I've heard they're gettin' up an army to come after us," someone suggested.

"Yeah, well, let 'em," another said. "An army comes at you in the open. We can fight an army. What we can't fight are these bastards who hide in the dark and shoot us down."

"Yeah," Nate said. He was the one who had found Eddie's body. "And you know what really pisses me off? It was the way whoever killed Eddie put that rock under his head. I mean, he did it like he was playing some sort of low joke or something."

Jake jumped when he heard what Nate said.

"What is it?" Laura asked him, feeling his reaction and looking over at him in curiosity. Lost in her own fears and her sympathy for Julie, she had not been following the conversation.

"What did you say?" Jake asked.

"I said let them bring an army. We can fight them," one of the cowboys said.

"No," Jake said, waving him off. He pointed to Nate. "You, Nate. Did you say something about a rock?"

"Yeah," Nate replied. "When I found Eddie, he was lying on his back with a rock under his head, like a pillow. And it was very obvious that it was no accident. Someone put that rock there. To me, it was just like pourin' salt into the wound."

"That's a strange thing for someone to do. I've never heard of anything like that," Curry said.

"My God, it's Tom Horn," Jake said. "They've set Tom Horn on us."

Jake's declaration stopped all conversation, for nearly everyone present knew of Tom Horn and of his reputation as a tracker and marksman.

"What makes you think the big cattlemen have hired Tom Horn?" Jim asked.

"They must have," Jake said. "What other reason would he have for killing Eddie?"

Laura gasped. "No," she said. "I don't believe Tom Horn is the kind of man who could kill Eddie like that."

"Laura, do you know Tom Horn?" Jake asked, surprised by her spirited defense of him.

"No, not really," Laura said. "But I have met him. Ella and I both met him."

"That's right," Ella interjected. "Some men, one named Payson and two of his friends, were getting most unpleasant with us when we were on the way up here from Casper. It just so happened that Tom Horn was in the saloon, too, and he called them out for it. When he did, they got real frightened, and left."

"I don't believe there is any one man in the world who could make me turn tail and run if I had two more with me," someone called out.

"Then you don't know Tom Horn," Jake said quietly.

"No, I don't. Who is he? A ten-foot giant with two heads and six arms?"

"That about sums it up," Jake said simply and without elaboration.

"Jake, you said you think Tom Horn was the one who killed Eddie Franklin," Jim said. "What makes you think that?"

"I don't just think it, Jim," Jake said. "I *know* Tom Horn did it."

"How do you know? Have you heard something the rest of us haven't heard?"

"It was the rock under Eddie's head that gave it away," Jake said. "Tom Horn and I are—or, rather, we were—friends. Close friends. I've known him for a long time, although I haven't seen him for several years. He and I were scouts together under Al Sieber, for General Crook and General Miles."

"Son of a bitch!" someone suddenly said, snapping his fingers and pointing at Jake. "I *knew* I'd heard your name before. It's been botherin' me all this time while

I've been tryin' to figure it out. But I've read about you, Jake Colby. You're a genuine hero! You were one of the ones who brought in Geronimo, aren't you?''

"I was there," Jake admitted. "But it was mostly Al Sieber and Tom Horn."

"I don't get it," Nate said. "What does the rock under Eddie's head have to do with all this?"

"That's what I was getting to," Jake explained. "You see, Tom has this peculiar habit. Every now and then, we would get into a little skirmish with the Indians. Whenever it was over, Tom would go out among the bodies of the Indians we had killed and put stones under their head. But he wouldn't do it with all of them. He would only do it with the ones that he, personally, had killed. It's like, some men carve notches into the butt of their gun, Tom Horn left a rock."

"Why did he do that?" Jim asked.

Jake shook his head. "I don't really know. He never told us why, and neither Al nor I ever asked."

"And you think he's the one who killed Eddie, just because he used to put rocks under Indians' heads?" someone asked.

"Yes," Jake answered. "He must be doing the same thing now."

"That could just be a . . . what do they call it? Coincidence."

"Then there were six other coincidences," Joe Curry said quietly.

"What's that?" Jim asked. The others in the room looked over at Curry.

"Are you saying some of the others who have been killed also had a rock put under their head?" Nate asked.

"Yes. Nobody has mentioned it before, because nobody knew what it meant," Curry said. "Until now."

Jim Averill took a swallow of his drink, then looked reflectively at the others. "That's seven now," he said. "Seven of our friends found dead with a rock under their head."

"Boys, I don't know about the rest of you, but I aim to get out of here until all this has blowed over," Joe Curry said. "I've stayed alive this long by not getting people like Tom Horn dogging my trail. And I don't plan to go back on that habit now."

"Jake, did you say this fella Horn was a friend of yours?" Nate asked.

"He was, at one time."

"Maybe you could go to him and tell him our side of the story. Maybe you could talk him into going away," Nate suggested.

"No!" Laura said quickly, putting her arms around Jake's arm as if to keep him here.

Jake smiled. "I'd be glad to do that, Nate, if I thought it would do any good," he said. "But if there's one thing I know about Tom, it's that he is loyal to the side he has signed on with. If he's working for the Wyoming Stock Growers' Association, we couldn't change him over to our side if we doubled the money they're paying him."

"You sound almost as if you admire the man," Jim said.

Jake was silent for a moment. "I do," he finally said. "I think Tom Horn is one of the most admirable men I have ever known."

AT A POINT HALFWAY BETWEEN CASPER AND BUFFALO

DISPATCH TO THE *CHEYENNE SUN*, FILED BY DAVID McCLOUD

When we offloaded the men and equipment at Casper, little did we know that the easy part of the expedition was over. We would now have to cover the 150 miles between Casper and Buffalo by horse and wagon. Buffalo, it is believed by all who are familiar with the situation, is the "rattlers' nest," the headquarters of all the nefarious activity that takes place in Johnson County and around Hole in the Wall.

Our first military act, therefore, was to see to it that the telegraph wires between Casper and Buffalo were cut, thus isolating the rustlers' headquarters. That was accomplished without difficulty, for we conducted a test to determine its success. Our next step was to begin the transit north, and it is here that we ran into our first problems.

To our discomfort and frustration, we discovered that melting snows from the winter just passed have left the ground soft and muddy. Thus our wagons, heavily laden as they are, have been bogging down, sometimes sinking hub-deep in the mud, making it almost impossible for the horses to draw them. In addition, one of our wagons actually fell through the floor of a bridge and had to be pulled from the gulch below by a system of ropes tied to saddle horns.

Another thing happened which would have been funny had it not caused a delay of several hours. Our hired mercenaries, being from Texas, were not aware of how shallowly rooted our sagebrush can be, especially when the ground is as soft as it is now. They tied their horses to the sagebrush, thinking it would restrain them, as indeed it would in their native state.

Not here, however, and soon the horses pulled loose and started upon their own way. It was indeed comical to see these men, armed to the teeth, proven fighters every one, reduced to the state of a "greased pig chase" as they ran out across the prairie, chasing down their mounts. Finally the horses were secured, the wagons hitched up, and locomotion was reestablished.

We are now two days out of Casper, and halfway to our destination. We are presently camped at the ranch of John A. Tisdale. Mr. Tisdale is a member of the Wyoming Stock Growers' Association and a very strong supporter of our effort.

During the journey of this last two days I have had the opportunity to examine this private "army" and confess to being most favorably impressed, despite the difficulties we have encountered. They appear to be dedicated men, for in their spare time they turn their attention first to their horses, and then to their weapons. And although their guns are already as clean as any utensil you might put on your serving table, even as I write this, I can look around the barn and see nearly all of these men paying laborious attention to detail as they disassemble, clean, and reassembled their weapons.

But, as in any army, there is also time for relaxation. And over in another corner of the barn, as I write this, four men are gathered around the fifth. The fifth is strumming a guitar and they are all singing a song with what, I must confess, are very good voices and well-established harmony.

Our supper tonight consisted of a rich and hearty beef stew, served from a very large pot which hangs suspended over an open fire. Even now a delightful aroma permeates the barn, reminding us all of the best meal we have had since leaving Cheyenne.

On a more serious note, we are an army, and we will be facing armed and dangerous men. Such a thought makes me melancholy, for I can't help but wonder if this may be the last decent meal some of these men will eat.

There has also been a great improvement in our sleeping conditions as well, for tonight we will bed down in the warm, dry hay of the barn.

Our two leaders, Colonel Frank Wolcott, and Colonel Frank Canton, do not always see eye to eye on the way things should be done. There is much discussion between the two, some of it quite heated. But I believe that such discord is to be expected when two powerful men are united for a common cause.

I am reminded that William Travis and Jim Bowie were at odds with each other during the siege of the Alamo. Despite this, all the world knows what wonderful things they were able to accomplish in that uneasy but historic partnership.

I feel that Colonel Wolcott and Colonel Canton,

joined as they are in the desire to raid Wyoming of the perfidious rustler, will also be able to put aside their differences in order to bring victory for this army of justice.

It is in the dry warmth of Mr. Tisdale's barn that I am writing this dispatch, but now I must bring it to a close in order that Vernon Peterson, the reporter for the *Chicago Herald,* and I may send our articles back to Casper by one of Mr. Tisdale's cowboys.

"Is that your first article?" Wolcott asked as McCloud was folding the paper and putting it in an envelope.

"Yes," McCloud answered.

"Do you mind if I read it?"

McCloud thought for a moment, then took the paper out of the envelope and handed it to Wolcott. Wolcott read through it quickly, then handed it back.

"What do you think?" McCloud asked.

"It makes us look a little like a bunch of bunglers, don't you think? I mean, telling about the horses getting loose, our wagons miring down, and one of them falling through a bridge?"

"Not at all," McCloud replied defensively. "On the contrary, I believe it shows our readers the hardships we are going through . . . and are willing to go through, to accomplish the mission. That we can endure such difficulty bespeaks the effectiveness of our leadership."

Wolcott thought about McCloud's words. Then he nodded. "Yes," he said. "Yes, of course you are right. This does prove that strong leadership is required to keep everything together. Oh, and one more point. In future articles, please refer to Canton as 'Mr.' Canton, for he is not a colonel. Only I am a colonel."

"Yes, of course," McCloud agreed, happy that Wolcott did not attempt to stop, or censor, his dispatch.

McCloud and Peterson called over the cowboy who had been designated to take his story to Casper.

"How soon will you be there?" McCloud asked.

"I'll ride all night," the cowboy answered. "I'll have your stuff there in the morning."

"And you'll take my piece directly to the telegraph office?" Peterson asked.

"Just like you said, Mr. Peterson."

"Good man, good man," Peterson said.

McCloud and Peterson watched the cowboy mount, then ride out at a gallop, as if delivering the pony express. McCloud chuckled.

"If he keeps that up, his horse won't last ten miles, let alone sixty-five."

"I think he was giving us a little of a show," Peterson suggested.

"I'm sure he was."

Again Wolcott came over to talk to McCloud. "Well, I see you two got your articles off."

"Yes, we did," Peterson replied. "And we appreciate your making arrangements with Tisdale to have one of his men act as a courier for us."

"Glad to do it. After all, we need to let the people know that their leaders aren't letting them down," Wolcott said.

"Colonel Wolcott, may I ask you a question?" McCloud asked.

"Yes, of course."

"What about Jim Averill?"

"What about him?"

"Jim Averill owns a saloon just outside Buffalo," McCloud said.

"Yes, I know who he is."

"And he has befriended the ranchers, cowboys, and outlaws of Johnson County to the degree that many look to him as their spokesman."

"I am aware of that as well," Wolcott replied. "What is your point?"

"My point is that Jim Averill has already written several articles stating their side in this dispute, and he is a very fine writer. In fact, our newspaper is now getting letters from readers who are beginning to question the WSGA. It would seem to me that if we are to succeed in this, we are either going to have to win Jim Averill over to our side or we are going to have to find some way to keep him quiet."

A small, conspiratorial smile played across Wolcott's face. "You need not worry about that, Mr. McCloud," he said. "Do you think we would undertake such a mission without silencing our most visible opponent? Events have already been put into motion to take care of the vocal Mr. Jim Averill."

The first pink fingers of dawn touched the mesa, and the light was soft and the air was cool. The last morning star made a bright pinpoint of light over the Big Horn Mountains, lying in a purple, ragged line to the west.

Tom Horn had come in the dark of early morning and, wrapped up in his blanket and poncho, waited for the sun to rise. He really wanted a smoke, but he knew that a cigarette could give him away, from either the glow of the tip or the smell of the smoke.

Though lesser men might give in to impatience, hunger, or discomfort, Tom Horn would not. He was effective because he was willing to be cold, wet, hungry, or thirsty, waiting for as long as it took to get the perfect shot.

A rustle of wind through feathers caused him to look up just in time to see a hawk dive on its prey. The hawk swooped back into the air, carrying a tiny field mouse that was kicking fearfully in the predator's claws.

People condemn me, Tom thought. They condemn me for what I am, and they call me a murderer. But how am I any different from the hawk? I am the hawk, and the people I hunt are the prey. The hawk is a part of nature, and so am I.

Tom Horn liked the analogy of the hawk and thought that he might use it sometime, perhaps to explain his position to the brothers of Sangre de Cristo. But for now he turned his attention to the little ranch house in the valley below, recalling what the representative of the Wyoming Stock Growers' Association had told him when he'd made this house Tom Horn's next target.

"I didn't get the name of the man that lives there," the representative had said as he'd pointed out the location on the map. "But I do know that this is one of the places on our list."

Tom had held up his hand. "It doesn't matter," he said. "I don't need to know a man's name to kill him. Sometimes it's better if I don't."

"It's probably just as well," the WSGA man said. "Anyway, according to the notes I've got here, this fella is callin' hisself a rancher, but ever' damned cow he's got on the place has been rustled."

"I'll take care of him," Tom promised.

"As soon as we hear that you have, we will make another payment."

*   *   *

The occupant of the house Tom was watching was just now waking up. For a moment Jake Colby was in that gray area between sleep and wake, commingling dream with reality.

In his dream Laura had been kissing him, touching him, holding him, arousing him . . . and now she was gone. He tried desperately to go back to sleep, to recapture the moment, and it almost worked, because he could smell her skin and sense her presence.

But when he physically reached for her, she wasn't there. Reality overtook fantasy, and the dream began sliding further and further away, until finally Jake was wide awake and knew he would not be able to recover the pleasure.

He lay in bed for a long moment after that, trying to remember the dream in order to hang on to its sweetness for as long as he could. But soon, even the memories began to fade, and with a sigh he sat up. He had to work on the roof of his barn today. It wasn't the kind of work he enjoyed, so the sooner he got to it, the sooner it would be over.

Running his hand over the bedside table, Jake located the matches, then used one to light the candle. A golden bubble of light pushed away the darkness, and Jake walked over to the little stove to get a fire going.

Fifteen minutes later the stove was putting out enough heat for him to make coffee, fry a couple of pieces of bacon, and scramble a couple of eggs.

From his position outside, and about seventy-five yards up the hill from the little house, Tom could smell the aroma of coffee and cooking bacon. It reminded him that he was hungry, and he reached into his shirt pocket and pulled out a piece of jerky. Wiping away the dirt and lint, he took a bite, then, because he didn't know when he would be able to eat again, he put the rest of the jerky back into his pocket and waited.

Half an hour later the back door to the shack opened, and Tom jacked a shell into the chamber of his Winchester .44-40 and raised it to his shoulder. But his prey—for Tom was now thinking of his targets in that way, himself as the hawk and the men he was hunting as prey—leaned far enough only to toss out a pan of water, then went back inside without ever affording Tom a clear shot.

Tom lowered the rifle. He was a patient man, he would wait for his opportunity. A few minutes later the back door reopened, and once again his prey came out onto the porch.

The prey stretched, then scratched himself. Tom raised the rifle to his shoulder, pulled back the hammer, and put the rifle site just behind his prey's ear. Slowly he began squeezing the trigger. He was just about ready to touch off the shot when his prey put on his hat.

"Son of a bitch!" Tom said aloud, lowering the rifle quickly. He had seen that hat before.

The hat was the round crown and narrow brim of a bowler. This wasn't prey! This was his old friend Jake Colby.

Tom waited until Jake went into his barn before he got on his horse and rode off. He left on the ground behind him the rock that would have marked what was to be his twelfth victim.

★★★

Thirteen

It was an especially quiet Sunday morning at the Hog Ranch, but the night before had been one of their busiest yet. Nearly three dozen cowboys and small ranchers had come calling, seeking the release of a week's worth of pent-up energy in the company of the girls of Hog Ranch. Several of the visitors, needing more extensive interaction with the young women than mere drinks and conversation could provide, arranged to spend the night. Most of them didn't leave until six o'clock this morning. As a result, all of the girls were upstairs, still sleeping.

Only Ella Watson was awake, and because she enjoyed quiet mornings like this one, she had come downstairs to share the time with Jim Averill. Ella and Jim were in the sitting room of the two-room apartment in which Jim lived, just off the back of the saloon. A fire was burning cheerily in the little potbellied stove, and the aroma of freshly brewed coffee permeated the room.

"More coffee?" Ella asked, getting up from her chair.

"Yes," Jim answered, holding out his cup. "Thank you."

Grabbing a handful of her skirt to use as a hot pad,

Ella picked up the blue pot from the top of the stove and poured a second cup for each of them. When she'd put the pot back down, she opened the door to the stove and threw in another stick of wood. The flames began licking around the new log, and it started popping and snapping as it caught.

Ella returned to her chair at the table. "This is nice," she said. "Sitting here, by a cozy fire, just the two of us."

Jim was reading a newspaper, and he looked up and smiled. "Yes, it is," he agreed.

They drank their coffee in silence for several more moments as Jim continued to be lost in the newspaper.

"It would be nicer, though, if I had someone to talk to," Ella finally said in exasperation. "What on earth have you found that is so interesting? You've barely said a dozen words to me since I came down this morning."

"I think the word is 'disturbing,' more than 'interesting,'" Jim said. He thumped the paper with the back of his hand. "According to this article, the big cattlemen have gone down to Texas to raise their own private army."

Ella laughed. "A private army? What in heaven's name are they going to do with a private army? Invade Kansas?"

"I wish I could laugh it off as easily," Jim said. "But to tell the truth, it worries me."

"Oh, Jim, what are you worried about? I mean, really, think about it. There's no way the law is going to allow the cattlemen to hire an army to run roughshod over Wyoming."

"The law? What law is this you are talking about, Ella? Is it the law that empowers the private detectives that work for the big ranchers, with all the authority of state officers? Is it the law that allows a notorious killer like Tom Horn to murder at will? I mean, everyone knows that he is out there somewhere, roaming around, killing without compunction, and leaving those grotesque markers of his strewn about. But has the law done anything to stop him? No, they have not.''

"Yes, but Tom Horn is only one man, and he is working in the shadows. I'm sure the law would stop him if they could find him. This article is talking about an army. I mean, suppose they do raise an army, what can they do with it? Who would they make war against? The outlaws in Hole in the Wall? You and I both know those boys can take care of themselves.''

"Yes, but can we?'' Jim asked ominously.

"What do you mean, we?''

"Let's face it, Ella, you and I are not very popular among the 'decent folk,' " Jim said. "And we make very easy targets since they know where we are all the time.''

"You worry too much,'' Ella said. "Why, I'll bet outside of Buffalo no one has ever even heard of us. Your articles and letters to the editor, maybe, but that's all.''

"You think not? Perhaps you should read this article.''

"What are you saying? That they mention us in the newspaper?'' Ella asked. Rather than being frightened, she was almost intrigued by the idea that her name was in the newspaper. "What do they say about us?''

"They say that we are behind all the rustling that's been going on up here,'' Jim said. "They say that I buy stolen cattle from the outlaws and you accept stolen cattle from the cowboys as payment for the services your girls render.''

"I've bought a few cows, just as you have. And I've loaned some money using cattle as collateral," she said. "But the fact that we aren't too particular about where the cows come from that we buy hardly means that we are behind all the rustling. Is that really what that paper says? That Jim Averill and Ella Watson are behind the rustlers?"

Jim chuckled. "Well, actually, they are calling you 'Cattle Kate.' "

"What? Cattle Kate? What an awful name!" Ella squealed in protest. "Let me see that article!"

Jim handed her the paper.

Ella began to read aloud: " 'The prostitutes who work at Ella Watson's Hog Ranch are a magnet for the woman-hungry cowboys and outlaws of Johnson County. And if the customers are short of cash, they pay in cattle . . . more often than not someone else's cattle. Cattle Kate, as Miss Watson is widely known, is said to be more than willing to accept stolen cattle as her price for the services of the prostitutes she supplies.' "

Ella handed the newspaper back to Jim. "Cattle Kate indeed," she scoffed. "If they are going to write about me, the least they can do is call me Ella Watson. If anyone is going to change my name, it's going to be me." She smiled coquettishly at Jim. "Or . . . you," she added.

Jim chuckled. "You're not going to start talking marriage again, are you, Ella?"

Ella shook her head. "No," she said. "You're right. It wouldn't set a good example for the rest of the girls. I mean, look at Laura, and how much she and Jake Colby are in love with each other. If I got married, she would want to get married, then the next thing you know they all would."

"Laura and Jake Colby are in love?" Jim asked.

"Of course they are. Are you blind?"

"Why, I don't think I even saw him last night," Jim said.

"That's because he doesn't like to see all the other men around her, so by mutual agreement he comes to see her on Thursday, when he can have her all to himself."

"Well, I'll be damned. I never knew that. So, you think if you got married, they'd want to get married, is that it?"

"Yes, and then I would lose her. I mean, he won't come in on Saturdays now, because he doesn't like to see other men with her. If they were married, there is no way he would be willing to let her continue working the way you would me."

"What makes you think I would let *you* go on working?" Jim asked.

"I . . . I just assumed you would," Ella sputtered. "I mean, you certainly don't mind my working now. And you are the one who asked me to come out here and get into this business in the first place. I always thought that if we got married, you would want me to continue."

"Well, you thought wrong," Jim said.

Ella smiled. "Why, Jim Averill. You're jealous, aren't you?"

"What do you mean?"

"I never realized it, but you don't like it when I go upstairs with one of the cowboys. I think that is very sweet."

"It's not as if you *need* to work," Jim said. "You have enough girls on the line, you don't have to do it yourself."

"Sometimes they get overworked and I help out,"

Ella said. "But . . . all right," she added coquettishly.
"All you have to do is say the word, and I won't do it
anymore."

"What do you mean, all I have to do is say the
word?"

"I mean it's up to you. If you don't want me to work
anymore, tell me."

Jim took another swallow of his coffee, studying her
over the rim of his cup. "I don't want you to work
anymore," he finally said.

"Then I won't work," Ella replied. "But what's in it
for me?"

Jim smiled. "You aren't going to let go of this, are
you?"

"No, I'm not," Ella said, returning Jim's smile.
"You're the one that opened this ball, Jim Averill.
We've come this far, and I'm going to play it to the end.
I think I've got you right where I want you."

"And where would that be?"

Ella got up from her chair and walked around to Jim's
side of the table, then climbed onto his lap. She put her
arms around his neck.

"Right here," she said quietly. "This is where I want
you." She kissed him, then pulled away from him, still
sitting on his lap, still with her arms around him and her
wrists crossed loosely behind his neck. She looked at
him with smoky eyes. "There," she said. "I've made
the first move. Now it is up to you, Jim Averill. What
is it to be?"

Jim took only a moment to decide what it was to be.
He pulled her face to his and kissed her again, much
more urgently this time. Ella made a strange little sound,
deep in her throat, and leaned her body into his.

After that, Jim stood up, picking her up as well. With

her arms still around his neck, he carried her into his bedroom. There he deposited her on his still-unmade bed and lay down beside her, kissing her again. He pressed against her, pulling her body to his, feeling her softness against him.

Their kisses became more urgent, and Ella writhed in pleasure. The tip of her tongue darted across his lips, then dipped into his mouth. The warmth she had generated in Jim now erupted into a raging inferno, and he started pulling impatiently at the hem of her dress and she at his clothes, until soon they were both naked and lying against each other.

Ella's body was not only soft and warm, but she was well schooled in the ways to arouse and please a man. And though Jim was aware of all that, and knew there had been many other men in this position before him, he felt, and believed—for the moment, at least—that this was all for him.

They began making love, and as they did so, Jim had no further thought of the men who had gone before him. There had never been anyone for her but him, and there had never been anyone for him but her.

Beneath him, Ella arched her body and rose to meet his thrusts so that they settled very quickly into an ever-increasing rhythm. What they were doing was strongly physical and immensely satisfying, but it was much more than that. It was mental and emotional, both a part of them . . . and beyond them. Their passions were perfectly orchestrated to move in harmony, and when their goal was reached, it burst simultaneously over them, affording each a tremendous sense of mutual fulfillment.

After their desires were satisfied, they lay side by side for a long moment. Outside, the sun rose higher in the sky, and from the stock pens they could hear the restless shuffle of the cattle. Jim's arm bridged the very narrow distance between them, his hand resting palm down on her naked hip. He could feel the smoothness of her skin, the sharpness of her pelvic bone, and the bush of her pubic hair. This feeling of intimate possession was, in a way, even more satisfying than what had gone before, and he knew there could never be anyone else for him but this woman beside him.

"Let's sell out," Jim said.

They were the first words spoken in several minutes, and they surprised Ella, who was lost in her own thoughts, because she thought he had drifted off to sleep.

"Sell the cattle? Didn't you say we should wait a while longer, to get the best price?"

"I'm not talking about just the cattle. I mean I want us to sell everything. The cattle, the saloon, your business. Let's sell it all."

"Why on earth would we do that?" Ella asked. "If we didn't have this place, what would we do?"

"Have you ever been to France?"

Ella laughed. "Jim, I've never been east of the Mississippi River. You know that."

Jim raised up onto his elbow and looked down at Ella. At the moment, she was lying with her hands folded behind her head, and it had the effect of pulling her breasts down so that, rather than prominent globes, there were long, soft curves in the slope of her body. Her nipples, highlighted by the morning sun, sat atop those curves. Jim moved his hand from her hip to the gentle rise, and he put the tip of his finger on her nipple. It hardened instantly to his touch.

"You would love it, Ella," he said as he worked the nipple between his thumb and forefinger. "They have cafés right out on the sidewalk. And the most wonderful food you have ever eaten. And the greatest saloons in the world . . . only they call them bistros.''

''Bistros,'' Ella repeated. She smiled. ''I like that word. Bistros. It sounds elegant.''

''We'll sell out here,'' Jim continued. ''Then we'll go to Paris. After that we'll come back to New York. I can make a living in New York. Hell, I can make a living anywhere.''

''I wouldn't want to think that we would leave the West forever,'' Ella said.

''We won't leave it forever. We'll come back. Maybe to Texas, or Denver, or San Francisco. Just not here, not where there is so much trouble.''

''What about my girls?'' Ella asked. ''Right now they depend upon me to make a living.''

''Nobody is mad at the girls. They'll be safe here. We'll give them their end of the business and they can make their own living,'' Jim said. ''What do you say?''

''Are you proposing marriage to me, Jim Averill?''

''Hell yes, I'm proposing,'' Jim answered. ''I mean, I've done everything except get down on one knee. But by God, if you want me to do that, I'll do that, too.''

Ella laughed. ''No,'' she said. ''I think the fact that you proposed to me while we were lying naked, next to each other, is the most romantic thing I can think of. I accept.''

''Good!'' Jim said, sitting up quickly. ''Now, get dressed. Let's go out front and get a pencil and some paper and start figuring out what we need to do.''

''Jim!'' Ella said in an agitated voice.

''What?''

''I said yes.''

''I know.''

''Well, doesn't that at least call for another kiss?''

"Oh," Jim said. "All right." He leaned over and kissed her almost perfunctorily on the cheek.

"Oh, my, be still, my pounding heart," Ella said sarcastically, fanning herself as she swung her legs over the edge of the bed to get up. "I don't know if I can handle the passion."

Half an hour later they were sitting side by side at a table in the saloon. Jim had a sheet of paper in front of him and they were going over figures, deciding the best way to dispose of their holdings. Although it was not yet noon, they had drunk a toast in celebration of their engagement, and the two empty glasses and a half-full whiskey bottle sat on the table before them. The room was also filled with the aromatic smoke of Jim's Cuban cigars, for both Jim and Ella were smoking.

The door to the saloon opened, and half a dozen men came in. Jim started to get up, but Ella put out her hand.

"No, I want you to keep doing exactly what you are doing," she said. "Now that I've got you, I don't want anything to come along that would distract you. I'll take care of them."

"All right," Jim agreed.

Smiling, Ella started toward the men. "Gentlemen, today is Sunday and we are closed. But since you are here, and I am in such a good mood, I'll make an exception and open just this once. Now, what can I get for you?"

"Are you Cattle Kate?" one of the men asked, his voice a low, rasping growl.

As he moved into the light Ella recognized him. It was Payson, the man who had been braced by Tom Horn back in Theresa. She didn't know why he was here, but her intuition told her that it wasn't good. Her ebullient mood began to fade.

"That's a name the newspapers made up," she said. "I'm Ella Watson. You're Payson, aren't you?"

For a moment Payson looked a little confused, then he, too, remembered the incident.

"Yeah, I'm Payson," he said. "I remember where we met now. You were bringin' in a new whore. Where is she now?"

"I'm afraid she didn't work out," Ella lied. "I had to send her back to St. Louis."

"Too bad," Payson wheezed. "She was a good-lookin' thing all right. All this time, I been aimin' to get up here an' pay her a visit. Just never got around to it before now."

"What can I do for you, Mr. Payson?" Ella asked pointedly.

Payson nodded toward the back. "The people I'm workin' for want to know if you own all them cattle out there."

"I own a few head," she said. "The rest belong to Mr. Averill."

By now Jim had gotten up from the table and come over to stand beside Ella.

"Something I can help you with?" he asked.

"Them your cattle?"

"Yes. Do you want to buy them?"

"Naw."

"If you don't want to buy them, then what do you want?"

"We want justice," Payson replied.

"Justice? And what do you call justice?" Jim asked.

"First thing is to see that them cows out there get returned to the people I work for."

"And who would that be?" Jim asked.

"Why, that would be the Wyoming Stock Growers' Association," Payson said with an evil grin.

"You go back and tell the Wyoming Stock Growers' Association that's not going to happen," Jim replied resolutely. "Those are my cattle, bought and paid for. I have bills of sale for every one of them."

"The people I work for don't care nothin' about your bills of sale," Payson said.

"The WSGA must be scraping the bottom of the barrel to hire someone like you," Ella suggested. "Though now that I think about it, I guess you are exactly the kind of person I could see working for them."

"Let's go," Payson said.

"Go? What do you mean, go? Go where?"

"Down to the Sweetwater, and a cottonwood tree that I know about," Payson said. "Before noon this day, I aim to see the two of you hanging, side by side from the same limb."

"What?" Ella gasped. "Jim!" Frightened, she leaned into him and grabbed his arm.

"Get out of here, Payson," Jim growled. "You don't frighten us."

"Hell, Averill, we don't want to frighten you. All we want to do is hang you," Payson said. He laughed a wheezing laugh, then spat a wad of tobacco out onto the floor, not even trying to hit the nearby spittoon.

Although Jim wasn't wearing a gun, he knew there was one behind the bar, and he took a quick step in that direction.

"Meechum!" Payson warned, and the man nearest Jim hit him on the head, hard, with the butt of his pistol. Jim went down like a sack of potatoes.

"Now, what about you, Miss Cattle Kate?" Payson

asked. "You goin' to give us any trouble?"

"No," Ella replied in a quiet, frightened voice.

Payson pointed to Jim's crumpled form. "Pick 'im up," he growled. "Let's get this done."

"Payson, are you really taking us out of here to hang us?" Ella asked.

"That's what we're going to do."

"Then, may I ask a favor of you?"

"What?"

"Jim and I were just talking about getting married," she said. "I have a new dress I was going to wear for the occasion. Would you let me change into it? If we're going to die together, I want to at least die in the dress I would have been married in."

Payson hesitated for a minute, then one of the other men spoke up.

"Why don't you let her do it, Payson?" he asked. "What's it goin' to hurt?"

"You know your problem, Meechum?" Payson replied. "You're too goddamned soft. Can't you see she's just tryin' to buy some time? Forget about the dress, missy. Just get on out there to the wagon like I tole you."

Ella didn't move.

"Let's go!" Payson said loudly and menacingly.

Laura was dreaming. In her dream she was back in Theresa, facing Payson again. Only this time there was no Tom Horn, and Payson, with an ugly, twisted smile and foul breath, was having his way with her.

"*Let's go!*" he said, reaching up to tear her dress from her.

Mercifully, Laura woke up at that precise moment, and she lay in bed, feeling her heart race, breathing hard, trying to convince herself that it had only been a dream after all, and she was here, safe in her own bed.

"Get them into the wagon," she heard a rough voice say.

That was no dream! She was wide awake now, but the voice she heard was the same voice she had heard in her dream. It *was* Payson! My God! He was here!

Her breath coming in hard, frightened gasps, Laura forced herself to get out of bed. Stealthily she walked over to look through the window, then gasped when she saw him. It was the same man she had seen in Theresa. She could never forget that ugly face!

She wondered what he was doing here, then her terror increased dramatically when she saw some men lead Jim and Ella out of the building and put them into a wagon. What caused her terror was the fact that Jim and Ella had their hands tied. Additionally, Jim looked as if he had been hurt.

Her first instinct was to call down to them, to ask them what they were doing with Jim and Ella; but fear restrained her.

"If you won't look after him to see if he is all right, then at least untie my hands so I can," she heard Ella say.

"We can always hit him over the head again and put him out of his misery," Payson joked gruffly.

"No!" Ella said. "Please, don't hurt him anymore."

"Oh, dear God! What is it?" Laura asked under her breath. "What are they doing with them?"

"Then you just sit there beside him and keep your mouth shut!" Payson said. "Drive on, Meechum."

Meechum climbed into the front seat, then snapped his whip over the head of the team. The horses started forward at a trot. Laura counted the number of men who had come for her friends. In addition to the driver, there were at least three other men in the wagon with Jim and Ella. Payson and another five men were on horseback, riding alongside the wagon.

Quickly Laura ran into Julie's room and shook her sleeping friend awake. "Julie! Julie! Wake up! Oh, please, wake up!"

"What is it?" Julie asked groggily. "What time is it?"

"I don't know," Laura answered. "Oh, Julie, please wake up!"

"Ohh," Julie groaned. "I had three of them spend the night with me. They took turns and I didn't get to sleep until they were gone, and that was after the sun came up," she said.

"I'm scared. Oh, God, I'm scared!" Laura said.

Realizing now that something really was amiss, Julie woke up fully and sat up. "Laura, what is it?" she asked. "What has happened?"

"Some men came," Laura said. "They took Ella and Jim."

Julie ran her hand through her hair, as if by that action to force herself into a greater stage of alertness. "They took Ella and Jim? What do you mean, they took them? Who took them?"

"It was Payson," Laura said. "He was the one I told you about, the one that Tom Horn frightened away down in Theresa. But I don't know why he took them, or where," Laura said. "I only know that Ella and Jim had their hands tied behind their backs. And Jim looked like he had been hurt. I think he had been hit over the head."

"When was this?"

"Just now," Laura replied. "Only a few minutes ago. Julie, what do you think this is about?"

"I think they are vigilantes," Julie said.

"What are vigilantes?"

"They are cowards who take the law into their own hands," Julie explained. "I'm afraid Jim's and Ella's cattle dealing have caught up with them."

"What will the men do to them?"

"They will hang them if they get the chance," Julie said.

"No! No, we can't let that happen!"

By now Sally had overheard Laura and Julie talking, and when she found out what was going on, she called in the others. Soon all of them were gathered around Julie's bed, trying to decide what to do.

"We've got to get someone," Sally suggested. "We have to get help."

"But who? Where would we go?"

"What about the Red Sash Gang?" suggested Linda Sue, one of the other girls.

Sally shook her head. "Nate Champion is the only member of the Red Sash Gang who doesn't live in Hole in the Wall. And he lives fifteen miles from here, too far away to get here in time."

"What about your friend?" Linda Sue asked Laura.

"Yes," Julie said. "Laura, you have to go see Jake. He's the only one who lives close enough to do anything."

"But there's only one of him," Laura protested. "There were at least ten who came for Jim and Ella. And there may be even more of them where they are going. What can one man do by himself?"

"Are you going to let Jim and Ella die without even trying to do something?" Julie asked. "You know Jake. Do you think he would appreciate it if you didn't at least give him a chance to help?"

"All right," Laura finally agreed. "All right, I'll tell him. But someone is going to have to help me saddle a horse. I've never done it before."

"Easterners," Julie scoffed, and nervously, because they needed some relief, the others laughed.

Jake's ranch was about five miles west of town. He was working on the roof of the barn when he saw Laura riding up.

"Hey!" he said, smiling broadly. "Isn't this a pleasant surprise? What are you doing out here?" Putting aside his stack of shingles, he stood up and walked down to the edge of the roof.

"Jake! They have Jim and Ella!" Laura called up to him, her voice catching in fear and excitement.

"Who has Jim and Ella?"

"Payson!"

"Who?"

"Payson! Remember the man I told you about? The one who was trying to make trouble for Ella and me at that place in Theresa. The one that Tom Horn ran off?"

"Yes, I remember."

"He came to the Hog Ranch this morning. Payson and several other men. I don't know what they wanted, or why they did it, but they threw Jim and Ella in the back of a wagon and took them off."

"Did Jim and Ella go willingly?"

"No! Jim looked as if he had been hurt, and they both had their hands tied behind their back."

Jake dropped down to the ground, then ran inside the barn. Laura dismounted and went inside with him. He asked more questions as he saddled his horse.

"Did you see which way they went?"

"All I know is that they were heading east when they left," Laura said.

"The Sweetwater," Jake said. "How many were there?"

"At least ten. I saw six men on horseback, and there were four in the wagon with Jim and Ella."

Jake slipped his rifle out of the saddlebags, then began dropping shells into its loading tube. When the Winchester was fully loaded, he put the rest of the shells from the box in his pocket. Then he pulled his pistols, spun the cylinders, and checked the loads in them as well.

"Get on back to the Hog Ranch," he ordered.

"But aren't you coming there, too? I mean, don't you need to start from there to track them?"

"No," Jake said. "I have to take a chance that they are going to the Sweetwater. If they are, I can get there quicker by cutting across country."

"Jake, you aren't going to try to do this alone! You are going to get help, aren't you?"

Jake shook his head. "From where? Hole in the Wall? There's no time. I'm going to have to go by myself."

"Oh, Jake! Please be careful! If you get hurt . . . if anything happens to you . . . I don't know what I'd do."

Jake looked directly at her. "You would survive, Laura," he told her. He put his hand on her shoulder. "This is rough country out here, darlin'. If we're going to build that life together that we've been talking about, we are going to be facing this same crossroads several more times over the next several years. If we run from it every time, it will eventually destroy us. You are going to have to learn to be strong, because if I am going to get through all of them . . . I can't be worrying about you."

Laura bit her lower lip, then nodded. "I understand," she said.

"I hope you do," Jake said. He pulled her to him and kissed her hard on the lips.

"Oh, Jake, do you have to—"

"Yes, I have to," Jake interrupted her. "Now, go on back to the Hog Ranch like I told you."

Jake swung into the saddle, then, with a shout and a slap of his feet against the animal's side, caused his horse bolt forward as if it had been shot from a cannon.

Jake held his horse at a gallop for ten minutes, then let it trot for ten, then pushed it into a gallop again. Twenty minutes later he saw what he was looking for— a wagon and several horses and men, just arriving at the mouth of a small canyon on the banks of the Sweetwater River. After slipping his Winchester out of the saddle sheath, Jake tied his horse to a tree, then bent over into a crouch and ran nearly fifty yards until he reached a rock outcropping that provided him both cover and a place from which he could watch the men down in the canyon.

"Shut your mouth, woman!" Jake heard one of the men say. "If you don't shut up right now, we'll throw you in the river and let you drown."

"You're going to drown me in that?" Ella taunted. "Why, there's not even enough water in there to give you hogbacks a bath."

"There's enough water there," the man said.

"Yeah, I take that back, Payson," Ella said. "No more often than you take a bath, I'm sure there is. You smell as bad as you look."

"I said shut up! We've heard enough of your sass!"

"If you've heard enough, untie us and let us go back

home,'' Ella said. "You won't even have to take us back.''

"What are we going to do now, Payson?'' Meechum asked.

"I'll be damned!'' Jake breathed. Of the ten men he could see, he recognized three. They were the same three who had killed his friends and burned the line shack that night.

"Get the hanging ropes,'' Payson ordered.

"The hanging ropes? What for?''

"Just get the goddamned ropes, Meechum,'' Payson growled. "We're going to do what we started out to do. We're goin' to hang 'em.''

"The woman, too?''

"Yes, the woman, too.''

"I thought we was just goin' to turn them over to Wolcott.''

"You thought wrong. Now get the ropes like I told you to.''

"Untie my hands,'' Ella said.

"I'm not untying anybody.''

"Untie my hands,'' Ella said again. "What's the matter, Payson? Are you afraid of an unarmed woman? I want to have another look at Jim. I'm afraid when you hit him, you hurt him bad.''

Payson laughed gruffly. "What the hell difference does it make how bad he's hurt? He's going to be dead in another minute anyway. You both are!''

"Please, Payson, I'm begging you. Let me go to him. Let me kiss him good-bye.''

"All right, untie her hands,'' Payson finally relented.

One of the men untied her hands, and no one stopped her when she untied Jim's as well. Jim stood there, rubbing his wrists, still dazed from the blow to the head and so groggy that Jake was certain he didn't have any idea of what was going on.

"Here they are," Meechum said, coming back with a couple of ropes.

"Throw them across that tree limb there," Payson ordered.

The two ropes sailed across the tree limb Payson indicated, then fell down the other side. Hastily formed nooses were put around Jim's and Ella's necks.

"Jim," Ella sobbed as the noose was slipped around her neck. "Jim, I love you!"

"Ella?" Jim replied. His voice was thick and confused.

Jake raised his rifle, trying to get a shot at one of the men holding one of the ropes, but he was too far away to be sure of his shot. From here he would be as likely to hit Jim or Ella as his mark. But if he was going to do anything, he would have to do it now. Pulling back the hammer, he aimed at the man nearest to him, then squeezed the trigger.

The bullet screamed across the canyon, and the posse man who was Jake's target grabbed his chest and fell.

"What the hell?" Payson called out in alarm. "Who is that? Who fired that shot?"

"There he is! I see him!" Meechum shouted. "There's only one of 'em!"

Jake's second shot dropped Meechum, but by now all of the vigilantes were shooting back at him. Bullets careened off the rocks in front of him and fried the air by his ear. He was trapped behind the rock, unable to improve his position, unable to get back to his horse. He was even unable to return fire, for to do so he would have to expose himself.

"Hang 'em!" Jake heard Payson shout. "Hang 'em now!"

"No!" Jim screamed. He rose up just far enough to see what was going on and saw the wagon team bolt forward, dragging the wagon out from under Jim and Ella. The tree limb sagged under their weight, and Ella and Jim, suddenly vaulted into open space, began swinging back and forth, kicking and clawing, trying desperately to ease the terrible constriction around their necks.

Jake rose up to get into position for another shot, but the higher he got, the better target he made and the more intense was the fire directed toward him.

Finally the shooting stopped, and Jake was able to rise up again to get another look. When he did, he saw that the wagon, with two men in it, was leaving at great speed, escorted by six riders. Behind the retreating men were four bodies. The two on the ground were the posse men Jake had shot. The other two, no longer jerking and twitching, but still swinging back and forth from the tree limb, were Jim and Ella.

Without regard as to whether the posse might turn around and come back for him, Jake ran from the rocks down to the riverbank. He had his knife out, and as soon as he reached the tree, he cut the ropes, letting the now limp bodies drop to the ground.

"Jim! Ella!" he shouted, hurrying over to see what he could do for them. He saw immediately that he could do nothing. It was too late. Jim and Ella lay absolutely motionless on the ground, their eyes bulging from the sockets and specks of blood around their grimace-pulled lips. Ironically, when they fell, their arms flopped out beside them, so that in death Ella's hand lay in Jim's.

Jake heard a groan from one of the men he had shot, and he went over to look down at him. He could see frothing bubbles of blood around the bullet hole in the man's chest. The wound was sucking air, and he knew that he didn't have long to live.

"Please, mister. You got any water?" the man begged.

For a moment Jake considered letting him die without water, but he couldn't bring himself to do it. With a sigh, he walked over to the river, scooped some water into his hat, then brought it back.

The man drank thirstily.

"You were one of the three who came to the line shack, weren't you?" Jake asked.

"The line shack?"

"At the Rocking H. About eighteen months ago. You and two others shot up the shack, burned it, then took all the cows."

The man coughed, and it was obvious that the coughing spasm was painful. "Yeah," he finally said. "Yeah, I was one of them. But how do you know that?"

"I saw you. I was in the shack."

"You couldn't have been. We killed everyone in the shack."

"I got away through the floor," Jake explained. "I watched you set fire to the shack, then take the cows. Now, I have to ask you, why are people like you and Payson riding for the Wyoming Stock Growers' Association? They represent the big ranchers, don't you know that? You're a rustler. You're one of the ones they're after."

The man began to laugh, and like the coughing, it caused spasms of pain. "You don't get it, do you?"

Jake shook his head. "No, I guess not."

"The big ranchers *wanted* us to hit Hunter's line shack. They figured that if rustlers hit him as bad as they were hitting everyone else, he would vote with them.''

''That's it? Three good men were killed just to get Hunter's vote in a stock growers' election?''

Jake's anguished question went unanswered. The outlaw took two more pain-racked breaths, then died.

★ ★ ★

Fourteen

DISPATCH TO THE *CHEYENNE SUN*, FILED BY DAVID MCCLOUD

Shortly after I filed my first dispatch yesterday morning, one of our scouts returned with the information that a band of rustlers had taken refuge at a place called the KC Ranch, about fifteen miles north of Tisdale's ranch. KC Ranch, we were told, belonged to Nate Champion, a small rancher who is known to be a member of the "Red Sash Gang."

There are some who insist that the Red Sash Gang is no more than a social or professional organization, much like the Wyoming Stock Growers' Association, though of course on a much smaller scale. Those who are really in the know, however, tell us that the Red Sash Gang is in reality a band of thieves, rustlers, and outlaws, bound together for mutual protection.

Although all agreed that the band of rustlers at KC Ranch should be dealt with, attacking them now would mean diverting our army from its course. Therefore Mr. Canton opposed the attack, urging that we stick to our original plan and proceed directly to Buffalo before anyone could get word of our coming. Colonel Wolcott, however, wanted to attack the rustlers at the KC Ranch.

A very spirited discussion ensued, in which everyone voiced their opinion, and ultimately, Colonel Wolcott's notion prevailed.

We waited until midnight, then started out. By first light we had the little cabin surrounded, finding concealment in the stable, along a creek bed, and in a wooded ravine behind the house.

Shortly after dawn the front door of the house opened, and two men, carrying buckets, came down to the creek to get water. They were immediately set upon by some of our group, and ropes were cast over trees, intending to make quick and quiet work of them.

But Mr. Canton, who is the former sheriff of Johnson County, and who knows most of its inhabitants, interceded on behalf of the two terrified men. He informed the others that the men they had captured were neither rustlers, cowboys, nor small ranchers. In fact, they had nothing at all to do with the cattle business. They were merely fur trappers who had spent the night with Nate Champion.

The fur trappers were sent on their way, but not before they provided us with the information that there were only two other men in the house, not a large band of outlaws, as we had been led to believe. According to the trappers, the two men were Nate Champion, who owned the house, and a friend, Nick Ray. Mr. Canton avowed that he knew both Champion and Ray on sight, and as the two were on the cattlemen's "Dead List," Major Wolcott pronounced them as legitimate targets.

The next person to exit the cabin was Nick Ray. He came outside, stretched, then looked around as if trying to determine where the two trappers had gone. Major Walcott gave the signal, and one of the Texas sharpshooters fired. Nick Ray was staggered by the first shot. That was followed by a fusillade from the Texans who were hidden along the creek bed. Ray went down, but, incredibly, he was not yet dead. He started crawling toward the cabin.

Bravery is not reposited only in those who abide by the law, for next I witnessed as brave an act as I have ever seen. The door to the cabin opened and Nate Champion ran outside with bullets flying all about him. Even as the bullets kicked up dirt around him, he bent over, grabbed his friend, and pulled him back into the cabin, slamming the door behind him.

As I pen these words it is late afternoon, and the stand-off has gone on all day. Nate Champion is an excellent shot, well protected by the thick logs of his cabin, and despite the best efforts of the Texas sharpshooters, we have been unable to effect dislodgement.

McCloud had taken up an observatory position in the bottom of the creek bed that ran by the front of Champion's house. Canton was there, directing the sharpshooters, and every now and then a Texan would rise from his protected position behind the creek bank, lift his rifle to his shoulder, aim, and fire. The rifle would roar, smoke would stream from the end of the barrel, and it would kick back against the shoulder of the man who'd fired it.

Sometimes, but not always, the shot would be answered from the cabin, and McCloud would hear the bullet whistle by, sometimes clipping tree limbs in its transit.

McCloud turned over on his stomach, then wriggled up to the top of the creek bank to get a better look. He could see pockmarks in the log exterior of the little cabin, but the walls were so thick that he doubted any of the bullets had actually penetrated.

At that moment one of the sharpshooters fired, and McCloud saw a little spray of shattered glass as the bullet popped through the window. The mystery was that there was any glass left anywhere.

McCloud returned to his more secure position just as Wolcott came running up the creek bed, bent over at the waist, an unnecessary precaution since in the bottom of the creek bed there was no way he could actually present a target.

"Can't these wonderful fighting men you brought from Texas get him out of there?" Wolcott hissed to the Canton.

Canton was sitting on the opposite side of the creek bed, whittling on a stick as if he were idly passing the time.

"Well now, Wolcott, you tell me how to do it, and I'll be glad to have them do it," Canton replied. Despite Wolcott's demand that everyone call him "Colonel," Canton never did, and now, four days into the operation, no one did.

"Well, we can't just stay here all day," Wolcott insisted. "There's only one of him. Why don't we have them all get together and rush the cabin? He can't get everyone."

"I know Nate Champion," Canton said. "He is a damn good shot. He'll get one or two of us. Maybe more."

"Yes, but he can't get everyone," Wolcott insisted.

"Wolcott, are you willin' to be one of the ones he gets?" Canton asked derisively.

Wolcott snorted. "We can't just stay here all day."

Sighing, Canton stood up. "Perry!" he shouted. "Get everything off that wagon . . . load it with straw and firewood, set it aflame, then roll it toward the house."

"Wait a minute! You can't burn that wagon!" Wolcott protested. "That's a hundred-and-fifty-dollar wagon!"

"You want him out of there or not?"

Wolcott was silent for a moment, then he turned and walked away, by his silence granting his consent.

McCloud crawled back up to the top of the embankment to watch. It took a few tries before not only the straw but the firewood and the wagon itself were burning. Then, with it in full flame, it was started down the hill toward the house.

For a few minutes nothing happened, then McCloud saw smoke coming from the roof of the house. Very quickly after that, the entire house was in flames.

"Get ready, boys," someone said. "Nobody can stay in there now."

Suddenly the front door of the house opened and Nate Champion, coughing from the smoke, ran out into the front yard. He had a pistol in each hand, and he was blazing away, though at this point they were no longer aimed shots.

At least a dozen Texans fired at the same time, and McCloud watched in morbid fascination as puffs of dust and sprays of blood marked the impact of the bullets. Champion went down.

Slowly, cautiously, and with their rifles trained on his still form, three men went out to him. They looked down at him for a moment, then one of them called back.

"He's dead!"

"Drag him away from the house," Wolcott called.

With a Texan grabbing hold of each leg, Champion's body was pulled across his front yard, leaving a swath of blood behind him. Someone leaned down and pinned a card to his shirt, then laughed.

McCloud went over to see what the card said. It read "Rustlers Beware."

"Let's go, men!" Canton called. "We've wasted enough time here!"

The "army" prepared to move out. That was when McCloud saw a bloody little notebook sticking out of Champion's shirt pocket. He reached down and removed it, then opened it to see what it was.

6:30 in the a.m. Me and Nick was getting breakfast when the attack took place. What happened was, they was two trappers spent the night with us and they went down to the creek to get water. When they didn't come back, Nick said he would see what happened to them. Nick went outside and all of a sudden there was a lot of shooting. I went outside and dragged Nick back in, but he was so bad hurt that he couldn't help me none in fighting back.

8:30 a.m. I think Nick is dead. He was breathing some while ago, but now there's no breath left in him. He was a good man and it's not right he should die like this.

9:30 a.m. Boys, there is bullets coming like hail. They are shooting from the stable and river and back of the house. I don't know who they are, or why they have come to get me, but they have sure done their damage.

Noon. Wish I could take me time out to fix myself a meal. Got some bacon that I didn't cook at breakfast because they commenced their attack then. Boys, I feel pretty lonesome just now. I wish there was someone here with me so we could watch all sides at once.

3:00 p.m. I seen a man in a buckboard and another on a horse go by the ranch but they was fired on. I seen lots of men come out on horses on the other side of the river but whoever it is that's shooting at me takes out after them too.

6:00 p.m. Well, they have just got through shelling the house like hail. I heard them splitting wood. I guess they are going to fire the house tonight. I think I will make a break when night comes, if alive. Shooting again. It's not night yet.

The house is all fired. Goodbye, boys, if I never see you again.

                                        Nathan D. Champion

☆☆☆

Fifteen

"Get that flour put into ten-pound sacks, will you, Neil?" Bob Foote called back to his clerk as he came outside and began sweeping the front porch. He ducked under the sign that read "Buffalo Mercantile, Supplies for All Mankind, Bob Foote, Proprietor."

"Yes, sir, Mr. Foote, I'll get right on it," Neil's disembodied voice answered from inside the store.

Moses was lying over in the corner, warming himself in a patch of sunlight. Nobody knew exactly whose dog he was, since he seemed to wander from house to business establishment with equal familiarity. He made no effort to move, knowing that Foote would sweep around him.

"You've got it made, Moses, you know that?" Foote growled. He tried to make his voice irritable, but Moses knew better.

Suddenly Moses lifted his head and looked toward the end of the street. Foote had neither seen nor heard anything, but when he saw Moses react, he knew that the dog had. Curious as to what it might be, he looked toward the edge of town.

A moment later Foote heard the drumming of galloping hoofbeats. It sounded as if there were at least two horses, and because it was unusual for even one rider to come into town at a gallop, Foote leaned his broom against the porch-roof support pillar and stepped out into the street for a better view.

By now he could hear a man shouting something, but whoever it was was still too far away to be understood. The two horses rounded the curve just outside town and thundered across the south gully bridge in full gallop. One of the riders was waving his hat over his head and shouting.

"They killed Nate Champion! A lot of men! We seen 'em gun him down!"

Foote held up his hand in a motion for them to stop, and though he wasn't sure they would do so, both men reined in their horses, bringing them to a halt in front of the general store. The horses were lathered and breathing hard from the exertion of their run.

Foote knew both riders. The one who had been doing the shouting was Ben Thomas, sometime cowboy and sometime employee at the flour mill. The other was Hank Ramsey, a wagon mechanic for the local freight line. They were generally sober young men, not given to creating any kind of a disturbance, and that was what made Foote so curious.

"They kilt Nate, Mr. Foote," Thomas said, somewhat calmer now.

"Who killed Nate?"

"I don't rightly know who it was," Thomas replied. "All I know is, there's a lot of 'em. We was comin' by Nate Champion's place when we seen smoke and heard shootin', so we rode over there to see what was goin' on."

"Just as we got there"—Ramsey took over—"we

seen Nate comin' out of his house. The house was bur-
nin' somethin' fierce behind him. Nate had a pistol in
each hand, blazin' away, but there must've been fifty or
sixty people shootin' back at him.''

"Fifty or sixty?" Foote asked in surprise.

"Maybe more," Thomas said, reasserting his right to
tell the story. "And they kilt him. Shot him down like
a dog.''

"Who was it?" Foote asked. "Who was shooting at
him?''

"I don't know who the fellas was," Ramsey said.
"All I know is they all had rifles, and they are damned
mean looking.''

"I seen Canton with them," Thomas said.

"Canton? Frank Canton? Used to be the sheriff
here?''

"Yes, sir. I seen him plain as day."

"Frank Canton has gone over to the big cattlemen,
working as chief of their detectives," Foote said. "I
know who they are, boys. There's only one thing they
could be. Those sons of bitches have done it. The
WSGA have hired that private army they've been talking
about. You fellas did the right thing by bringin' us the
warnin', but now we've got to get the word out to the
whole county. Go over to the livery and rent yourselves
a couple of fresh horses . . . charge 'em to me, then start
spreadin' the warning. Will you do that for me?''

"Sure thing, Mr. Foote," Thomas said. "But what
about the folks here in town?''

"I'll take care of letting them know," Foote promised.

As the two men took their exhausted horses over to
the livery stable, Foote hurried back into his store, then
reached under the counter and pulled out a red sash. He

wrapped the sash around his belly, then strapped on his pistol belt.

"What is it, Mr. Foote?" Neil asked. "What's going on? What did them men want?"

"Neil, get my horse saddled, will you?" Foote said, not directly answering the question.

"Yes, sir," the young clerk replied, starting out the back.

Foote's wife, Meg, came into the store from their living quarters, which were attached to the back of the store. She had been baking bread, and her hands and apron were dusted white with flour.

"Bob, what is it?" Meg asked wiping her hands on a towel she had carried with her. "What's going on?"

"It's the Wyoming Stock Growers' Association," Foote replied. "You know that army they have been talking about in the newspaper? Well, by God, they've gone and put it together, and they are attacking us."

"Attacking us? What do you mean?"

"Attacking us! Like wild Indians from the plains! I should've known this was comin' yesterday, when those men took Jim and Ella out and hung 'em. Today they killed Nate Champion and burned his house."

"Oh, Bob, they didn't kill Nate," Meg said sorrowfully. "He was such a nice young man."

"You mark my words, Meg. They don't intend to stop there. They aren't going to be happy until every house in Buffalo is razed to the ground and every man, woman and child is lying dead in the street."

Meg gasped and put her hand to her mouth, getting flour on her cheek as she did so.

"Well, by God, I don't intend to let them do that," Foote said.

"Mr. Foote, your horse is saddled," Neil said, coming back into the store at that moment.

"Thanks," Foote replied. "Meg, you and Neil break out rifles, ammunition, blankets, whatever people might need. If anybody needs anything, give it to them."

"Give it to them?" Meg asked.

"The rifles and blankets and stuff we'll get back later. The expendables we won't worry about. If we don't defend ourselves, we won't have anything left anyway. When that private army gets here, I intend for us to be waiting for them."

For the next half hour Bob Foote rode up and down the main street of Buffalo, cupping his hands around his mouth and shouting out, both a warning and a challenge, to his fellow citizens:

"Citizens of Buffalo! My friends! The high-and-mighty Wyoming Stock Growers' Association has declared war upon all of us . . . the small rancher, the cowboy, the merchant, the common man! An armed body of assassins has entered our county, and with bullet and fire have destroyed the lives and property of our people!

"Some of our fellow citizens, our neighbors, our friends, are already dead!

"This murderous gang is now marching on our village. . . . Men, citizens, as you love your home and families, I call upon you to shoulder arms and go to the front to battle the approaching foe!

"Come to my store and get whatever you need for this battle: guns, knives, ammunition, food, blankets. It is all free! Your manhood and mine demands action! Fall into line! Don't let these cowardly assassins go unchallenged!"

From all over town men and women began answering

Foote's call to arms. The smithy left his forge, draymen abandoned their wagons, clerks ran out of the stores, the barber abandoned his shop with his draped and lathered client following him, bartenders and customers poured into the dusty street from saloons.

"Where are they?"

"They are south of here," Foote called back. "If we arm ourselves and act quickly, we can meet them before they reach our town!"

Back in Foote's store Meg and Neil were already tossing out Winchesters and filling outstretched hands with boxes of ammunition. Tobacco, slickers, food, and blankets were loaded into wagons.

Men appeared in the streets, leading saddled horses and wearing red sashes. Many of them put on the sash whether they were members of the Red Sash Gang or not.

Down at the far end of the street, at the Hog Ranch, the girls, still in mourning for Ella and Jim, gathered in the parlor to watch through the windows in fascination as the town prepared itself for the upcoming battle.

"Did you hear?" Julie asked. "These people who are coming here have already killed Nate Champion."

"Nate is dead?" Sally replied. She began to cry, and Laura, who knew that Nate was a particular favorite with Sally, went over to put her arm around her and comfort her.

"Look at them out there, grabbing guns and loading wagons," Linda Sue said. "My God, what's happening to us?"

"I'll tell you what is happening," Julie answered. "We are finally fighting back!" She reached for her shawl. "And I'm going to join the fight!"

"You? What are you going to do? What can any of us do?" one of the other girls asked.

"I don't know," Julie answered truthfully. "I could make coffee, or hand out ammunition, or load guns. If it's the only thing I can do, I'll spread out a buffalo blanket and give free fucks to the fighting men!" she said resolutely. "But by God, these people coming toward us are the same ones who had Eddie killed, and who killed Ella and Jim, and I'm going to do something!"

"And Nate. Don't forget, they stopped by Nate's ranch and killed him," Sally said.

"Oh, my God!" Laura suddenly shouted. "I just thought! Jake is out at his ranch all alone and he doesn't know about this!" She started toward the back of the house.

"Where are you going?" Julie asked.

"Help me saddle a horse," Laura pleaded. "I've got to get out to Jake's ranch and warn him! I mean, if they attacked Nick Champion, they might attack him as well!"

"Just a minute," Julie said. She hurried around behind the bar, then leaned down. When she rose a second later, she was holding the double-barreled shotgun that Jim had kept there. She held it across the bar. "You'd better take this."

Laura shook her head. "I don't know anything about guns," she said.

"Then learn," Julie ordered. "There's nothing to it." She cocked both hammers. "All you do is pull back on these things, then pull the triggers." She eased the hammers back down. "Take it," she insisted. "You never can tell when you might need it."

Nervously Laura nodded, then accepted the proffered

weapon. Afterward she and Julie went out to the stable to saddle one of the horses.

"You'd better take Belle, she's the fastest horse here," Julie said. "She belonged to Ella, but Ella won't be needing her anymore."

"Thanks," Laura said.

"Just get out there before those bastards from Cheyenne do," Julie said.

Laura wasn't sure why she stopped just before she reached Jake's house. It wasn't anything she saw or heard. It was more like something she *felt*.

After dismounting, she pulled the shotgun out of the saddle sheath, then started walking quietly through a little path in the woods toward Jake's house. Just before she reached the clearing, she heard angry voices coming from the back of Jake's house, and she knew someone was there.

Although she was alert to the situation, she was, surprisingly, very calm under the circumstances. She moved quickly to get across the open space that lay between the thicket of trees and the side of Jake's house. When she reached the house, she pulled back the two hammers just as Julie had showed her and held the gun very close to her chest. Then, with her back pressed against the wall of the house, she crept along sideways until she reached the back. Very carefully she looked around the corner.

Jake was standing at a distance of about ten yards from his back porch. His hands were tied in front of him, and he was bare from the waist up. Bright red streaks of blood were running down his stomach from several knife wounds slashing across his chest.

Payson was standing in front of Jake, holding a knife.

The tip of the blade was moving back and forth like the head of a coiled snake. Payson laughed, an evil, raspy laugh.

"I just been playin' with you so far, Colby, that's why they ain't none of 'em deep. But one of these times I'm liable to slip . . . I might cut you too deep and that would mess up some of your innards. You'd do best by tellin' me where at you keep your money."

"What makes you think I've got any money?"

"Well, you're tryin' to run a ranch here, ain't ya? You can't do that without money. I know you got to have some, some'eres so where at do you keep it at?"

"You go to hell."

Payson slashed at him again, but this time Jake managed to catch Payson's wrist, even though his own hands were tied. There was a moment of silent struggle, then, as Payson perceived that he might be losing the struggle, he called out in a strained voice.

"Shoot him, boys!"

Laura knew that she could wait no longer. At that precise moment she stepped out from the corner of the house with the shotgun already raised to her shoulder. Without so much as a word, she shot the man nearest her, and the blast of buckshot spun him around.

"What the hell?" the other called, and he turned his pistol away from Jake toward the source of his own danger.

He wasn't fast enough. As in one motion, Laura swung the shotgun from the first man to the second, and she pulled the other trigger. She saw this man's face turn to red pulp as he went down.

Jake wasted no time in taking advantage of the situation. With Payson distracted by the two shotgun blasts, Jake was able to seize the moment. He forced Payson's hand around so that the knife was pointing toward Payson's chest. Then he began to shove.

Payson felt the point of his own knife blade begin to penetrate the skin just over his heart. He looked first at it, then at Jake. In one instant his eyes went from hate, to surprise, to fear.

With one final thrust, Jake forced the blade, hilt deep, into Payson's chest. Payson let out a long, foul-breathed, life-surrendering sigh as he went limp, then fell at Jake's feet.

"Jake!" Laura called, throwing the shotgun aside and running toward him. "Jake, are you all right?"

Jake raised his arms and let her come to him, then lowered them so that even though his wrists were still tied together, he was able to hold her in an embrace in the circle of his arms. He could feel her trembling against him.

"It's all right now," Jake said, trying to comfort her. "Don't worry, everything's going to be all right."

"I killed them, Jake," Laura said in a small, awestruck voice. "I killed them. I took their lives."

Jake pulled her more tightly into him. Both were oblivious of the blood from his chest wounds.

"What makes you think they were human? Besides, you had no choice," he said. "It was them or me. You saved my life."

"I know, I know," she said. She took a deep breath. "And I would do it again and again, a thousand times if necessary. It's just that . . . I never thought I would ever have to do anything like that."

Jake held her to him for a moment longer, then he lifted his arms away from her and bent to withdraw the knife from Payson's chest. "Can you cut the ropes?"

he asked, handing her the knife and holding his wrists in front of him.

"Yes," she said. The knife was slick with blood, Jake's and Parson's, but she overcame her revulsion as she worked to cut the ropes.

"I don't know why you chose this moment to come out here," Jake said. "But it's a lucky thing for me that you did."

"Oh, Jake!" Laura said, remembering then. "An army has come into Johnson County to attack us."

"An army?"

"The Wyoming Stock Growers' Association. They've put together an army of fifty to a hundred men. They've already killed poor Nate Champion, and people are saying that they are headed for Buffalo to burn the town! All the townspeople have gotten together. They're going out to meet them before they get here."

"If the townspeople are going out to meet the cattlemen . . . then I'm going, too," he said.

Sixteen

When the Texans and the cattlemen left Nate Champion's ranch, Wolcott, in at least one sound military move, sent a rider out ahead to act as a scout. They had been under way for a couple of hours when the rider came galloping back.

"What's with him?" Wolcott asked. "What is he so excited about?"

"Men ahead!" the rider was shouting as he approached. "There's a large body of men ahead!"

"Who are they?" Wolcott asked when the rider drew to a halt alongside.

"I don't have any idea," the rider answered, trying to calm his horse, which was twisting about nervously now after the fast run. "But they're all wearin' red sashes, and ever' damn one of 'em's got guns."

"How did they find out about us so fast?" Wolcott asked.

"That's not hard to figure out," Canton replied. "We've made every amateurish mistake in the book. We announced our intention in the newspapers, and if that wasn't enough, we took a whole day just to kill one man.''

"We killed two," Wolcott corrected, bristling at the suggestion that he might be an amateur.

"Hell, the first one don't count. He was dead before the day even began," Canton growled.

"All right, so the nesters up here know," Wolcott snorted. "How many are there?" he asked his rider.

"There's at least a hundred 'n fifty of 'em. Maybe more," the rider reported nervously.

"One hundred and fifty?" Wolcott gasped, amazed at the number. "Are you saying there are one hundred and fifty men coming toward us? Can there be that many rustlers up here?"

"You damn fool, don't you understand?" Canton said. "We aren't fighting just rustlers up here. We are fighting the homesteaders, the small ranchers, the townspeople. Don't forget, we are invading their land. You'll have every citizen between the ages of sixteen and sixty armed and ready to defend their homes. This isn't an expedition against rustlers anymore. This has become a patriotic war . . . and they are the patriots!''

Wolcott looked at Canton for a moment, then he nodded, coming to the reluctant realization that Canton was telling the truth.

"All right, I'm asking you, Canton," he said. "You know this country . . . and these people. Do you have any suggestions on what we can do now?"

"We have to head over to the TA Ranch," Canton suggested. "The fella that owns it is sympathetic to our cause. The TA is pretty close, and if we have to make a fight, it would be an easy place to defend."

Wolcott twisted around in his saddle to look back over

the men he had led this far. The Texans were sitting stoically on their horses, ready to advance or dig in, whichever was asked of them. The cattlemen who had come along were a little more nervous.

At that moment, another rider came toward them at a full gallop.

"Who the hell is that?" Wolcott asked. "I don't have any other scouts out!" He pulled his pistol.

"Hold it, hold it!" Canton shouted, reaching up to push Wolcott's hand down. "Don't you recognize him? That's James Craig. Hell, he's a member of the WSGA, for God's sake. I know you've seen him before."

"Yeah, I remember. He lives up here, though, so I was just being cautious."

"He's a good man," Canton said. "We can count on him."

"Turn back, turn back!" Craig shouted as he drew within earshot. "Everybody in town is aroused. The rustlers are massing from every direction! There are more than three hundred men less than a mile away, and the number is growing!"

"Three hundred? My God, only a few moments ago it was one hundred and fifty!" Canton said.

"We have to get to cover as quickly as we can," Wolcott shouted. "Retreat! Retreat!"

Even as he was ordering the retreat, Wolcott had turned his horse and started it at a gallop toward the TA Ranch.

"Wait!" Canton shouted to him. "Wolcott, our wagons! What about our wagons?"

"Leave them!" Wolcott called back excitedly. "There is no time!"

DISPATCH TO THE *CHEYENNE SUN*, FROM DAVID
MCCLOUD

Our situation has taken a somewhat ominous
turn. After leaving the KC Ranch, where we
successfully engaged and killed the two rustlers,
Nate Champion and Nick Ray, we started toward
Buffalo. However, when we were but a few miles
south of Buffalo, we encountered a large body of
men coming to meet us.

The irony of all of this is that I, and many others
in this expedition, believed we were coming to
liberate the citizens of the towns of Johnson
County from the oppressive yoke of the rustlers.
It seems, however, that the good citizens up here
do not look at us as an army of liberation. Instead,
they see us as an invading army of would-be
conquerors. We are not fighting for the common
man as we thought . . . rather, we find ourselves in
the position of fighting against the common man.
It is not a position with which most of us are
comfortable.

Unfortunately, we have come too far to turn
back. We now must engage the army that has
come after us if we are to save our lives. And what
a magnificent army it is. Its ranks are filled with
the likes of cowboys and cooks, mill hands and
mechanics, lawyers, and teachers, fathers, sons,
and brothers. In short, it is exactly the kind of
army that, but one generation ago, saved our
Union. And now, perceiving a threat just as real,
such an army has been formed again, this time to
combat us. In but a few short hours, we have gone
from the hunters to the hunted, and Colonel

Wolcott has brought us to the TA Ranch, from which position we shall conduct our defense.

To an admittedly untrained military eye, the TA Ranch seems well suited for a defensive operation. It is nestled in a bend in Crazy Woman Creek. The main buildings, which are blockhouse-type buildings, are themselves surrounded by a log fence seven feet high, with a barbed-wire fence beyond that. The ranch house is protected by a windbreak of trees and is flanked by several outbuildings—a stable, an icehouse, a small chicken coop, and a dugout for storing potatoes. We have also located a stack of very thick timbers that were purchased for a new building, but which Colonel Wolcott has confiscated for the construction of breastworks.

All day and all night, Colonel Wolcott has directed the building of our defensive fortifications. These, I have dubbed "Fort Wolcott."

I shall attempt to describe them for you.

On a small hill about 50 yards away from the stable, we have constructed a log barricade, measuring some 12 by 14 feet, with openings through which our sharpshooters will be able to cover approaches to the ranch. Trenches have been dug inside the barricade, and breastworks have been raised around the ranch house. Now, all is ready, save for one thing. In our hasty retreat from our forwardmost position, we left the wagons behind. The wagons contain all our supplies: weapons, ammunition, blankets, water, and a commodity the absence of which we are rapidly becoming quite aware.

Food.

If the townspeople lay siege to us, and if the siege is a long one . . . we are going to be very hungry and very thirsty before it is all over.

Night had fallen by the time Jake and Laura returned to town, and much had already been done in preparation for meeting the invasion. The men of the town and county had been formed into companies of twenty men each, each company led by a deputy sheriff. The ladies of Buffalo—and this included the girls from the Hog Ranch—had set up kitchens and under the flickering light of several torches were preparing wagonloads of food to be sent into the field with their men.

Laura found Julie, Sally, and Linda Sue working at one of the kitchens, and, perhaps buoyed by the excitement of knowing that Jake was no longer in danger, she was able to make a joke.

"They didn't like your idea of following the men into the field with buffalo robes?" she teased.

Julie laughed. "I haven't made the suggestion yet," she said. She reached around to grab her back, as if it were hurting her. "But if I have to knead much more bread dough, I'm going to."

It wasn't until then that Julie noticed the blood on Laura's blouse, for although she had washed her hands, the stains were still on her dress.

"Laura, what happened to you? Are you all right?"

Laura had almost forgotten, and when she looked down at herself, she dismissed it with a nervous laugh. "I'm fine," she said. "And so is Jake."

A tall, bearded man named Arapaho Brown rode through the street of the town then.

"All right, men, to horse and wagon!" he shouted,

standing in the stirrups of his horse. "We have word that they are fortifying the TA Ranch. If we start now, we'll have the superior position by dawn. Let's go kick those sons of bitches out of Johnson County!"

With a roar of approval, scores of men ran to their horses or climbed into the waiting wagons and, with cheers and waving hats, started south into the night.

Without giving it so much as a second thought, Laura mounted Belle and rode alongside Jake. She was happy to see that Jake made no effort to send her back.

All that day and far into the night, even as the Johnson County defenders were pouring south of Buffalo to meet them, the Texans and ranchers worked hard to turn the TA Ranch into a fort. When they were finally finished they sat, exhausted, where they were. Canton thought that the cattlemen, wealthy men who were used to dining on lobster and steak in sartorial splendor at the Cheyenne Club, made quite a sorry sight. Their hands were blistered and their shoulders bruised from working with the ten-inch-thick timbers. Along with the Texans, the cattlemen were having a supper of potatoes, the only edible commodity at their disposal. Afterward they posted guards and turned in to try to get some rest.

It was a long, reflective night.

At dawn the next morning, from inside the fortifications at the TA Ranch, the Texans and cattlemen could see their attackers in the distance. The homesteaders from the town and county had reached the position in the wee hours of the morning. Since that time they had busied themselves digging rifle pits and constructing breastworks on the hills and ridgelines around the ranch.

When it was light enough to see, Wolcott and Canton climbed into the hayloft and stood looking through the firing holes that had been augured into the wall the night before.

"We are surrounded by a bunch of ribbon clerks and mill hands," Wolcott scoffed. He shook his head. "My God, who would have thought it?"

"What is your plan now?" Canton asked.

"My plan is to sit tight, right here," Wolcott answered. "We're in a good defensive position. We should be able to hold them off almost indefinitely."

"What about food and water?"

"We have an entire storage room of potatoes," Wolcott suggested. "We can live on that for a while. Surely, when our people down in Cheyenne don't hear from us, they'll send people up here to see what is going on."

"Yes," Canton said. "But I decided not to wait on that."

Wolcott looked over at his co-commander. "What do you mean? What did you do?"

"Last night I slipped a man out of here," Canton explained. "I sent Buck Garret over into the next county, where the telegraph wires are still intact, with instructions to wire the governor, to let him know what is going on."

Wolcott stared at him for a long moment, then he nodded.

"Thank you, I'm glad you did. That was a very smart thing to do," he said. It was the first time either of them had given the other credit for anything.

At that moment, from the hills surrounding them, they heard the sound of rifle fire. The Johnson County folks had opened fire as soon as it was light enough to see . . . even though none of the Texans or cattlemen were in position to make themselves a target. Shortly after the opening fusillade, Canton saw one of the horses in the

corral fall. He was puzzled for a second, then he saw
another go down, and this time he saw a mist of blood
from the strike of the bullet.

"The sons of bitches are shooting our horses!" Canton shouted, starting toward the ladder. He went down
the ladder quickly, then called out to the men who were
taking refuge among the bales of hay. "I need a couple
of men to go out into the corral with me!" he said.
"They're shooting our horses!"

Those sons of bitches!" one of the Texans cursed. He
and another got up then, and the three of them went out
the back door, using the log fence as cover. From the
end of the fence they were able to dash out into the
corral, gather up a few of the horses, then bring them
back. It took them several trips, but eventually they had
all the surviving horses moved into the relative safety
of the stable.

With the horses denied them as targets, the men of
the county started firing at the barn, where most of the
Texans and cattlemen were holed up. For the most part
they were merely wasting ammunition, for the bullets
buried themselves in the thick timber walls. A few of
them penetrated, but when one did it had so spent its
energy that it represented no danger to anyone inside.

The exception was in the bullets that were fired
through the windows. These, still deadly missiles, careened and whizzed around the rafters, raising dust and
causing the defenders inside to seek shelter behind
stacked bales of hay and cling to anything they could
that would provide some protection.

One of the bullets hit one of the cattlemen in the ear-
lobe, taking off a piece of his flesh and leaving a shred-
ded, bloody piece of skin hanging from the bottom of
his right ear.

Several of the defenders in the barn, not content just to be targets, began firing back at their attackers, using the firing loops they had drilled in the walls. All day long the men inside the barn and the three hundred men who were on the hills surrounding the barn exchanged long-range rifle fire.

Late in the evening of the first full day of the siege, the firing subsided. A few of the defenders inside the barn continued to shoot back, but Canton stopped them, reminding them that the only ammunition they had was what they had on them.

"You may recall," he said, "that you all hightailed it into here, leaving the wagons and supplies outside."

Sheepishly the men looked at each other, realizing the truth of Canton's statement. As a result, all the firing stopped. With the cessation of gunfire it grew very quiet, so quiet that those in the barn could hear the conversation being exchanged by those who were outside.

"That fire ready to get them steaks on yet?"

"I got some biscuits here. Anybody want any biscuits?"

"Hey, Brown, pour me a cup of coffee, will you?"

The talk of food was augmented by the smells as, within the barn, the men caught the aromas of steaks being grilled over an open fire and coffee brewing. Their stomachs growled in protest, and the raw potatoes they had did little to assuage their discomfort.

"Hey, you fellas in there!" someone called from outside. "Any of you hungry?"

One of the Texans had managed to bring into the barn with him, in addition to his Winchester, a heavy-caliber, long-range buffalo rifle. After loading the rifle carefully, he walked over to one of the firing loops, then lifted the rear site, slid the gate up the track to compensate for distance, took careful aim, and fired.

The heavy boom of the rifle echoed across the open space between the two forces. On the top of the hill opposite the barn, a large black kettle was suspended over an open fire. The Texan's big .52-caliber bullet crashed into the pot, knocking it off its suspension cradle and spilling its contents onto the fire, which hissed and then went out.

Those in the barn who had seen it cheered lustily.

"That there's one pot of soup those bastards won't get!" someone said, laughing, and as word reached everyone else in the barn, they all came to congratulate the Texan on his shot. It had accomplished nothing, of course. The homesteaders obviously had a lot more food where that came from. But it made the Texans and the cattlemen feel good.

"You think they'll try to rush the barn tonight?" Wolcott asked nervously.

"No," Canton said. "They've got us trapped in here, they know we aren't going anywhere. Why should they take such a risk?"

"I wonder if Garret got through?"

"Buck's a good man," Canton said. "He'll get through."

"If he didn't, we're the same as dead," Wolcott said.

CHEYENNE

"It's nearly midnight," the butler told Doyle Hunter. "You can't see the governor now. He is asleep."

"Wake him up," Hunter demanded.

"No, sir. I'm not going to wake him up. Not at this hour of the—"

"I said, wake him up!" Hunter said again, this time enforcing his argument with a drawn pistol.

The butler looked at the pistol for a moment, then nodded. "Yes, sir," he said. "If you put it that way, I suppose I could wake him."

Less than a minute later the governor, still tying his robe around him, came down the stairway to meet Hunter in the foyer.

"What is it, Mr. Hunter?" he said. "What is so important that you had to frighten my servant with a drawn pistol?"

"Governor, our men are trapped," Hunter said.

"Our men? What men?"

"Don't pull that on me, Governor," Hunter hissed angrily. "You know what men. You are as aware of the army we sent up into Johnson County as if you had called out the militia and sent them yourself." He showed the governor the telegram he had received less than half an hour ago.

The governor read it, then sighed. "How in the name of all that is holy did they ever get themselves into such a fix?" he asked. "I thought this was going to be a quick and clean operation. I was told that a private army would go up there and clear out the rustlers. But now, according to this telegram, the entire town of Buffalo has mobilized themselves to go out and meet them."

"Yes, sir."

"And not only meet them, but to hold them at bay in a ranch somewhere."

"Governor, you are going to have to do something and do it quickly," Hunter said. "Otherwise our men are going to be slaughtered, and you are going to be the laughingstock of the nation.''

"There are troops at Fort McKinney," the governor said. "They could go down there and end this thing in an instant. But I don't have the authority to call them out."

"Who does?"

"Only the president has the authority to do that."

"Then get in touch with the president. You are both Republicans," Hunter reminded him. "Surely you have some pull with Harrison."

The governor was standing by a nearby table, and he began drumming his fingers on it as he thought about the situation. "You're right," he said. "That's our only hope. All right, I'll send a telegram to the president."

"Tell him if he is going to do anything, he had better do it immediately," Hunter cautioned. "Our men are trapped in there without food or water. I expect the John-son County people could move in today, if they wanted to."

Back at the TA Ranch, Wolcott and Canton were starting their second night without sleep. As there was no firing now, they stood at the open door of the hayloft, looking out toward the hills that lay between them and Buffalo. Scores of campfires flickered and glowed along the Crazy Woman River, and the aroma of the suppers, long since eaten by the Johnson County army, still lingered in the air.

Somewhere in the hills beyond, coyotes bayed at the moon.

"Tomorrow morning," Wolcott said.

"What?"

"If Buck got through, we should be relieved tomorrow. If no one has come to relieve us tomorrow, we're pulling out."

Canton nodded without speaking.

★★★

Seventeen

Fort McKinney

The commandant's house seemed exceptionally white in the bright silver moon. It was so bright, in fact, that it appeared to Second Lieutenant Peabody Andrews to have an almost spectral glow about it. That made it even more difficult for him to bang on the front door at this hour. But he was the duty officer, and the telegraph message was for Colonel J. J. Van Horn. And, most important, the message was from the president of the United States.

After pulling down the hem of his jacket, then checking to make certain that his uniform was buttoned properly, Lt. Andrews walked up to the front door and knocked.

Inside a dog started barking. At first the barking dog startled the young lieutenant, but he realized that the dog would help him awaken the colonel, and he welcomed it.

When the dog stopped barking, Andrews knocked on the door again, once more soliciting the dog's help.

Then, looking through the window of the door, he saw a dim light at the top of the stairway. The light began descending. Finally he could see the colonel, carrying a lantern toward the door. The young lieutenant braced himself for what he was sure would be an outburst.

"I'm sorry to awaken you, sir," Andrews said.

"Don't be ridiculous, Lieutenant," Colonel Van Horn replied, reaching for the message. "You are the duty officer. It is your duty to awaken me when required."

"Yes, sir," Andrews said, thankful that the colonel was taking it so calmly.

Colonel Van Horn read the message, then handed it back to the young lieutenant. "Awaken Captain Barber and Captain Fitzhugh," he ordered. "Tell them I want their entire companies turned out in full array, mounted, and ready to march in one hour."

"Yes, sir," Lieutenant Andrews replied. "They are both with Third Battalion, sir. Shall I also awaken Major Forbes, the battalion commander?"

"No, Lieutenant," Colonel Van Horn replied. "I will assume command."

Captains Barber and Fitzhugh were less gracious about being awakened in the middle of the night. But when Andrews told them that this was in response to a special order from the president of the United States, and that Colonel Van Horn, and not Major Forbes would be leading them, their irritation was replaced quickly, first by a degree of curiosity, then by a sense of ambition. After all, if this was a special order from the president, and Van Horn chose them from among ten other cavalry troop commanders, it could only bode well for them.

The troopers were considerably less ambitious than their commanders and much more irritated at being awakened in the middle of the night. Some, who were sleeping off a drunk, were more irritable than others. But all of them were very curious as to what was going on, and within half an hour the irritation was gone and most were actually looking forward to whatever adventure was before them.

"You think it's Indians?" a young soldier asked. He had only recently come to the fort, and though it had been a long time since there was any Indian trouble, many of the old-timers had been teasing him about it.

"If it is, sonny, you'd better hang on to that red hair of yours," one old sergeant said. "A Sioux will pass up ten brown-haired men to get to one young man with red hair."

The young redheaded soldier grimaced, and several others laughed, grateful that someone was the brunt of the sergeant's taunts.

"Bugler!" a voice called from somewhere in the darkness. "Sound Boots and Saddles!"

The bugler lifted the instrument to his lips, then the crisp, musical command reached every corner of the fort. Exactly five hours and twelve minutes after Buck Garret sent his urgent telegram to Doyle Hunter in Cheyenne— three hours and forty-six minutes after the governor telegraphed Wyoming's two senators in Washington, D.C.; two hours and twenty-one minutes after the two senators awakened President Harrison; and one hour and three minutes after Second Lieutenant Andrews knocked on the front door of Colonel Van Horn's quarters—the massive front gates of the fort swung open and the cavalry, riding by fours, started toward the TA Ranch.

When Jake Colby and Laura Place woke up the next morning, by the blackened ring of a spent fire, they were lying side by side in the blankets of their bedroll. They had slept together, but there had been nothing sexual about it. As it turned out, Laura was not the only woman who had come from town. Meg, the storekeeper's wife, Julie, Sally, and Linda Sue from the Hog Ranch; and several others had as well. During the exchange of fire the day before, Laura and the other women had remained safely in defilade behind one of the hills.

Laura had spent the night with Jake, snuggling against him for warmth against the cool air. And when they awoke in the morning, they found themselves in an embrace.

"Good morning," Jake said, smiling at her.

"Good morning," she replied.

"Last night was . . . nice," he said. He didn't know quite how to explain it, but there was something very intimate about having spent the night with her without the necessity of sex. It was as if they had the right to be together, not because he had paid for that right at the Hog Ranch, but because they belonged together.

"We've got breakfast, folks!" one of the other women shouted. "Coffee, bacon, and biscuits, over here!"

Jake and Laura got a cup of coffee and a biscuit-and-bacon sandwich, then moved over to sit on the tongue of a nearby wagon. As Jake drank his coffee, he began to look at the wagon.

"Where did this come from?" he finally asked.

"It was one of the wagons they brought up here," Sheriff Angus answered. Sheriff Angus and Arapaho Brown had assumed the co-leadership position of the impromptu army. Ironically, Sheriff Angus had twice defeated Arapaho Brown in the race for sheriff, and though they were political enemies, they were allies in this cause, and they, like Jake and Laura, were sitting on the tongue of one of the invaders' wagons.

"Have you seen what all is in these wagons?" Arapaho Brown asked.

"No, I didn't even notice them yesterday," Jake answered.

"Well, it's where your breakfast came from," Brown said chuckling.

"Yes. And guns, ammunition, even dynamite," the sheriff added. "It is very obvious that these people didn't come up here to put on a parade for us. They came up here with murder in their hearts and hands."

"Dynamite?" Jake replied, his curiosity piqued by the sheriff's words. Still sipping his coffee, he stood and walked over to the wagon, then pulled back the tarpaulin to look inside. There he saw six cases of dynamite.

"My God, there's enough dynamite in there to bring down a mountain," Jake said.

Arapaho Brown nodded, then took another swallow of his coffee. "You know, I think we ought to give this dynamite back to them," he suggested.

Angus looked at Brown. "Give it back to them?"

Brown smiled, then nodded. "Yeah," he said. "Only first, let's light the fuse."

Inside the barn, Wolcott and Canton were at their lookout posts up in the hayloft, at the open, hay-loading door.

"What in the hell?" Canton said. "Wolcott, look over there! What the hell is that?"

The subject of Canton's curiosity was a large ark, made by connecting two wagons together. The wagon in front was fortified with heavy timbers and bales of hay. The result was a moving breastwork, for it was being pushed toward them by half a dozen men.

"I don't know what kind of contraption they've put together there," Wolcott replied. "But they've built it upon our wagons."

"Our wagons?"

"Yes, look at the wheels."

"Damn, Wolcott, there's dynamite on those wagons!" Canton shouted.

Wolcott's eyes grew wide as he realized not only the truth of what Canton was saying . . . but its meaning.

"They mean to dynamite us!" Wolcott replied.

Quickly Canton ran over to the ladder and shouted to the men who were in the area below.

"Men, get on your guns!" he called. "They're pushing a barricaded wagon toward us . . . filled with dynamite! We've got to stop them!"

There was a flurry of activity as every Texan and cattlemen in the barn, exhausted now for lack of sleep and weakened by two days of hunger and thirst, moved to the holes, windows, and other firing positions in the barn.

Without any specific order to fire, they began shooting at the wagon, thirty or forty rifles banging away. Puffs of dust, splinters of wood, and bits of straw flew from the wagon as the bullets struck, but still the wagon creaked through the grass.

"We can't stop them," Wolcott cried in alarm. "They're going to blow us all to hell and there's not a damn thing we can do about it."

"Unless we can blow them to hell!" Canton suggested. Cupping his hands around his mouth, he shouted down to the riflemen. "Men, shoot at the second wagon! The second wagon! The dynamite is on it! Try and hit it!"

The word was spread around, and all the riflemen began concentrating their fire on the second wagon.

Jake was one of the twelve men pushing the two wagons forward. He had one stick of dynamite in his hand and three stuck in his belt. The other men were similarly armed, and the idea was to get the wagon close enough to the barn to allow them to light the fuses, then hurl the sticks toward the barn.

If that didn't do the job, they had one more option, and that was to light one fuse that led to all the rest of the dynamite on the wagon. Once that fuse was lit, they would give the wagon a huge push and let it roll downhill into the side of the barn. The result of that many cases of dynamite going off at the same time would be to make splinters of the barn and corpses of its defenders.

There had been some discussion about the second part of their plan, as there was always a possibility that a random bullet could set off the dynamite. If it did, then the wagon would be splinters, and those pushing it would be corpses.

Jake knew immediately when the defenders in the barn changed their tactics, because the bullets that had been crashing into the front wagon were now hitting the rear wagon. Of course, by design, the rear wagon did not present as good a target. Still, a few of the bullets got through, and Jake cringed when he saw a large piece of wood splinter off from the corner of one of the dynamite cases.

"Faster, boys!" Brown shouted, having seen the same thing Jake saw. "If they hit one of these cases, we're done for!"

Jake and the others started pushing faster. There was

going to be one hell of an explosion soon. The only question was, where would the wagon be when it exploded?

"Canton! Canton! Look!" Wolcott shouted. He pointed to the north, and there, coming over the hill, with flags and guidons flying in the breeze, was the United States Cavalry!

"It's the army! We're saved!" Canton shouted happily. "He got through! Garret got through! Cease fire!" he shouted to his men downstairs. "Everyone, cease fire! The cavalry has arrived!"

"The army?" one Texan said. "Glory, we can't fight the army!"

The cattlemen, who knew immediately that the army was their salvation, laughed, then began shaking hands all around, patting each other on the back.

"Look at them," Canton said derisively. "From the way they're carrying on, you'd think we won."

As soon as the shooting from the barn stopped, the men pushing the dynamite wagons could hear the high-pitched notes of the bugler and the approaching army.

"Hold it!" Brown said, standing up. "What is that?"

"It's the army," another said, and the men behind the wagon watched as the cavalry, led by Colonel Van Horn, rode boldly right down into the little bit of space remaining between the wagons and the barn, positioning themselves squarely between the two fighting groups. Colonel Van Horn held up his hand, then shouted at the top of his voice.

"Cease fire! Cease fire! By the authority of the president of the United States, I order both sides to cease fire at once!"

From behind the wagons, and from the barricades and breastworks on the hills, the Johnson County men emerged. They began walking toward the barn, and though they were carrying their weapons, they were not in a threatening position.

From inside the barn, a dirty white rag, tied to one of the tines of a pitchfork, began to wave back and forth.

"You men inside there! Come on out!" Van Horn called. "It's all over now."

The Texans and cattlemen, licking lips that were chapped and cracked for lack of water, stepped outside cautiously, their eyes shining brightly from tired, deep-set sockets on powder-blackened faces.

"Who is in charge here?" Colonel Van Horn asked as the men came out of the barn.

"I am in charge, sir. Colonel Frank Wolcott at your service," Wolcott said, saluting Van Horn.

"Colonel?" Van Horn asked.

"It is a temporary rank granted by the governor of Wyoming."

"My rank is permanent, and granted my by the president of the United States," Van Horn replied. "I take it, Mr. Wolcott, that you recognize my authority?"

"I do, sir."

"And you surrender yourself and your men?" Van Horn asked.

"I will surrender to you, sir, and to the U.S. Army," Wolcott responded. "For it is a body I once served, with great pride." He looked at the armed men from the town and county, and at the women who had accompanied them and were now by their sides. "I will not surrender to these people."

Colonel Van Horn looked at Sheriff Angus. "Does it matter to you who they surrender to?" he asked.

"No," Angus replied. "As long as the sons of bitches are turned over to civil authorities."

"Agreed," Van Horn said. "Captain Fitzhugh, collect these men's weapons and put them under arrest."

"Colonel . . . for my men," Wolcott said. "Could we have some water?"

"Yes, of course. Forgive me for not making the offer sooner. Captain Barber, provide each of them with a canteen," Colonel Van Horn ordered.

Hastily, and without any resistance, pistols and rifles were exchanged for canteens. The Texans and cattlemen appeared oblivious of the whoops and taunts of the grinning homesteaders, rustlers, and townspeople, who leaned on their rifles and squirted tobacco juice toward the would-be invaders.

FINAL RESULTS OF THE GREAT STOCKMEN'S WAR
SPECIAL FOR THE *CHEYENNE SUN*
By David McCloud

Afraid that the citizens of Johnson County would organize a lynching of the prisoners, the cattlemen and the Texas volunteers were removed from Johnson County and taken to Cheyenne to spend ten weeks at Fort Russell, awaiting trial. Although the citizens of Johnson County wanted them tried for making an illegal war, the only indictments that were handed down were for the murders of Nate Champion and Nick Ray.

Because they were Johnson County's prisoners, even though they weren't being held in Johnson County, that political body was ordered to pay the costs of the confinement at Fort Russell. This was a rate of 100 dollars per day, per man, and within a few weeks, Johnson County's treasury, already one of the poorest in Wyoming, went broke. With no more money to pay for their confinement, the judge ordered the prisoners released without bond.

The Texans, after a wild party of celebration during which they became very intoxicated and started fighting among themselves, were the next morning put on a train for Texas. Once they departed, they were no longer in the jurisdiction of the court of Wyoming, and as the governor has stated that he has no plans to seek extradition from Texas, the case against them has been, in effect, dropped.

There remained then only the cattlemen to face charges, but as everyone agrees that it was bullets from the Texans' guns that killed Champion and Ray, it was not practical to continue the prosecution of the cattlemen. Therefore, and with the overwhelming approval of most of the citizens of Cheyenne, the case against the cattlemen has also been dropped.

The war some are calling "the Cattle Barons' Rebellion" is over.

Eighteen

"Horn?" Deputy Sheriff Richard Proctor called, sticking his head back into the cell blocks. "Tom Horn, you awake back there?"

Tom Horn had been lying on the cot in his jail cell, but he hadn't been sleeping.

"I'm awake," he said.

"You have some visitors."

Tom Horn sat up, then swung his legs over the edge of his bunk. "All right, Dick," he said. "Send 'em on back."

The visitors, Doyle Hunter, George Perry, and two other members of the Wyoming Stock Growers' Association, were directed by Proctor back into the cell block, though no directions were actually needed, as they had visited Tom before. They walked back to his cell, then stood in the corridor, looking through the steel bars at the most famous prisoner in the jail.

Tom was in jail for murder. He wasn't arrested for killing rustlers. The fact that he had left a trail of dead rustlers behind him, with their heads resting on a rock, was not only well-known, but was publicly approved and quietly sanctioned. But when the head resting on one of those rocks turned out to be that of fourteen-year-old Willie Nickell, there was a sudden public outcry to "bring the killer to justice."

Responding to the demands of the public and orders from the officials, Deputy U.S. Marshal Joe Lefors undertook the case. Tom was in Denver, but Lefors, who was an old friend from Tom's own law enforcement days, wrote Tom a letter, telling him that there was "more work to be done, and the cattlemen were interested in renewing their contract with him."

Tom came back to Cheyenne and, in response to an invitation from Lefors, visited him in his office for "a few drinks and some talk of old times."

Lefors was generous with his whiskey, refilling Tom's glass every time it got down to the half mark. Tom got very drunk, and the drunker he got, the taller became his tales. One of his tales related to the death of young Willie Nickell.

"Did you shoot that kid?" Lefors asked.

Tom wagged his finger back and forth, smiling at Lefors. "Now, why would I answer a fool question like that?" he asked.

"Somebody shot him," Lefors said. "And they left his head on a rock, just like you always do. Also the distance between the empty casings and the body indicated that whoever did it was one hell of a shot. You're about the only one I know who could've hit him, dead center, from that far away. What would you say if I told you I thought you did it?"

"I'd say it was the best shot I ever made, and the dirtiest trick I ever done," Tom replied, sloshing down another glass of whiskey.

What Tom didn't know was that behind a partially

opened door in the next room, Lefors had hidden a stenographer. The stenographer was making a transcription
of everything that was being said.

During the trial that followed, Tom Horn denied that
he actually made a confession, claiming that anything he
might have said that sounded like a confession was actually no more than the kind of bragging and "spinning
of yarns" that old friends who have both been in the
law business do when they get together.

"We were each one trying to outdo the other one, so
to speak," Tom explained. "Joe would tell some big lie,
then I would tell another. When you are into one of those
drinking, bragging bouts, you don't really expect anyone
to take you serious."

But Tom Horn was taken seriously, and despite the
fact that he denied everything he had said while under
the influence of drink, the jury found him guilty, and he
was sentenced to hang. He was now awaiting the exe-
cution of that sentence.

"Any news about my appeal?" Tom asked his visitors.

Perry took off his hat and stood looking at it for a
long moment without saying anything.

"Hell," Tom said. "You don't have to answer that
question. I can see in your face that it's been turned
down."

"We're sorry, Tom," Perry said.

"To tell the truth, I didn't much expect anyone to
listen to a poor old cowboy like me. What about the
governor? Any chance of a pardon? Or of him com-
muting the sentence?"

Perry shook his head, once. Once was enough.

Tom smiled. "No need for you boys to stand there
with such hangdog looks on your faces. I didn't really

expect anything, anyway. By the way, Mr. Hunter, I've got that rope I told you I'd make. It's a damn good one, too.'' Horn went over to his bunk and picked up a coiled rope, which he brought back to hand through the bars to Doyle Hunter.

''Thanks,'' Hunter said.

''That may be worth somethin' someday, after I'm gone,'' Tom said.

''Tom, I want you to know, we can't begin to tell you how grateful we are for what you have done for us,'' Perry said. ''The . . . war . . . we launched against the rustlers of Johnson County was, in every respect, a disaster. But you have been very effective. The number of rustlers you took care of has certainly paid off handsomely for us.''

''I'm glad I was able to be of some help.''

''If only you hadn't . . . uh . . . that is, if only that fourteen-year-old boy hadn't been killed. A few more months of your, uh, special services, and we would have been rid of the rustlers forever,'' Hunter added.

''Special services?'' Tom said. He chuckled. ''Is that what I did for you, Hunter? Perform special services?''

Hunter cleared his throat. ''Well, uh, yes,'' he said. ''I mean . . . what else would you call it?''

''I would call it killing,'' Tom Horn said easily. ''You had some killing you wanted done, and I did it for you.''

Hunter shook his head. ''No, I would rather not think of it like that. We are cattlemen, not killers.''

''Is that a fact? Tell me, Mr. Hunter, did you or did you not pay me a fee for every rustler I killed?''

''Taken care of . . . not killed,'' Hunter said.

Tom made a scoffing sound. ''Please, Hunter, at least have the guts to tell it like it is. You are killers, all of you.''

"How dare you call us killers?" Hunter protested. "You are the one who rode out onto the range, staying gone for days at a time, going without rest, eating your meat raw so as not to give away your position, going without water, enduring every hardship, just so you could get your man."

"Yes, but only after you aimed me toward the target," Tom insisted. "I was the weapon you used. But I am no more personally responsible for the deaths of those men than the rifle and bullets that killed them."

"I suppose you are going to say that we directed you to kill that fourteen-year-old boy?" Hunter challenged.

"You directed the killing of his father," Tom replied. "And from the time the boy put on his father's coat and hat, then rode his father's horse through the gate of their place, he was a dead man, regardless of who killed him."

"Suppose I accept this premise," Perry suggested. "Will you answer a question for me?"

"If I can."

"Why didn't you shoot Jake Colby? He was on your list of people to 'take care of.' I know you must have had the opportunity. But you let him live."

"Yes."

"Why?"

"I chose not to kill him."

"You chose not to?"

"Yes."

Perry smiled. "Then you have made my point, Mr. Horn. If you chose not to shoot Jake Colby, that means you could have chosen not to shoot the others. That you did shoot them means that you chose to do so. Weapons don't have the power of choice, Mr. Horn. If a rifle is aimed and the trigger pulled, it will shoot anyone."

Horn was quiet for a moment, then, with an almost imperceptible nod of his head, he turned away from the bars and walked over to sit on his bunk.

"Damn, Perry, the way you can argue a point, I should have used you as my lawyer," he said. "I guess I hadn't actually looked at it like that."

"Yes, well," interjected Hunter, "now that you have, you needn't be so high and mighty with—"

Perry put out his hand to shush him. "The truth is, Tom, there is enough guilt to go around," he said. "And you are right. My colleagues and I are at least as guilty as, and perhaps even more guilty than, you. But the question is, what are you going to do about it?"

Tom looked up from the bed.

"Do about it?" he asked.

"You're going to hang tomorrow, Tom," Perry said flatly. "There is nothing we or anyone else can do to prevent that. You have to understand that the governor's back is up against the wall now. If it hadn't been for that fourteen-year-old kid, he could have commuted the sentence—hell, he could have granted you a full pardon. But not now. You understand, you are going to hang tomorrow and no power on earth is going to prevent it."

"Yeah," Tom said. "I've pretty well figured that out by now."

"So, the question remains. Are you going to do the right thing?"

"I think what you are asking me is, am I going to tell the rest of the world about our arrangement?"

Perry nodded and licked his lips. "Something like that, yes," he admitted.

Tom looked straight at them without batting an eye. "Boys, you may think you made a deal with the devil, but you didn't. You made a deal with Tom Horn. And

Tom Horn doesn't go back on his word. I told you I would keep quiet about it, and that is how I am going to the hereafter.''

''Bless you, Tom Horn,'' Perry said with a grateful sigh. ''I will personally see to it that your name becomes synonymous with one who honors his word.''

The next day, thirty minutes before he was due to be led out to the gallows, Tom Horn finished writing his autobiography. He gave it to Dick Proctor with the instructions that Proctor deliver it to John Coble, a friend. Silently Proctor nodded.

''Well,'' Tom said. ''It's about time for my show, isn't it, Dick?''

Again Proctor nodded, though he said nothing.

''Well, let's do it,'' Tom said. ''I sure don't want to keep those good folks waiting.''

Working quickly, other deputies began strapping Tom down, securing his arms to his sides by use of leather straps that connected to a leather belt. They didn't secure his legs until he was already outside, until he had actually mounted the gallows. There they strapped his legs.

By Tom's special request, two men began singing, their voices blending in perfect harmony.

''Damn, Dick, where's the hangman?'' Tom asked, looking around.

''There isn't any,'' Proctor replied. ''You'll be hanging yourself.''

Tom chuckled. ''I'm goin' to have a hell of a time doin' that, strapped in like I am,'' he replied.

Proctor looked toward the trap door. ''When you step on that door, your weight will activate a hydraulic device,'' he explained. ''Water will start pouring out of one bucket and into another. When the second bucket is full enough, it will spring the door.''

"Well, I'll be damned," Tom said. He grinned broadly. "We sure do live in some amazing times, don't we?''

"Do you want a hood?" Proctor asked.

"I reckon not," Tom replied. He looked out over the assembly of witnesses. Most of those who were gathered in the front row were lawmen, many of whom he had worked with at one time or another.

"I've never seen such a pasty-faced bunch of sheriffs in my life," he said as he stepped onto the trap door.

Below him, he heard a spring snap open, then water started pouring.

He waited.

In the distance a hawk called, and Tom looked toward him and saw him flying free. Then an amazing thing happened. Tom felt that, somehow, he and that bird had exchanged places, so that he was the one flying around, looking down on these proceedings.

The water continued to pour, cascading from one bucket into the other.

Tom wanted to laugh. He wanted to tell all of the assembled witnesses that they weren't actually going to see anything; that only his body would feel the noose, but he wouldn't be in his body. However, he knew that wasn't what they wanted to hear. He was being hanged, and those who were hanging him wanted to get their money's worth.

"Tom," Proctor said, "if you'll let your neck be relaxed, it'll snap like a twig and be over in a second. Tighten it up, an' it's likely to take a little longer. I've seen 'em kick for near half an hour.''

The water continued to pour, the sound changing pitch

as the volume in one bucket decreased while that in the other increased.

The time that was left until the second bucket was full was all that remained between Tom and eternity. It was a brief moment in the lives of those who stood on the ground, watching, but it was a lifetime for Tom Horn. Tom used it to think about the mountains of Arizona. He had been his happiest there, and he wanted to fix that impression upon his mind, so that if any impression survived this transition, it would be of that.

It was obvious by the sound of the pouring water that the second bucket was just about full. Suddenly there was the loud sound of an opening mechanism, and the trap door fell out from under Tom's feet, dropping him off into space and launching him into eternity.

THE CIRCLE H RANCH

Laura was sitting in her favorite chair on the front porch. The afternoon grew long, and in the west, the sun, in golden splendor, dipped behind the Big Horn Mountains. Purple shadows began to work their old familiar way up into the draws and canyons.

From here she could see the house where their oldest son, Eddie, lived with his wife and two sons. Nate, their second son, who had been a flyer in the U.S. Army Air Services, had been killed in France, fighting a war that was so far away that Laura still had no idea why America had gotten involved in the first place. Jim, their youngest, was a lawyer down in Cheyenne, though he and his wife and daughter had driven up in his Ford V-8 to spend the weekend in celebration of Jake's sixtieth birthday.

Jake had gone out for a ride an hour or so earlier. He'd said he needed to "check the herd," though with Eddie as his foreman, and the dozen cowboys they now had working for them, Laura knew it was more something Jake wanted to do than anything he had to do.

She saw Jake coming back, and she smiled and breathed a little prayer of thanks. She knew she had no right to the life she had enjoyed. She had come west as a whore, she had lived through cattle wars and droughts, blizzards and market failures, the advent of the telephone, automobile, airplane, motion picture, and radio. She had buried one son and watched the other two marry and start families of their own. And she had seen her husband, once considered an outlaw, be honored by the governor of Wyoming as one of the state's leading cattlemen.

But for all of that, the blessing she was most thankful for was the fact that her love for Jake, and his for her, had grown stronger with each passing year.

Jake dismounted, and one of the hands hurried out to take his horse back to the stable. Jake thanked him, then walked up the brick walkway toward the house. He was carrying a rock.

"What in the world do you have there?" Laura asked with a little laugh.

"I found this," Jake said. "Just up the hill. Last night's rain exposed it. It's been there for forty years."

Laura laughed again. "That's a rock, Jake. It's probably been there a million years."

Jake shook his head. "Not this rock," he said. "There was also a letter, stuck down in this bottle."

"A letter? Who is the letter to?"

"To me."

"A letter to you, that's been there for forty years? What in the world does it say?"

Jake took his glasses from his shirt pocket, put them on, then unfolded the letter and began to read:

Dear Jake,

This rock was to have been your pillow, and you would have been my twelfth. You are still alive because of that dumb hat you are wearing.

Somehow or other, old friend, you and I have wound up on different sides of this battle. But I'm the kind of man who doesn't have so many friends that I can afford to lose them. And I sure as hell don't intend to start killing them off.

You used to tell me about the ranch you wanted to build someday. I hope this one is it. If it is, have a drink someday in the future, and remember your old friend,

Tom Horn

Without a word, Laura got up from her chair and went into the house.

"Laura? Laura, where are you going?" Jake called after her.

When Laura didn't answer, Jake followed her. When she reached the hall closet, she pulled down a box off the top shelf. From the box, she took Jake's old hat.

"Well, I'll be," Jake said. "I thought that hat had been thrown away years ago."

"No one is ever going to throw this hat away, Jake," Laura said. "You were wearing this the first time I ever saw you." She looked around to make certain no one could overhear her. "In fact . . . this was the only thing you were wearing. It has always been special to me, and now that I know it once saved your life, it is even more special.''

Jake put it on, then they kissed. At that precise moment, their youngest son, Jim, his wife, Mary, and their daughter, Ella, came into the house.

''Oh, Momma, Daddy,'' Ella said, laughing. ''Look at Grandpa wearing that funny hat.''

Jim laughed also, then he got a closer look at the hat. ''Wait a minute,'' he said. ''I think I've seen that hat before. Yes, I know I have. You used to keep it on the top rung of the hall tree, but you never wore it, and when we were kids, you would never let us wear it. I'll just bet you there's some sort of a story behind that hat.''

''That's right,'' Jake said.

Jim was silent for a moment, then he said, ''Well?''

''Well what?'' Jake asked.

''Aren't you going to tell me the story?''

''Maybe someday,'' Jake said.